The Lost Ring

J. Galliano

Copyright © 2020 J. Galliano

All rights reserved.

ISBN:

DEDICATION

I dedicate this book to Nadine & Kimberly, and to all my friends, who like books, enrich my life.

"Everyone is a moon, and has a dark side which he never shows to anybody."
— Mark Twain

Prologue

Then

Blood.

There was so much blood.

A painted scene where the artist had used too much crimson. It covered the sheets and soaked steadily into the mattress and even dripped onto the floor.

Drip-drop, drip-drop.

Who would have thought that a single human body could hold so much blood?

Her screams slashed like knives through the stillness and silence of twilight. On any other night, the darkness outside of the Hacienda would be full of sounds: the hoot of an owl, the plaintive cry of stray cats in heat, the wind rustling through the leaves, the dogs barking in the courtyard... but tonight all that we could hear were Lucia's cries, as contraction after contraction tore through her body.

This was to be Lucia's and Francisco's first child, but even in her agonised, semi-delirious state, Lucia knew the agony she was experiencing was not the usual pain of labour. She had witnessed her two elder sisters give birth years before, and of course there had been pain, but this was more than that, this was like being ripped apart from the inside and she could almost feel her life's blood escaping her.

Please don't let my child die, Lucia thought as she cried out, the burning pain in her abdomen intensifying as she struggled to push. Labour had come hard and fast and it was too early; she had not expected the child to be born for at least another month.

It was too soon.

Francisco had sent the stable boy to fetch the town's doctor, but Lucia feared he would not arrive in time, or if he did, there would be little that he could do for her. She would put her faith in God to see her through. She prayed that God might give her strength and keep death at bay. Rosa, her maid, wiped the sweat off her brow with a cool flannel and made soothing sounds to try and quell Lucia's fear, but her eyes could not mask her distress.

The light of the numerous candles illuminated the opulent bedroom. The smell of wax as it burned, mingled with that of blood. A sudden breeze from the open window made the candles flicker, threatening to extinguish them. Lucia feared her life and that of her child might be snuffed out just as easily.

She could hear Francisco pacing just outside the door, whispering prayers.

"Francisco *mi amor*, my love, come and stay by my side," Lucia called out to him, then she let out another wail of agony.

Francisco rushed into the room. His usually tanned face was pallid but turned ghastly white as he saw the blood which coated her nightdress and the mattress.

"Lucia, the doctor is on his way. Just a little longer, my love," Francisco told her, his eyes filled in equal measure with love and fear for his beloved wife and the child he had yet to see.

Each contraction wrapped around Lucia's body, reaching from her back to her torso and abdomen, like a blade searing through her flesh. She felt lightheaded and her long, blonde hair was matted with sweat, her blue eyes filling with tears. Rosa, who had known Lucia since she was a child, knelt by her bedside and held her hand. Francisco sat on the other side of the bed, gripping Lucia's hand tightly as if he could somehow will strength from his body to hers.

As the next fierce wave of pain flowed through Lucia's body, she yelled like a woman possessed by the devil himself, and pushed as hard as her weakening body would allow. She felt relief as the child left her womb, even more so when the welcome sound of a newborn's cry filled the air. Lucia wept as Rosa quickly but carefully cleaned and wrapped the child in a soft white cloth and laid her against Lucia's chest. Rosa held the child there, as Lucia was too weak to even move her arms.

"A beautiful baby girl, *mi senora*, my lady." Rosa told her, her brown eyes filled with emotion and unshed tears.

"As beautiful as her mother," Francisco added softly as he laid his hand on his wife's forehead and touched the baby's cheek.

"Isabel..." whispered Lucia, looking adoringly into her daughter's eyes. The tiny newborn stared back, as if she too were transfixed.

Lucia smiled beatifically for a moment, but her face soon contorted in anguish once more as another spasm flooded her abdomen.

"*Mi senor*, another child. Take Isabel," Rosa said, her voice tinged with fear. She handed the child to Francisco and placed an arm around Lucia's back to lift her up slightly. "*Mi senora*, you must find the strength to push again. You have another child yet in your belly."

The instant and all-encompassing love Lucia had felt for her daughter filled her with renewed strength, and she managed to push once more. The pain was like nothing she had ever experienced before, nor did she wish to ever again. She prayed for it to end. A guttural scream erupted from deep in her throat as her second child came into the world, and then she was silent.

Rosa couldn't help but gasp as she saw the child, which lay as still and quiet as its mother, in a pool of crimson red. She picked up the child quickly and wrapped her in cloth, but not before Francisco had seen the babe and recoiled in horror. Rosa tried to pass him the child, who now mewled softly at being handled, but Francisco shook his head savagely and took an unconscious step back, holding Isabel even closer to his chest.

"What is wrong with it?" Francisco managed to utter, averting his eyes from his second daughter. "It matters not, Rosa. Help save my Lucia – she is what matters now."

Reluctantly, Rosa set the child, who was so small, down on the bed, close to her mother. Rosa tried to stem the bleeding with numerous white cloths, which too quickly turned scarlet. Lucia lay still, her breathing shallow. Rosa's tears fell in earnest as her beloved mistress passed from this life into the next.

"Lucia, no! You cannot leave me! Please come back to me!" Francisco begged, his pain so raw and crippling that Rosa could not bear to look at him. "My beautiful Lucia, *mi amor*." Francisco wept as he stroked her soft hair and kissed her full lips which were already tinged blue.

Upon hearing her father's despair, Isabel began to cry, as if she too lamented the loss of a mother she would never know. The second child, perhaps in response to her twin sister's call, began to wail weakly.

"Take it away!" Francisco yelled at Rosa.

"*Mi senor*, your daughter..." Rosa entreated, carefully picking up the small bundle from the bed.

"I have only one daughter," Francisco said angrily, holding Isabel to his chest. "Now leave me, Rosa – leave me with my Lucia!" he shrieked like a deranged man.

Rosa had never seen him like this, and so she turned and hurried out of the room, leaving her master in pieces as he held onto his dead wife.

Beth

Chapter One

Now

The plane touched down in Malaga Airport, with just a light thud, then thundered to a halt. I looked out from the small cabin window at the sun-bathed mountains and blue skies, then picked up my Michael Kors bag, which I had placed carefully underneath the seat in front me. It was a birthday present from Nathan.

Nathan was already removing his seatbelt. He and I had been dating for over three years and this was our first holiday abroad together; we were both looking forward to spending a relaxing week at the beach. Correction: I was equally excited and terrified.

Do you think it is possible to yearn for something and be frightened of it at the same time? It doesn't make much sense, I know, but that is exactly how I felt as I stood up and shuffled my way to the front of the plane.

Since as far back as I could remember, I had had a phobia of the water, so a trip to a Spanish coastal town may not seem like an ideal choice – but I was taking this trip for two reasons. One of them was Nathan. He loved to surf and, back home in Bristol, he spent his free time at the Wave, or taking weekend trips to Sennen Cove, Bournemouth and Watergate Bay. I wanted to be able to share in his hobbies and his passion for the ocean. The second reason was that I wanted to overcome this irrational fear, because although I was filled with a deep sense of unease and panic at the thought of a large body of water, whenever I came across an image of the ocean, part of me also felt drawn to it in a way I could neither explain or describe.

I had spent countless hours at therapy discussing my aqua-phobia– amongst other issues –and had made great progress. I had even forced myself to learn to swim, albeit always in the shallow end of the pool, my body in no more than a metre of water, and having taken my anti-anxiety medication.

Nathan and I had been planning this beach trip to Tarifa for over six months, and I had been psyching myself up to it. It would be my first trip to the seaside in almost twenty years, ever since...

But I didn't want to think about that now. I forcibly stopped those memories from surfacing. At this point in my life I was happy, and I wanted it to stay that way. I was eager to feel the warm sand beneath my feet, the sea breeze in my hair, to eat delicious food and to spend a few days away from it all.

I had also brought my camera with me, stored carefully in the overhead compartment. In fact, I was hardly ever without it. It was my most treasured belonging. I was a freelance photographer by profession and I hoped to add some stunning photographs from our trip to my portfolio. I hoped to start a travel blog one day, as Nathan and I ventured further around the world.

The air-stairs were soon attached to the plane, and as we stepped outside we were hit immediately by a wave of hot air. Even for late September, the morning heat was stifling, radiating from the tarmac. My new flip-flops clicked noisily against the ground as we made our way inside the air-conditioned terminal.

Nathan winked at me from under his Adidas baseball cap and I grinned at him and held his hand. He looked so relaxed in his cargo shorts and blue Rip Curl T-shirt, which hugged his toned chest and arms.

Nathan had been working so hard that I felt he needed this break more than I did. He had started his first job as a barrister six months ago, at the offices of Philips and Morgan, in a swanky office building in Bristol's city centre. Ever since, Nathan had been putting in crazy hours to get himself noticed by the partners. With his sandy blonde hair, permanent grin and muscular physique, he looked more like a full-time surfer than a lawyer.

We first met in a posh wine bar in Clifton called The Cascade, which my best friend Samantha –Sam for short –had dragged me to, tearing me away from the essay I was trying to finish early. According to Sam, who had a tendency to exaggerate everything even when not intoxicated, the gorgeous, tall, blonde stranger in the corner had been eyeing me up since we'd walked in.

I'd had a couple glasses of wine and was already feeling a little lightheaded, so when Sam dared me to go speak to him,

I did. Sam had a vivacious, outgoing personality which drew people to her, for which I envied her. So I decided to emulate her, striding more confidently than I felt, to speak to this stranger.

For once, Sam hadn't been exaggerating. The closer I got, the more I realised just how good-looking he was, and I felt my false self-assurance crumbling with every step. But he had noticed me heading towards him; to turn back now would make me look completely foolish, and Sam wouldn't let me live it down for the rest of the evening. So I forged ahead and simply said "Hi" with a nervous smile.

I was surprised when Nathan told me he was studying to become a lawyer. He just didn't seem like the type of guy that would chose to be stuck in an office all day. I didn't think we'd hit it off, as I naturally gravitated towards men who shared my passion for the arts, but his wicked sense of humour and the mischievous look in his clear blue eyes soon proved me wrong. We spent the entire evening sitting on stylish but uncomfortable steel stools, drinking too many cocktails, as the soft jazz music served as a backdrop to our constant chatter. Sam had left hours earlier with a guy she'd hooked up with, giving me a not very subtle wink before she kissed me goodnight.

By the end of that evening, I felt I knew Nathan more than some men I had dated for weeks. When the bar had kicked us out to close up, he kissed me softly and asked for my number, and I hadn't looked back since. In the three short years we'd been together, I had come to love this man more than anything else in the entire world.

I tore myself away from the memory of that night and

focused on the present. We continued walking hand in hand to our flight's allocated luggage conveyor belt and waited for our bags to appear. Is it only me that feels panicky at the thought that your bag has been lost or stolen and you now have no clean underwear or make-up for the rest of your trip?

Instead of focusing on all the bags that weren't ours, I studied the other people milling around the terminal. It had always fascinated me how some people expressed so much of themselves in their facial expressions, whereas I had learned to keep my identity deep under my skin.

I played with the strap of my camera, which now hung around my neck, and watched the other passengers on our flight as they waited for their luggage. Most of them where English, like me, and would now venture to various corners of Spain's famous Costa del Sol, or perhaps a little further afield. July and August were the country's busiest months for tourists, but September was extremely popular too. Nevertheless, I hoped the beaches in Tarifa wouldn't be jam-packed.

I enjoyed solitude; it was part of the reason I loved my chosen profession so much – or perhaps it had chosen me. With photography it was just me, the camera and my subject of choice. No office politics or bitchy co-workers.

A couple with four kids, who had sat in front of us in the plane, looked utterly exhausted. Who could blame them? I could never imagine having more than one, maybe two, children. The two older boys, no more than five and seven, ran around the trolley onto which their dad was hoisting their suitcases. Their laughter and happiness was contagious, and their younger twin sisters looked on in admiration of their older siblings.

The two girls, who I guessed to be around two years old, wore pretty yellow dresses dotted with white daisies, which almost touched the floor. Their little toes peeked out from the sandals they wore. They caught me smiling at them and both gave me a cheeky grin.

I took a quick photograph of their small white feet, against the black slate of the airport's tiles. One of my favourite photography projects, and one of my most successful, was capturing a small aspect of a person's body: an arm, a leg, hands or feet, in various lighting constructs and undefined backgrounds. It invited the viewer to create a whole world for that person from just a little glimpse of them and their environment. An elderly hand clasped in a grandchild's, a child's legs as they ran, the shadow of a kite next to their pounding feet, the scuffed shoe of a homeless person. Everyday motions and activities captured for all eternity in an image, as well as all the emotions they evoked.

I looked at the photograph I had just taken on the LCD screen. I was happy with the shot: two sets of feet with matching sandals and dresses, close together, looking oddly vulnerable.

Thoughts of Helena came unbidden into my mind, but I pushed her away; far, far away into the recesses of my mind. I would allow nothing to dampen my mood today.

With a sigh of relief, I spotted our two blue and white suitcases coming into view on the carousel. Nathan lifted them both off with ease. With our cases now trailing behind us, we made our way to the car hire desk. We'd pre-booked our car along with our flights and after a short wait, we had the keys to our rental Seat Ibiza and headed to the designated car lot to pick it up.

The sun was brilliant and unforgiving in the cornflower blue sky. I reached into my bag and pulled out my sunglasses. The heat of the day seemed to burn our unprotected skin in mere minutes, my pale skin turning slightly pink. Nathan opened the car boot and placed the suitcases inside, then we opened the windows to let some of the accumulated heat escape and turned the air-con as high as it would go.

Using a map I had downloaded to my phone, we made our way towards the Costa De La Luz – the Coast of Light. We listened to Ed Sheeran and Boyce Avenue, as we drove for a couple of hours to reach Tarifa.

As we came off the motorway and neared the coast, the roads began to wind and twist as we drove over and around the hills. I was starting to feel a little carsick as we crested the final ridge and the vast and stunning beach of Tarifa stretched out before us. The deep blue ocean shimmering like broken glass, rolled onto the fine golden sand. Huge sand dunes and pine forests rose up behind the beach.

The view was utterly breathtaking. I revelled in the stunning landscape without fearing the kilometres of Atlantic Ocean which framed it. I made myself focus solely on the sea's beauty, not giving any thought to its depth, or the billions of gallons of water it held. I asked Nathan to make a quick stop at the next lay-by, so I could take a photograph to mark the first moment of our little break in this seemingly unspoilt part of the world. The giant white turbines of wind farms dotted the hillsides above Tarifa like sentinels, adding to the landscape's character.

Around twenty minutes later, we found our hotel, which was located next to the long main road that ran adjacent to the coastline. We parked on the sandy earth that served as the hotel's car park and made our way inside.

The hotel, aptly named Diamante del Sur – Diamond of the South – was a small, square, whitewashed building, with large glass windows which glinted in the sun. It was only three storeys high, with large balconies which overlooked the vast sand dunes and the sea beyond, and it was backed by rolling hills covered in colourful wildflowers and shrubs.

The foyer was cool thanks to its thick stone walls and open space, and was supported by white columns which reminded me of Greek temples of old. The smell of fresh flowers in earthen clay vases filled the air, and I took a deep breath as I looked around me.

The inside of the hotel was modern and minimalistic. People visited this part of Spain for the ruggedness of its windswept landscape; fanciful and unnecessary decor was neither needed nor wanted here. At the reception desk, a young pretty woman with dark skin and even darker eyes greeted us and took our passports and details.

"*Bienvenidos*, welcome, Mr Nathan and Miss Beth. Your room is ready for you –number thirteen. Just take the lift to the second floor. It's the last room on the corridor to your left. Here at Diamante del Sur we hope you enjoy your stay with us, and just let us know if you need anything more. Reception is open from 7am to 9pm," she told us in near-perfect English.

"*Gracias*." Nathan and I said in unison as we made our way towards the lift.

My Spanish wasn't great, but better than Nathan's – he knew nothing apart from *gracias* and *cerveza,* beer. Growing up, my nanny had been an elderly lady, who had moved to the UK from Spain many years before. She had taught me quite a bit of Spanish but over the years I'd forgotten much; I hoped this trip would jog my memory enough to get by.

Our room was spacious, and a king-sized bed with turquoise bedding dominated the room. A small, dark mahogany wardrobe and matching coffee table, two large comfy seats, and a tiny kitchenette, made up the rest of the living space. A door to our right led to a white and blue tiled bathroom, nautically themed with decorations of seashells, starfish and seahorses, and a large walk-in shower with a stone grey floor.

The room was perfect. I threw myself on the bed and let out a contented sigh, enjoying the rays of sunshine which streamed through the window onto my face. Nathan laid down next to me and put his arm around my waist. The bed was soft and the bedding cool, and I closed my eyes.

I felt myself falling, sinking deeper and deeper, and soon I was unable to breathe. I was surrounded by water. I opened my eyes but it was too dark and murky to see much. I sunk to the bottom and felt sand and pebbles against the bare skin of my arms and legs.

It was cold too, the kind of cold that permeates into your bones and slows the beating of your heart. My lungs burned with the desire to breathe but I kept my lips pressed firmly together; the sea water stung my eyes but I couldn't let it fill my lungs. I tried to kick my legs, to swim to the surface, where I could see ebbing rays of moonlight. I tried using my arms, too, but it was as if I was made of stone, too heavy to move. I could no longer contain my panic – I was going to drown. In mere moments my body would involuntarily take a breath.

When it did, I felt the frigid water force its way into my airways. I coughed and spluttered, taking in even more water. I could feel my throat start to constrict and my vision waver, but it didn't prevent me from seeing something move in the water just a few metres away. It was big and glided swiftly through the water.

Even in the gloom I could see it was a shark. A great white shark, huge and prehistoric-looking. A real-life dinosaur, deadly, with too many teeth and which was now heading straight towards me.

I jolted up in bed, gasping for breath, a thin film of sweat covering my whole body. I was shaking. I wiped damp hair from my forehead. The eyes of the shark, ancient and primeval, fixed on me, like an afterimage in my mind's eye. I took a very deep breath to calm the racing of my heart. It was only as I heard the door to the hotel room open that I realised I had been alone.

"Oh, sorry Beth, did I wake—" Nathan began, but stopped mid-sentence when he saw the look on my face. "You OK? Did you have another bad dream?"

I nodded rapidly, willing myself to smile. "Yeah, I must have dozed off. The usual bad dream – must be being so close to the ocean," I replied, trying to keep my tone light.

"You were fast asleep when I came out of the bathroom, so I thought I may as well pop to the local supermarket and get us some supplies. I got us plenty of bottled water, some *vino*, some crisps – apparently garlic flavoured, which sounds weird, but gotta be good, right? And some chocolate-filled croissants. How about a glass of wine to get you back in holiday mode?" Nathan asked with a cheeky grin.

I nodded again gratefully. Nathan was used to my bad dreams. During our first few weeks together, when we started sleeping over at each other's apartments, it had freaked him out to find me thrashing and turning, struggling to breathe or having a full-blown panic attack in the middle of the night. His concern for me, and the way he had cuddled me after such episodes, made me realise how much I welcomed his presence in my life. I had had a couple boyfriends before Nathan, of course, but I always seemed to push them away, never wanting to get too close. It had been different with Nathan. He was the one who had encouraged me to go back to therapy, which I had given up on, to overcome these night terrors and my aqua-phobia.

I couldn't remember the last time I had had a bad dream in which I was drowning, but it had been a few months at least. I felt I had made so much progress, but I guessed that being so close to the ocean would set me back a couple of steps.

Nathan handed me a glass, half-filled with delicious *rioja*. I sipped it gratefully. It was rich and silky, with a hint of red fruits and berries. I savoured its taste and almost instantly felt more relaxed.

"Thanks babe, just what I needed," I told him, taking another long sip.

"We can always spend the rest of the afternoon in bed," he said with a wink, "if you don't feel up to venturing down to the beach just yet?"

"That's OK, I'm feeling fine really. I actually do fancy a long walk on the beach, stretch my legs after the plane ride and car trip. I want to dip my toes in the water – baby steps," I said with a smile. I meant it. I was tired of letting the past and these irrational fears hold me back.

"If you're sure? That sounds like a good plan."

We opened up our suitcases and packed away most of our stuff in the small cupboard and bedside tables. We found our swimsuits, removed the clothes we had been wearing for travelling in, and placed them in a laundry bag I'd packed.

I slipped on a recently-purchased red, revealing swimsuit from Oasis. It was bold and daring, just as I was willing myself to be. It earned me a wolf whistle from Nathan, who looked every bit the hot surfer in his blue Animal swim-trunks, which brought out the colour of his eyes. I shoved him playfully and finished off the rest of the glass of wine in a single gulp. I didn't normally drink much alcohol but, as they say, *when in Rome*. I planned to spend the week drinking almost exclusively *sangria* and *tinto de verano*.

We covered up with copious amounts of factor fifty-plus sun-block. I had purchased two bottles in Boots before flying over. Although my hair was black and thick, my skin was quite fair, although not as light as Nathan's. I would have to keep on top of him to make sure he didn't end up looking like a typical lobster-coloured English tourist in the Mediterranean.

I put on a white crochet beach cover up, with yellow and blue embroidered flowers, some flip-flops, and a pair of oversized sunglasses which completed the beach look.

"Wow, you look absolutely stunning. Spain suits you," Nathan whispered as he wrapped his strong arms around me, kissing my neck softly and caressing my waist. "I'm starting to think my original suggestion was way better."

"Hey, plenty of time for that later, you," I admonished him jokingly. "Let's get down to the beach and enjoy what's left of the afternoon sun."

I felt good. Sexy. Alive. Young. Free and loved.

I picked up my beach bag and pushed down the image my mind had conjured of an ocean - cold, dark and deadly.

Chapter Two

We walked under the dense, protective canopy of the pine forest and onto the mountainous sand dunes. The world's colours were illuminated vividly by the sun's intense rays, the green and brown hues of the tall grass, the golden yellow sand, the royal blue of the Atlantic Ocean and the white wispy clouds suspended in an azure sky.

The cool sea breeze was a welcome respite from the sweltering heat. We hurried down to the sea, to the lapping waves which caressed the shore, and dipped our hot feet into the chilly water.

I felt my chest tighten a little as the water swished over my ankles. Nathan clasped my hand tighter, giving me a reassuring squeeze and I felt the tension leave my body. I closed my eyes, turning my face up to the warmth of the sun, and took a deep breath of clean sea air, which invigorated my senses.

The wind picked up even more. Kite-surfers and wind-surfers drifted through the landscape, like colourful birds across the sky and sea, as if dancing with the air and water.

From my beach bag I took out my camera– a Nikon D750, a birthday gift from my father – and took a few shots. I also took a few candid pictures of Nathan, his eyes fixated on the surfers who swam far out from shore to catch the biggest waves and swells.

When we first started dating, Nathan hadn't liked me taking his picture, but over the months he had gotten used to it and, I think, had secretly come to like the attention. I must have taken over a thousand pictures of him in the time we'd been together.

As a Christmas gift for his parents, I had framed one my favourite pictures of Nathan, one I had taken at his friend's wedding. He had been wearing a dark grey suit, and in his hand he held a glass of champagne. His face was angled to the right, and he stood in an open field, waiting for the bride and groom to arrive. His parents had loved it.

"Can't wait to get out on the water tomorrow," he said, turning to face me. "You don't mind, do you? I won't be out too long, I promise. I plan to enjoy every moment of this holiday with you."

"Of course I don't. Part of the reason we chose Tarifa was so you could surf. Plus, I always have my camera to keep me company."

Two young kids came running up beside us and splashed each other in the water. I took a photo of their tanned, skinny arms as they flung the crystal-clear water into the air, capturing the brilliant sunshine in the droplets. I checked the image; it invoked a sense of fun, of carefree youthfulness and life.

I put the camera back into my bag and we continued walking hand in hand along the shore, until we came to a deserted part of the beach. Here we laid out the turquoise hotel towels with large white anchors embroidered in their middle, and stretched out, enjoying the warmth of the sand through the fabric.

"Gonna have to dive in – boiling my nuts here," Nathan exclaimed. He stood up and dusted the fine sand off his arms.

"Charming," I laughed.

"You coming in?" Nathan asked hesitantly.

"Tomorrow I will try, I promise."

Nathan gave me a broad grin before running off and diving straight into the water. He didn't fear anything; he had an almost childlike belief that he could be or do anything he set his mind to. How freeing that must be.

"What's the water like?" I called out to him, once he had reappeared from under the surface.

"Ahh – colder than it looks!" he called back with a laugh. "Gonna do a few laps, before my balls turn blue!"

"Stop talking about your balls!" I shouted as I took out an empty spray bottle from my bag.

"Only if you promise to give them some attention later!" he retorted. He turned around and began swimming into deeper waters.

Anxiety tugged at my chest as he swam further out, and I had to repeat in my mind that Nathan was a strong swimmer and would be fine. I went down to the shoreline and filled up the bottle, spraying the mist onto my face and chest to cool down.

I continued watching him cut through the water with

ease. I knew he felt safe and at home in the water. He was a natural born adventurer: he enjoyed hiking up mountains, cycling, and he had tried bungee jumping, paragliding and even skydiving. His fearless attitude to life was one of the many things that attracted me to him.

Tomorrow I would step into the sea and swim.

Tomorrow I would prove to myself that I had no reason to fear the water, that my trepidation was irrational and unfounded and could therefore be overcome.

I stayed by the shore – it was cooler here – and watched the other beachgoers. A group of older women were huddled under an umbrella playing a board game. Two men played bat and ball. A group of kids built sandcastles and dug moats; others frolicked in the shallows as the waves peaked and crested before dissipating onto the beach.

After a few minutes I headed back to our towels and lay down on my front, to allow the sun to tan my back. I blinked as I saw, in the distance, a young woman dressed in a long, dark grey dress. She faced the ocean, her back to me. Her waist-length, auburn-brown hair hung over her slim shoulders, unmoving in the wind.

Although I couldn't see her face, she emanated a feeling of sadness that I couldn't quite explain. Her figure also seemed incongruous with her surroundings. Her dress covered most of her body, so alien compared to the other women on the beach, with their skimpy bikinis or were topless, their breasts and toned bodies glistening in the heat. She would make for a great photograph, though.

I loved capturing moments in which one particular aspect or person stood out from the rest of the scene. A homeless person in a street of high-end boutiques, a piece of litter in a field of green, a lone child in a crowd of adults.

I reached into my bag and brought out my camera once more, but when I turned around, the woman was gone. I looked up and down the beach, thinking that she may have just continued on her walk, but she was nowhere to be found. I began to wonder if I had even seen her at all.

I settled back on my towel but then cried out as a very wet and very cold Nathan laid himself on top of me.

"You're *freezing*! Get off me right now!" I laughed.

"Hey, just thought I'd help cool you down," he said brightly as he rolled onto his towel, his face turned up to the sun, his eyes closed, a smile on his face. "This is exactly what I needed. I can just feel the stress of the past couple months drifting away."

"That's what I wanted to hear. You deserve a break. You've been working so hard lately – I was actually getting a little worried about you," I said, trying to sound casual but unable to hide the concern in my voice.

"Seriously? Well, no need to be – we knew the first two years as a trainee would be tough. I just didn't realise how difficult it would be to keep on top of the workload, or how many hours I'd need to put in. I don't know where the day goes, between carrying out due diligence, legal research, drafting board minutes, filing documents, drafting submissions, helping with graduate recruitment… and that's just half of it. I'm just trying to prove that I'm one of the best trainees they've got."

"I'm so proud of you," I said, kissing him on the cheek. "How's about we go back to the hotel room and I help you get rid of any remaining stress?" I murmured suggestively.

By way of a reply, he kissed me deeply. I'm not sure if it was the wine combined with the sun, or just his kiss, but I wanted Nathan right there and then. We quickly dusted the fine sand off our towels as best we could and rolled them up. I packed up the beach bag and we headed back to the hotel.

The wind had picked up even more; I felt like my skin was being lightly sand-blasted and I was glad for my beach cover up. Seagulls shrieked overhead and bulls grazed lazily in the tall grass beyond the hotel.

The hotel receptionist took our towels and gave us fresh ones, as well as offering us glasses of chilled orange and mint infused water, which I drank gratefully. Once back in our hotel room, we took off our bathing suits, leaving them to rinse in the sink, and stepped into the spacious walk-in shower.

The cool water felt invigorating against my sun-kissed skin. I lathered up generously with watermelon shower gel, wiping away the sweat and sunscreen, then squeezed out a generous blob of coconut shampoo and began to wash my hair.

Nathan wrapped his strong arms around me and kissed me again, and soon I was lost to the feel of his mouth and his muscular body on mine as he ran his hands up and down the length of me. He picked me up easily and I wrapped my legs around his waist, gasping as he entered me. The water continued to rain down upon us and I dug my nails into his back as we continued to make love.

"That was amazing. *You* are amazing," Nathan whispered to me once it was over.

"We are amazing together." I told him.

I held onto him for a few moments longer, relishing feeling so close to him. We finished showering and stepped back into the room, wrapped in our bath towels, and lay down on the bed. We were a little tired but as soon as Nathan kissed me again, I unfurled the towel from my body and revelled as he continued to touch, caress and lick every inch of my skin. I moaned deeply as he entered me again, and closed my eyes, allowing the world to disappear to just the feel of Nathan.

A short time later, when we were both satiated, Nathan lay next to me and soon dozed off. I got up from the bed and tiptoed into the bathroom, closing the door behind me. I ran a brush through my damp hair, applied some leave in conditioner, allowing it to air dry into its natural curls.

My hair was one of the things Nathan said he loved about me, and I had always taken great care, not to mention a fortune, in keeping my long locks glossy and healthy. I picked up my make-up bag from the counter next to the sink, rummaged through it, and picked out the items I'd need. I brushed on a drop of foundation and a little blusher and bronzer to highlight my cheekbones. I opened up my new eye-shadow palette and coloured my eyes in smoky shades of pink. I applied black eyeliner and black mascara, which emphasised the hazel-green of my eyes. I placed a small silver locket around my neck and ran my fingertips lightly over it. I finished with a light nude lipstick, then stepped quietly back into the room and slipped on a sea-green maxi dress and silver sandals.

"Nathan," I whispered softly, nudging him. "Honey, time

to get up. We better go get some dinner."

"What time is it?" he murmured, barely opening his eyes.

"Gone eight."

"Wow, no wonder I'm starving..." he said, finally opening his eyes. "You look really beautiful in that dress."

"Thank you. I'm ready to go, so I'll wait for you out on the terrace."

I stepped out onto the balcony. Night had descended and the sky was now freckled with stars. The wind, now softer and cooler, blew against my bare arms like a caress. The trees of the forest were black, silhouetted against the velvet night sky. I stared at the dark mass of the ocean, illuminated solely by the cold light of the moon, which cast a silver beam across the water, like a path. A path which seemed to beckon me to its infinite watery depths, where I would be lost forever.

"Beth," I heard Nathan say, distracting me from my reverie. In that moment it wasn't the fear of the water that frightened me, but rather that the sea beckoned...and I wished to go to it.

We weaved through the crowds that filled Tarifa's walled old town. Like the sea, it sparkled, but with tapas bars, trendy shops and nightclubs. People spilled into its narrow pathways, the coolness of the night a reprieve from the day's heat allowing the streets to come alive. We wandered through the cobbled passages, flanked by beautiful white houses with typical Andalusian courtyards, bright blue doors and window frames. The small, intricate iron balconies were adorned with pots of colourful flowers, their perfume filling the night air. The air also thrummed with the energy of people looking to have a good time, their chatter and laughter as intoxicating as the alcohol they've consumed.

We passed the town square, where young pretty women in colourful and extravagant costumes danced flamenco, cheered on by the crowds. The sounds of the dancer's shoes, which had nails driven into their soles, resonated across the square, their rhythmic movements perfectly in step with the guitar music that accompanied them. The women swirled and shook their long, full-flowing skirts with colourful ruffles. Shawls tied around their small waists accentuated the curve of their buttocks, and the dancers' lace-trimmed fans accentuated their hand movements.

I was transfixed. I had been in Spain for less than a day but I felt as if I had come home. It was a sensation I couldn't describe, almost like a sense of belonging.

"I could imagine you dressed and dancing like that," Nathan commented, making me smile even more.

"So could I," I replied wistfully.

As we walked away from the square, I turned back to catch a final glimpse of the dancers. From the corner of my eye, I saw a woman in a floor-length ash-grey coloured dress, her back to me. The same woman from the beach. Again, she seemed to stand out from her environment, like a dark smudge in an otherwise colourful picture, I tried to keep her in sight but she was soon lost in the crowds.

Then the bells rang out from the tower of the church that presided over the square. It had old stone walls and stained glass windows, with a spire that reached the heavens. This church at the centre of the town – at its heart – was lit by floodlights, as if to remind everyone of its importance and the values it represented. The heavy door, fortified with iron bars, was closed and sealed, as if the house of God was beyond our reach at night – but isn't that when we may need God the most? When we are alone and scared and lost in the dark?

Nathan led me down yet another narrow street, filled with numerous tapas bars. Their owners had ingeniously created seating for their establishments in the limited space, with miniature tables and bar tops. The enticing smell of food made my stomach rumble, and we managed to find a free table in one corner of a busy-looking restaurant.

"I don't know about you, but I could eat for England just about now," Nathan stated as we perused the menu.

"Me too. That's what I love about tapas –you get to try a little of everything."

"Well, how about you order for both of us? Let's be adventurous."

An extremely tanned guy, with a mop of black hair, approached us a couple of minutes later to take our order. "*Buenas noches*. What can I get you both for tonight?" he asked us, his voice deep and melodic.

"We'll have some *raciones, por favor*. Croquettes, *calamares*, seared tuna, chips with ham and a mixed salad. *Gracias*."

"Excellent. And to drink?" he enquired.

"We'll have a couple of local beers," Nathan told him.

A few moments later, we were sipping chilled beers with a lemon wedge and helping ourselves to huge green, juicy olives, as we waited for our food to arrive. Latin music filled the small space. It was such a sensational mix of friendly people, which added to the communal atmosphere that could be felt like a beating heart throughout the town.

As we tucked into the delicious food, we talked about the future, the many places we wished to travel to, and our career aspirations. I loved these conversations, especially while away in a foreign land, where everything seems possible and within reach. I've found it is only when you distance yourself from the rat race, from the day to day monotony, that you allow yourself to dream and to focus on what you really want from life.

We drank some more beers and ordered some flan with cream for dessert. We paid the bill and walked back into the heaving streets. We found a cluster of small nightclubs and wandered in and out of them, drinking *sangria* and *mojitos* as we danced to the music. I felt energised by the happiness and laid-back attitude of the people around me. We chatted with numerous people, both locals and other tourists, learning more about the local culture and the activities not to miss out on during our visit.

It was hot inside the Rubix Club, a writhing mass of bodies moving with the beat of the thrumming music. I excused myself from the Dutch couple we were talking with, to get some fresh air, and stepped outside into the cool night. Taking a band from my clutch bag, I tied my hair up in a loose, messy ponytail, allowing the tendrils of curls to cascade freely. From my bag, I also took out some moisturising lip-gloss and applied it generously to my dry lips.

I was just about to go back inside and tell Nathan we could perhaps call it a night, when I saw her again, the young woman in the grey dress. I felt a slight chill run up my spine as I stared at her. She stood at a distance and, once again, she stood with her back to me. I lost her in a crowd of people for a moment, but there she was again, standing a little further away in an empty side street. Before I even realised what I was doing, I was moving towards her, but even though she stood completely still, it seemed as though it was taking too long to close the distance between us.

"Hello – are you OK?" I called out without thinking.

She gave no indication of having heard me, and she remained motionless still staring away from me. *What I am doing? Why am I chasing this stranger? Perhaps she's just the town fruitcake or drug addict – that would explain the heavy clothing at this time of year.*

I hadn't caught a glimpse of her face, but there was something about her that seemed familiar. Perhaps her hair, her build, the way she held herself? I didn't know, but I had seen her three times today already. Granted, Tarifa was not a big town, but it still seemed like one more time too many. And why did she seem so out of place? Something jarred in my mind when I looked at her.

"I don't want to bother you, it's just... I thought you might need some help," I said when I was closer, my voice sounding uncharacteristically loud as it reverberated off the walls.

It was then that I noticed the silence that had enveloped me. I could no longer hear the music blaring from the bars and clubs, or the loud voices of people who had drunk too much. Maybe I had drunk too much, too. I felt like I was moving in a kind of bubble; I couldn't even hear the sound of my own footsteps on the cobbled streets. Even the colours seemed muted, duller, as if the world had suddenly been cast in shades of grey.

I took a few more steps towards her, I was now only a short distance away, but suddenly I felt so cold that I stopped in my tracks, feeling as though my body had been engulfed in a block of ice. It was then that the strange girl began to turn around slowly. All at once, I didn't want to see her, or look upon her face. I was gripped by an inexplicable panic. The air seemed thinner, and I struggled to take a breath. I wanted to turn away and run back to Nathan, put some distance between myself and this strange girl, but I was rooted to the spot and couldn't move.

Something grabbed my arm as I felt myself toppling forwards. As I did so, I caught a glimpse of her face, but the shadows made it look all wrong.

"Hey, *someone*'s drunk too much. I came out looking for you when you didn't come back," Nathan said as he steadied me. "You're shaking – did something happen?"

"No. I think you're right – a little too much alcohol," I answered hurriedly. "I just need to sleep it off... I suddenly feel exhausted."

I glanced at the end of the narrow street, relieved to see that it was deserted.

"Yeah, me too. Let's get a taxi back to the hotel," he said, and I agreed gratefully.

I didn't look back at the empty street as we headed to the taxi rank, but instead focused on the bright colours and sounds in front of me, bringing the world back to life.

Chapter Three

I am lying at the bottom of the sea bed, looking up at the vast, dark waters which enclose and press down upon me. The surface seems too far away, unreachable.

But it doesn't matter, because I am dead.

I know I am dead.

I don't feel the need to breathe and I'm not gripped by heart-wrenching panic. Instead I am calm, floating at the mercy of the ocean and its tides, like the fronds of seaweed which grow around me.

The waters were murky and gloomy in the half-light, but there was something else here with me, something that was swimming towards me…a shark, perhaps? Again I did not react – what did I care if the shark ate me up? There was no life left in me. There was an upside to this: I could no longer feel pain. Instead I would become one with the sea. I longed to be one with the sea…

A bright beam of sunlight flashed across my face and I opened my eyes hesitantly to the morning light. My head throbbed like a bass drum. I sat up in bed gingerly as Nathan continued to open the blinds.

"Morning, gorgeous! I thought you wouldn't want to sleep in too late on our first full day. Here, drink this, and take this," Nathan said softly, as he handed me a glass of water and a couple of paracetamols.

"Thanks – you're a star," I told him as I gratefully took a long gulp of cool water and swallowed down the pills. "I'm thinking I should stick to water today."

"Speaking of water, you sure you're ready to try getting into the sea today? You know there's no rush, right?" he asked, his apprehension evident in his crystal-blue eyes.

"A couple of years ago I would have told you I'd never set foot in the sea, or any large body of water, but seeing Dr Roberts has really helped." I recollected the many images of people in the deep sea he had shown me. "Between the exposure and Morita therapy techniques, I feel I've made great strides. I don't have it half as bad as some of his clients – I've even managed to learn how to swim, so as long as I stay in the shallows I'm sure I'll be fine," I continued with more conviction in my voice than I felt.

I was loathe to admit to Nathan that I had taken mild sedatives during my swimming lessons, but I was committed to doing away with this fear and learning to love the ocean as much as he did.

"I hope you know how proud I am of you, of how far you've come," he said seriously. He sat next to me and kissed me tenderly on the lips.

"I know you are. Perhaps one day I'll be an even better surfer than you," I teased.

I remembered one of our first dates at Nathan's apartment. We had ordered in Chinese food and we were going to sit down to watch a movie together. I wasn't aware that he'd chosen *The Meg*, and our relationship was so new, and I liked him so much, that I didn't want him to think I was some sort of weirdo that would get freaked out by a simple movie.

So, I plonked myself down on the sofa, made excuses to go to the bathroom or make popcorn as often as I could, and tried to look elsewhere – anywhere other than the sea of blue and the enormous shark on the 55-inch flat-screen TV. But as the movie went on I felt myself pale, then begin to sweat. I even felt my legs go weak, and still I said nothing. My heart began to race and I found myself taking in large gulps of air. I decided it was best if I just left the room for a while, but after taking no more than a couple of steps, I became dizzy and fainted. I came round to see Nathan looming over me, his face pale and hair dishevelled, having run his hands through it in panic.

I had had no choice but to come clean and tell him of my aqua-phobia. As with the other few people I had confided in, he asked if I had had a bad experience with water, but I explained that I hadn't. I couldn't really explain the reasons behind the phobia, which made it all the more frustrating, but I guess most people with phobias couldn't explain theirs either. Not all fear can be justified or rationalised. I mean, people are afraid of all sorts of weird things, like buttons, balloons or clowns…although I guess clowns *can* be pretty creepy – we can blame Stephen King for that one.

I tore myself back to the present and had a quick shower, which eased the thrumming of my head and changed into a strapless black swimsuit and yellow sun dress. We headed to the hotel restaurant for breakfast, which was bustling with other guests eager to start their day. The smell of coffee reached my nostrils as we were led to our table on the terrace, which faced picturesque meadows and the mountains of Tarifa, I took a few shots with my camera. The challenge was to capture all this beauty in the limited view of a camera's eye.

Nathan helped himself to a full English breakfast from the buffet. I remembered a quote from some actor: *you can take the boy out of England, but you can't take England out of the boy*, and smiled to myself. I decided on a couple of thick slices of wholemeal bread and drizzled them generously with extra virgin oil, crushed tomatoes and a little sea salt. The coffee was freshly ground and delicious. I took it black and soon felt the caffeine kick in.

I had brought my beach bag with me, so once we were done with breakfast, we headed straight back out to the beach. It was another beautiful day, the sun high in the sky, framed by fluffy white clouds. The wind was calmer and the beach was covered in a blaze of colourful parasols like oversized flowers. The warm sand shifted with every step I took as we made our way to the shore. We walked along the damp sand, past the seaweed and driftwood that had been washed in by the tide. We peeked into rock pools, the cool water lapping at our feet, crabs scuttling to safety in nooks and crannies. I could almost taste the salty air as the seagulls cried and flew over the sun-speckled water.

After about an hour, Nathan went to the wind-surf hire shop and hired a surfboard. I watched as he donned his wetsuit and jogged happily down to the water and jumped in, though not before kissing me profusely and asking if I would be OK on my own. I reassured him that I would be fine and that I would very slowly paddle in myself, and only stay in the shallows so I would be in no danger of drowning.

Once alone, I sat close to the lapping waves, listening to the percussive sounds as rounded stones were rolled up and down the beach. I dug my fingers into the sand as I watched Nathan expertly and powerfully swim further out to where the other surfers lay in wait for the next big wave.

After a few moments, I stood up purposefully and took a couple of steps into the cool blue-green water. I scrunched my toes into the wet sand, grounding myself. I felt a stirring of unease, but this was tempered by the anti-anxiety medication I had taken with breakfast.

The dream of the previous night pervaded my thoughts. I had come to stay right next to the Atlantic Ocean, which stretched on forever into the horizon. It was bound to trigger my fears, no matter how much I thought I had overcome or suppressed them.

I pushed the images of the nightmare away and instead visualised myself swimming in the cool ocean. I imagined myself confident in my strokes and enjoying the feel of the water on my skin as I swam. With only a little hesitation, I took a couple more paces into the shallows, the water now passing my knees. I took deep breaths, allowing my body to adjust to the temperature of the water and begin to relax. I filled my mind with happy thoughts and memories.

With a tiny step or two more, I let my fingers caress the surface of the water. My body thrummed with adrenaline, enticing me to run and flee, but I knew I could do this. I could and I would swim in the sea, much like I had forced myself to learn in the kid's pool. My swimming instructor, Margaret, a strong woman in her fifties, had been patient and understanding with me, even though at times all I could manage was to sit in the water like a heavy stone.

I lower myself slowly, allowing the water to rise over my stomach, now taut with tension, and above my breasts, my nipples turning hard due to the cold, and finally up to my neck. I was now kneeling completely in the shallows.

I let out a long, slow breath and closed my eyes. I allowed my other senses to take over, inhaling the briny smell of the ocean, relishing the feel of the water as it moved around my body, covering every inch of my skin, and listening to the sound of the wind as it blew towards the shore.

Without opening my eyes, I stretched out my arms and began to swim. I swam parallel to the shoreline, calming my mind by telling myself that the seabed was just beneath me and I could stand and walk out whenever I wanted to. After a number of breaststrokes, I opened my eyes. My world was now aquamarine blue as I frog-kicked through the water. I allowed myself to smile. I was doing something I never thought I would be able to do. I began to swim a little faster.

I soon learned that swimming in the sea and swimming in a pool were two very different things. Although I was more buoyant in the salt water, a pool had no cresting waves or currents to swim against. I soon found myself tiring.

With the broadest grin on my face, I stood up and strode out of the water and back onto the warm golden sand. I had done it – I had overcome my irrational fear and swam in the ocean. Not only that, I had loved every second of it. There was a sense of freedom, of weightlessness and abandon, when gliding through the sapphire waters of the wild sea, that a pool simply could not offer.

My euphoria was short-lived, ebbing away as quickly as the sea recedes with the tide. There she was again, that strange young woman in the long dress. She was just standing there, less than thirty metres away, her back to me once more.

I was glad she was facing the ocean. I didn't want to see her face. She continued to exude a sense of sadness and pain. I couldn't explain it, I could only feel it, just as I could feel the sun on my skin. The image of this woman stirred something within me, something I did not wish to examine or explore so I quashed it.

Throughout most of my adult life, I had learned to become a master at suppressing emotions and experiences I did not want to relive. I turned my back on this strange woman and continued to walk down the beach, focusing instead on the beauty of the landscape that surrounded me. A short while later, I heard Nathan calling. I turned round to see him jogging towards me.

"How did you get on, beautiful?" he asked me, placing his cold hands on my hips and kissing me softly.

"Better than I could have hoped for. I mean, I swam –I enjoyed it, and I definitely plan to do it again," I replied unable to suppress a self-satisfied grin.

"Awesome! Maybe next year we could go surfing together?"

"One step at a time, but sure – next year I'll give it a go, just for you!"

"I don't know about you, but I'm starving!" Nathan said, just as his stomach gurgled.

"You're *always* starving." I said, laughing and giving him a playful shove.

"Hey, I'm a growing man who needs constant sustenance. Actually, there seemed to be a nice *chiringuito* by the windsurf shop, wanna check it out?"

"Sure, it will be good to get a break from the sun, too. We don't wanna end up with sunstroke."

It was only just gone 1pm, so the *chiringuito* was busy but not heaving, as it would surely be in an hour or so when the locals had their lunch. We found a small wooden table, shaded by a nearby cluster of palm trees, and took our seats on the green cushioned stools. I ordered us some *gazpacho*, some fried fish and *ensaladilla rusa* Russian salad –which Nathan found peculiar but enjoyed. We rounded off the meal with some mouth-watering, thick slices of watermelon.

We decided to head back to the hotel and have a siesta. We slept for over an hour, then played cards on the shaded terrace until the sun began it's journey to the horizon. The sky held the promise of a beautiful sunset, so we had a quick shower and got dressed for the evening. I wore a blush-pink gypsy skirt and a figure-hugging white laced top, earning me another wolf whistle from Nathan. It was just another of the reasons why I loved this man so much, the way he always made me feel beautiful.

We decided to head back out to the beach before dinner, to watch the sunset. We strolled, arms around each other's waist, along the twilight beach, which was now tinted sepia, the sand more orange than golden and the water darker and less inviting. The mountainous sand dunes rose and fell across the landscape, its hills sculpted by the winds like ocean waves.

We noted the trails of beetles, birds and lizards criss-crossing the sand, evidence of their passing soon to be covered over as if they had never been here at all.

We sat on the crest of a dune, my skirt ruffling in the *levante* wind that blew from the east, to watch the rich red hues blend with the orange, purple and pomegranate pink that dyed the sky. The horizon stretched into the distance as if into eternity, as if time no longer mattered here. I watched the line where Heaven touched the earth. Sunsets heralded the promise of a new day, full of possibilities, of another day of life. As the minutes ticked by, the mauve of the sky intensified, then darkened to give way to thousands of stars and to highlight the brightness of the moon.

We kissed under the night sky and whispered words of love and promises of a lifetime together. I could not recall ever being as happy as I was in that moment. The winds rustled through the tall grass of the sand dunes like hushed whispers, but then I heard a voice in the murmur.

The voice was both simultaneously familiar yet unknown, carried in the wind like fallen petals. At first I could only hear the faintest of melodies but then the words became clearer, reminding me of a lullaby which I hadn't heard in many, many years and which threatened to bring tears to my eyes.

Duermete mi nina, de mi corazon, ya no llores mas,
Duermete ya, que viene el cuco y te comera,
La, la, la... la, la...

It was the same lullaby my nanny had sang to me as a child. My father, unable to cope with me or Helena after my mother's death, had soon hired a nanny, Dolores, to look after us. She was in her fifties, which at the time seemed ancient to me, and she had a big bosom and a heart to match. From the Spanish she had taught me and from what I remembered, the words translated as:

Sleep now my child, love of my life, don't you cry no more,
Sleep now, for the bogeyman this way comes and will eat you up.
La, la, la... la, la...

I had thought the tune was hauntingly beautiful as a child. When I hadn't understood the words, I even found it soothing.

Now, not so much.

Reluctantly, I pulled away from Nathan's embrace and scanned the dunes behind me. I could see no one in the gloom. The trees behind us stood like watchmen against the night sky. The landscape I had so adored and admired during the light of day now seemed threatening and unwelcoming. A suddenly inhospitable place where dangers lurked.

"What's wrong, Beth?" Nathan asked.

"Just thought I heard someone."

By his blank expression I knew he hadn't heard anything.

"Why don't we go get some food?" I said. "I'm feeling a little chilly, actually."

"Sure, you know me—"

"I know – always hungry!" I finished for him with a laugh.

We stood up and headed back down the beach, across the darkened shoreline, our footprints swallowed up by the surf. We were just about to walk up the beach, to cut through the pine forests onto the main road, when something caught my eye. I stopped and squinted at the now black waves, the cold water lapping at my toes.

There.

There it was again.

Something glinted in the shallows: a flash of red in the silver moonlight. I took a few steps further into the water, the swash and backwash of the tide obscuring my view, leaving a foamy trail on the damp sand.

"Whatcha doing, hun?" Nathan asked.

"Nothing. I just thought I saw something—"

I caught another quick glimpse of red, and quickly shot my arm into the water, putting my entire hand around the object. As I stepped back and opened my hand, seawater and sand fell away to reveal a gold ring, adorned with a single large crimson ruby. It was old and had clearly spent many years in the sea, but it was beautiful.

"What'd you find?" Nathan enquired, peering into my open palm. "Wow – well spotted! It looks old and expensive too"

I could barely speak. The waves rolled onto the shore, their sound like a drumbeat that echoed the pounding of my heart. I lifted the ring, almost reverently, and placed it onto my index finger on my right hand. It fit perfectly. The ruby stone was radiant, like a speck of blood in the bleached moonlight.

Chapter Four

The next day, we decided to go on a whale-watching tour. We had spent the previous evening at a quaint tavern we had discovered just off the main road, where we had feasted on fresh grilled fish and sliced potatoes drizzled in olive oil and green peppers, accompanied by plenty of crisp white wine. That morning we had had another hearty breakfast before setting out towards the old town and down to the port to be picked up by the boat.

I was looking forward to the trip and hoped we would catch sight of some whales. I had my camera at the ready and longed to see and capture the beauty of the marine life in the area. In the past I had always stayed clear of boats, when I had allowed fear to rule my life, but that was before. Now I was determined to embrace the sea and all it had to offer. Still, I had taken an anti-anxiety tablet with breakfast, and I would most definitely not take off my life jacket for the whole trip, but my sense of unease was manageable.

The boat sailed a few kilometres from the coast. It was packed full of tourists who jostled to get the best seats. Nathan and I found a good spot on the top deck and settled in for the ride, my eyes scanning the horizon for signs of life.

The sun shone on the water, creating a pale band of shimmering light. There are only fourteen kilometres of sea dividing Tarifa from Africa, and I stared at the Atlas Mountains, which seemed to float on a white bed of low-lying cloud.

Around the Straits of Gibraltar, where the Mediterranean Sea meets the Atlantic Ocean, we spotted three minke whales, a breathtaking sight as they rose up from the deep blue to breathe, and a large pod of bottlenose dolphins, which surfed the bow waves the boat created. This was the way people should experience whales and dolphins, in the wild, in their natural habitat, not kept imprisoned in tanks and concrete pools.

When we sailed closer to Tangier, we even saw orcas, which were following the migratory routes of tuna fish. I even managed to get a few good shots of the huge tuna as they raced to escape.

Three hours later, and with more than a hundred new photos in my camera's SD card, the boat docked into port again. We had lunch within the ancient city walls, in a tiny pizzeria with a wood burning stove and pints of pear cider.

As we left the small establishment and continued along Tarifa's characteristically narrow streets, past the charming jumble of shops and secret corners, we came across an elderly woman selling her wares on the street. She sat on a small hessian-covered stool, and before her lay a navy-blue cloth covered in bracelets and other colourful trinkets.

I picked out a brown leather plaited strap bracelet for Nathan, which suited his surfer look and his now tanned skin.

I reached into my purse and brought out a ten-euro note, handing it to the ancient lady, who sat hunched over, her face covered by a white laced shawl. She raised her eyes to meet mine, her aged face wrinkled and weathered by the sun. She gave a small nod and reached to take the proffered money, but then stopped midway, staring at my hand.

The ruby glowed cardinal red in the brilliant sunshine. The night before, I had cleaned up the ring as best as I could and placed it on my finger as soon as I was out of the shower.

"*Ese anillo no es para ti!*" the old woman hissed at me.

She quickly withdrew her arm and shrunk away.

"I'm sorry—" I uttered, unsure of what had just happened, and a little shocked by the venom in her voice.

"Away. Away, go!" She shooed me off, waving her arms frantically.

I was so embarrassed to see other people turn round to look at us, wondering what the commotion was about, that I stepped away quickly and let myself be swallowed up by the crowd not even sure where Nathan was. It was only when I'd made it to the end of the street that I realised I still held the bracelet in my hand.

"What was that all about?" Nathan asked when he'd caught up with me.

"I have no idea, I think she said something about the ring. Something about it not being mine or not for me... At least, something like that."

"Maybe it was hers?" Nathan joked.

"God knows. Finders keepers, as they say. I love this ring. It may have belonged to someone else before, but now it's mine," I said, feeling strangely possessive about it. "Oh, I got you a bracelet – well, I guess I stole it," I added, handing it to him.

"Thanks, I guess." he said, laughing softly, then putting it on. He checked his watch. "We've got about another hour before we're picked up at the hotel for cheese and wine tasting."

"Yum, I'm looking forward to that!" I replied, the incident with the old woman already fading from my mind.

I stared out at the rippling sea from the hotel room's balcony. The sun was beginning to drift towards the horizon, setting the landscape aglow in an array of oranges and reds. I could hear the hoot of an owl and the high pitched squeak of bats as they prepared to hunt at dusk.

We had had an amazing afternoon together, sampling glasses of delicious red wines from vineyards from all over the country, from Galicia, Catalonia, Aragon and Andalusia, accompanied by a selection of delectable fresh cheeses and Iberian hams.

We had been given a tour around a beautiful hacienda surrounded by rolling hills, vineyards, olive and orange groves, and deciduous woodlands. We had been shown the wine-making process from start to finish, as well as how the various cheeses were aged to perfection. The large and stunningly beautiful white-washed hacienda had stood proudly on the mountain top, as if watching over its lands.

As the hours ticked by and we were allowed to wander freely around the grounds, I took various photographs, attempting to capture the beauty of a tradition and livelihood which has remained largely unchanged for centuries.

I felt at ease here, with a sense of belonging I hadn't experienced until I had met Nathan. I loved Bristol, but living there reminded me of everything I had spent years trying to suppress and forget. Perhaps that was why I yearned to see the world, so I could be someone else and part of something else, far away from where I began.

After a quick shower back at the hotel, and now dressed in a cream lace maxi dress and rose-gold sandals, I sat out on the balcony and enjoyed the stillness and coolness of the night. I could hear the water running as Nathan had his shower.

A short while later, he joined me. In his hand he held a small box. It was a lovely turquoise colour – a shade I recognised instantly. Without preamble, Nathan got down on one knee and opened up the Tiffany & Co. box, to reveal a stunning three stone engagement ring in platinum. Even in the light of dusk it shone resplendently. Before I could utter a word, Nathan took hold of my hand in his.

"Beth, the three years we have been together have been the best years of my life. Since the day we met, you have been it for me. I couldn't imagine my life without you, and whatever life has in store for us, I know I want you by my side as my wife. Will you marry me?"

For a few moments I was speechless. All I could do was stare at his earnest face and the wonderful ring he had picked out for me. We had, of course, spoken of getting married before, as I'm sure many young couples do, but never too seriously. We were so young still, and had so much to learn and discover... but we would do that better together. I felt that deep down we were meant to be. No one else would ever come close to Nathan, in my eyes.

"Nathan... Yes – a million times yes. Of course I will marry you!" I exclaimed, kissing him. I felt I could laugh but also cry at the intensity of my feelings.

"Thank God for that. I think the rest of the holiday would have been more than a little awkward if you'd said no," he joked.

Nathan took the precious ring out of the box and slipped it onto my ring finger. I hugged him close, and soon we forgot all about dinner and returned to bed together. Slowly and teasingly, we removed each other's clothes and made love. We fell asleep naked, our bodies intertwined and our lust satiated.

I am walking barefoot through orange groves. It is night-time, the darkness thick as if cast by an evil enchantress. Pale stars fill the night sky but provide little light, so it is only by the cold silver beam of moonlight that I make my way through the rows of trees. The wind is like icy fingers on my skin, penetrating through my cloak. My feet are numb as they step on the sparse grass, which appeared black. My hair falls loose about my face, tousled and tangled, and I push it away. I pull the hood of my cloak further over my face.

I move languidly through the crepuscular world which surrounds me. In the distance, on top of the hillside, a magnificent pale white hacienda seems to glow against the backdrop of the night sky. Here amongst the groves I am free to do as I please.

A twig snaps.

I turn around in surprise. The trees, which had previously seemed to offer me protection and cover, now seem alien and hostile.

I am no longer alone. Someone else is out here lurking in the darkness.

Following me.

My footsteps quicken on the hard, cool earth as I hurry towards the house on the hill. The flames from the torches on its exterior act like beacons, whether in warning or to welcome me back, I can no longer be sure.

Whoever is out here with me hastens too.

My heart beats faster as I glance around, but whoever is here with me remains hidden.

I instinctively feel that I am in danger and that I need to get back. The other person somehow senses I am going to run and, before I manage to break away, a cold, slim hand encircles my wrist tightly, and—

I woke up suddenly, my heart racing and sweat prickling my skin. The dream had been so vivid and disorienting that it took me a few moments to realise I was lying in bed in our hotel room. I glanced to my right to see Nathan sleeping on his front, snoring softly, his tanned torso exposed. I welcomed the cool breeze that streamed in through the open window. Moonlight created a diffuse glow in the room, much as it had done in the dream. I stared at the ceiling, watching the shadows until the night surrendered and the light of dawn filled the room.

The next morning, a strong wind was blowing, the sea a mix of blue-grey and white, the waves tempestuous as they smashed onto the seashore. The kite-surfers and wind-surfers were out in full force, like birds of paradise filling the sky with a multitude of colours. It was a good day for surfing, and my fiancé kissed me lightly and strode off confidently into the turbulent waters, the board held under his arm.

I laid out my towel, then took my Kindle from my beach bag and continued reading the book I had started on the plane, *A Mother's Confession* by Kelly Rimmer. It was my first book by this author and I was hooked. Before I got stuck in again, I applied a generous amount of sunscreen, aware that on breezy, cloudy days, you can very easily get burned without even realising it. I laid back and tapped away, page after page. The protagonist had lost her husband and was struggling to cope, and also had a child to look after.

Even though I didn't want to, I couldn't help but think whether my father had struggled as much, when my mother passed away. He must have done, because Dolores was soon in our lives to help raise Helena and me.

Perhaps it was because I was far away from home, or perhaps it was due to the story I was immersed in, that I peeked into the chest in which I had securely locked away most of my childhood. For so many years, I'd tried to act as if I'd miraculously appeared from thin air as an eighteen-year-old, fully grown woman at university. As if I could somehow start my life from a point of my choosing.

But there is no peeking into Pandora's Box without all hell breaking loose. I was eight years old when my mother died. I wished I had more memories of her. The ones I did have were faded and blurry, like an overexposed photograph, too bright and lacking in distinguishable detail.

It was my fault she was dead.

Tears stung my eyes and I felt my chest constrict – but I wouldn't do this now. Not now, not ever. No matter how much you want to, you cannot change the past. It is what it is, and the scars of the past are mine to bear until the day I die.

I switched off my Kindle, placed it back in the bag, and stood up to face the sea. I allowed myself to be mesmerised by the movement and ever-changing hues of the waves as they crashed rhythmically into the shallow. The turbulent sea mirrored my thoughts and, before I had a chance to talk myself out of it, I began walking towards it.

The surf splashed forcibly against my legs as I took step after step into the water, which sucked at my feet hungrily, pulling back to prepare for another onslaught of rolling waves. I felt a flutter of panic rise in my chest, like a bird struggling to take flight. I may have learned how to swim in a swimming pool, but I was by no means a strong swimmer. Also, in a pool you don't have to worry about rip currents.

I stopped when the water reached my mid-thigh, fear preventing me from going any further. I was proud of how far I'd come. I might never be fully comfortable in the sea, but at least I could enjoy it, be part of it and so be part of something bigger than myself. I only wished I could overcome my past as easily as I had overcome my fear of the ocean. But I was slowly coming to realise that, as William Faulkner once said, *The past is never dead. It's not even past.*

Over the rush of the ocean waves, I thought I could hear a soft voice, singing. I felt coldness spread across my body.

The song was like the lullaby I had heard the other night whilst on the dunes, the one from my childhood.

Sleep now my child, love of my life, don't you cry no more,
Sleep now, for the bogeyman this way comes and will eat you up.
La, la, la... la, la...

I turned to face the beach, but there was no one close by. The wind had kept most of the other beachgoers in the shelter of the sand dunes. The song faded in and out with the ebb and flow of the sea, like a badly tuned radio, haunting and melancholy, yet so light I could make myself believe I was simply imagining it. I turned back to the sea, trying to make out Nathan from the other surfers clad in wetsuits.

Something brushed against my leg. I looked down, expecting to see a piece of seaweed, or worse, the tendrils of a jellyfish – but it was something much more awful than that.

I cried out as a hand, as white as a bride's gown, circled around my ankle. My stomach clenched painfully, as my gaze trailed over the hand, along its arm and into the *face* that stared up at me from below the surface of the water.

I barely registered the long tattered dress that floated around the figure that lay beneath the water. In that moment, as she fixed her eyes on me, the rest of the world ceased to exist. There was no doubt in my mind —at least, in the small part of my mind that wasn't frozen in terror —that this was the woman I had been seeing since my first day on the beach. Now, for the first time I laid eyes on her face properly, and immediately wished I could *un-see* it.

Her bloodless face, skin stretched across her skull, sallow and wax-like, was slightly distorted by the swirling waves. I couldn't move. Her hair floated around her like a grotesque halo. Her thin blue lips pressed firmly closed. Her eyes were those of a cadaver, the corneas blue-white and opaque.

As she stared at me, her formerly expressionless face morphed into hate and spite as the grip around my ankle intensified. It was the pain that propelled me to move – I stepped back forcefully with my free leg, trying to wrench myself away from her and out of the water.

But the dead thing would not let me go so easily. Instead, as if angry that I had dared to flee, she pulled me under. In shock, I barely had time to close my mouth, as I swallowed mouthfuls of salty water which burned my throat. Despair flared across my whole body.

I could feel her decaying hands and body climb across my own as she pressed me down to the seabed. I opened my eyes and she stared at me from mere inches away.

I was actually going to drown in a metre of water.

I closed my eyes. I couldn't bear to look at her face any longer and instead flailed at her with my arms and legs – but she was too strong. Maybe I had been right to fear the water after all. Perhaps this sense of foreboding had stemmed from a premonition of my death.

Abruptly, strong, muscular arms grabbed me beneath my own arms and pulled me up from under the water. I sputtered and gulped air, my body shaking as I began to cry. Nathan hoisted me into his arms, much like someone might hold a child, carrying me out of the water and putting me down smoothly on the warm sand.

"Jesus, Beth are you OK? I was making my way towards you when I saw you got swept in... The currents are too strong. You really shouldn't try to go swimming today."

Nathan told me gently as he wiped the hair carefully away from my face.

He then placed both hands on my arms as he gazed down at me. I couldn't respond. I was too stunned to speak; all I could do was tremble as tears continued to work their way down my face. Nathan looked as panicked as I felt. If he hadn't been so close, I don't know how I would have made it out of the water.

"It's OK, Beth. I got you. Don't worry, it's OK," he murmured soothingly as he wrapped me in a hug.

I wanted to speak, to tell him what I had seen, but would he think I was crazy? That my misgivings of the ocean had resulted in my distressed mind conjuring something that couldn't possibly exist? I couldn't risk alienating him, I couldn't risk him finding out who I really was. If he knew, he would walk away from me forever.

I felt another jolt of fear course through my mind. I checked my hands but was relieved to note that both rings were still safely on my fingers and hadn't been lost to the sea. As the sun emerged from behind a cloud, the diamonds glittered beautifully on one hand, as did the scarlet ruby on the other.

Chapter Five

The last few days of the holiday passed in a blur of walks on the beach, *sangria,* copious amounts of food, sun and sex. I only ventured back into the water with Nathan. I'd given him quite a scare, so he was more than happy to stay close as I took quick dips in the sea to cool down from the unrelenting heat.

I didn't see that woman again, and if I did have dreams, I didn't remember them, for which I was thankful. We had made the most of our week away, but before I knew it, we were back in the rental car, driving away from the windswept landscape of Tarifa and towards Malaga airport.

I watched the sea until we reached the motorway. There was something special about this place, not just because Nathan had proposed to me here, but something that tugged at me, something which I couldn't quite explain.

The motorway was busy with both tourists and locals. I connected my phone to the car's audio system and played the soundtrack from *The Greatest Showman,* both of us singing along. Neither of us could actually hold a tune to save our lives, something we often laughed about.

At the airport we checked in our luggage and headed towards security, then through to the departure gate. As the plane took off, I allowed myself a final glance at the endless sea, the sun shining upon it like liquid gold, and then I closed my eyes and rested my head against the seat back.

The image of the face I'd seen in the water flooded my mind, suppressing everything else. I grabbed the armrest and forced her away, deep into the recesses of my mind, to dwell with all my other unwanted recollections.

"Honey, you OK?" Nathan asked, taking in my face which must be pale.

"Yep, sure, just a little travel sickness," I replied, forcing a weak smile.

"Here, have some water –you may just be a little dehydrated."

As soon as the seatbelt sign had been turned off, I stood and walked to the bathroom facilities at the back of the plane. I splashed cold water on my face and stared at my reflection. For a split second I felt I wasn't the only one staring back at me, and the small space suddenly felt claustrophobic.

I rushed back to my seat and took a sleeping tablet, even though it was only early afternoon. Around twenty minutes later I had dozed off, with Nathan's hand in mine. A couple of hours later, we touched down in Bristol Airport. I was a little groggy, but happy to have slept through most of the flight.

We picked up my car from the car park and headed towards our rented apartment in Sunningdale, Clifton. I loved our flat. It had been a new build when we moved in, giving us the opportunity to decorate it in our own style. The owner was a good friend of Nathan's dad, Alex, and it was Alex who had let us know that this place was available.

It was a compact two-bedroom home, with an open plan kitchen and living room, one large family bathroom, an en-suite in the master bedroom, and a tiny terrace which overlooked the street. We had painted most of the walls dove grey, our bedroom in a light mauve, and I had decorated with throws, pillows and colourful curtains.

We lumbered in with our suitcases, unpacked and loaded the washing machine. I then took a long, hot shower, as travelling always made me feel icky and I was keen to wash away the day and slip into my cosy flannel pyjamas.

Once dressed, I took some garlic bread from the freezer and placed it in the oven, then boiled some pumpkin ravioli and drizzled olive oil and chopped walnuts on top. A quick but satisfying dinner. Tomorrow I would have to go do a big food shop. I was inspired to try and recreate some of the mouth watering dishes we had tried in Spain. This made me recall how Dolores would make us *gazpacho* soup in the summer, and Spanish omelettes stuffed with peppers and onions when we wanted some comfort food.

I didn't think of Dolores often. It wasn't that I had bad memories of her necessarily –after all, she had helped raise me and my sister – it was just that in thinking of her, I couldn't help but think of my mother.

I had always thought Dolores' name peculiar: *dolores* meant pain and sorrow. I recalled once asking her why her mother had named her so. She had replied that her mother had told her that her birth had been terrible and excruciating, lasting for almost 36 hours, but that she had chosen her name because of the Virgin Mary of Sorrows. Her name was a reference to the love that Mary felt for her crucified son and of the love a mother feels for her child, which is the greatest love that exists.

Her response had only left me questioning if my mother had loved *me* like that. Or whether, in her final moments, she wished she could have chosen her life over mine, and in that way at least she would still have had Helena, her favourite child. I know parents say they don't have a favourite child but I don't believe this. Helena was both my parent's favourite, this hurt all the more because Helena and I were identical twins.

I sat down and picked at my ravioli, my unhappy thoughts ruining my appetite. After Nathan and I had cleared up the dishes, we sat down to watch some TV. We scrolled through a number of channels but could find nothing we wanted to see, and in the end just settled on the comedy channel and watched re-runs of *Impractical Jokers*. Nathan loved the show, and often watched a couple of episodes to unwind after a particularly hard or serious day at the office.

On this night, I was in no mood for such trivial entertainment; my thoughts were too dark. I told Nathan I was heading off to bed for an early night. I kissed him goodnight and curled up in bed alone in a foetal position, much as I did as a child. Once it finally came for me, I welcomed the deep oblivion of sleep.

The sound of rain tapping lightly on my window stirred me

awake. Reluctantly, I opened my eyes as soft grey light filtered through the narrow gaps in the blinds. I reached over and was surprised to find the bed empty. My fingers touched upon a small piece of paper; I picked it up and read the note aloud.

"Went to the office early. Didn't wanna wake you, you looked so beautiful. Will try not to be back too late, your fiancé xx"

I loved these little notes from Nathan. They reminded me of our early dating days, when we would leave messages for each other around the flat, in our chocolate stash, pinned on the fridge, on the sofa. Just silly little things like *Have a good day, I'll miss you* or *There's a piece of cottage pie in the fridge with your name on it.* They felt so much more personal than a text message. I'd never told him, but I kept every single note he'd ever left me, in a cardboard box at the back of the wardrobe, along with birthday cards, torn tickets to movies or plays we'd seen, and, most recently, our plane ticket stubs. It was like a little time capsule of our relationship, one I envisaged us shifting through when we were old and grey.

I traced my fingers lightly over the word fiancé. On the night he had proposed, Nathan had called home to tell his parents, his sister and his best friend Sebastian, that we were engaged. I could hear their voices over the line, offering us their congratulations, their joy and love for Nathan obvious.

It's the normal thing to do, isn't it? To share good news with the ones you love. Especially when the big stuff in life happens, like getting engaged. I didn't call anyone. I had told myself I would simply let them know once I was back home, but I knew I wouldn't call my father or Helena today, or even Sam. I would let them know if and when the opportunity arose. After all, there was no rush – it wasn't as if we were planning to get married next month or anything. Also, it's easier to share good news with people you know will be genuinely happy for you. Sam I guessed would be thrilled but I figured my father would probably be pleased for me, but pleased isn't quite the same as happy, is it?

I don't have what you would call a close relationship with my father. When my mother's body was placed six feet underground, it was like part of him was buried alongside her; the better part. All that remained was a husk, a shadow of the man he had once been. He threw himself into his work to survive, whilst Helena and I struggled to keep going, feeling almost like orphans.

I wish I could say that our lonely childhoods had made Helena and I even closer, but that would be a lie. I thought of Helena, which was something I tried to do as little as possible, but childhood memories rose to the surface of my mind like pieces of driftwood. The time she pushed me down the slide whilst I was still standing at its precipice and I fell, the time she pulled the head off my favourite doll. The time she tore my homework book to shreds, the time she yelled at me that she hated me and that she wished I had died instead of our mother. One of the worst memories was when I found my kitten in the bathtub, water trickling over the sides, the sound of each drip on the tiled floor as loud as gunshots.

I shook my head forcefully at that last recollection, surmising that Helena probably wouldn't care if I was engaged or not and that was fine. I was no longer a child, and neither was Helena, and my mother had been dead for almost twenty years. The past was in the past, and I refused to be a prisoner of it.

I treated myself to a few more minutes in bed, allowing the soothing sound of the rain on the window to ease my troubled thoughts. Then I got out of bed and went straight into the shower, allowing the slightly-too-hot water to cascade over my skin. I needed to wake up and get on with my day.

I towel dried my hair and applied some leave in conditioner, running my hairdryer over it for a couple minutes before allowing it to dry naturally. I dressed in my comfiest pair of jeans and trainers and a light sweater. After a quick breakfast of whole-wheat cereal, I grabbed my camera bag and handbag, and headed out into the streets of Bristol.

I was currently working on a new project. One I had been hired to do by the Water-Well Media Centre, as part of its latest concept for its next exhibition, succinctly titled *The Old and the New*. The theme sought to explore and showcase the contrast, or equally the harmony, between modern life and the past within the city of Bristol. I had decided to focus my contribution to the project on churches and contrast them with the new, ultra-modern architecture popping up around the city: a juxtaposition between modern life against that of centuries-old religion. Bristol's architecture included medieval, Gothic, modern industrial and post-war construction, and there was no short supply of churches.

I was standing on College Green, outside Bristol's beautiful cathedral, which had stood for over a thousand years and I decided, a great place to start my assignment.

Narrow shafts of sunlight pierced the greyness of cloud cover above, the shifting light levels served to deepen every hue, lending a boldness to the scene, which emphasised the Cathedral's vertical lines, characteristic of Gothic architecture and the large, ornate stained-glass windows.

I took numerous shots from the outside. It was such a large building that it was difficult to capture all of its beauty in a single composition, but I hoped to create a collage, using photos taken at different times of the day and in various weather conditions, to highlight how the world may change around it but the church always stood in defiance of time.

One particularly good image was that of a policeman on horseback, a typical sight around Bristol's city centre, against the stone wall of the church: the new and the old. The green tones of the grass and foliage served as splashes of colour against the tall horse's black flank and crest. The horse neighed gently at me several times before the policeman turned and they cantered off towards the waterfront.

It began to drizzle – lightly at first, just a raindrop on my hand and forehead, but then with more force, and I decided to take my work indoors. The beauty found within the cathedral always made me pause.

Today it was almost empty, quieter and seemed graver somehow; perhaps it was just the bleak weather. Such architecture inspired awe; awe at what man could create, and of history itself, which seemed to permeate from its walls, if only they could tell what they had witnessed over centuries. I lost myself, viewing the world through my camera lens, taking in the columns, arches and buttresses, which dwarfed me. I took shots upwards towards the ceiling, the columns rising up from the lower corners of the frame so as to draw the eye upward, a sense of motion captured in a still frame, highlighting the symmetry. The mid-morning light, although weak, painted the interior in a rainbow of colours from the stained glass. The angled light cast patterned shadows across the vaulted ceilings. The images I was capturing were beautiful and I couldn't help but be pleased.

In the chapter house, a Romanesque build dating from the 1100s, I focused on the intricate, patterned carvings. The sculptures of beasts dressed as people within the elder lady chapel caught my attention. I looked at my watch, surprised that I had spent a whole two hours wandering around inside the cathedral. I had taken over a hundred shots, which would be more than enough to make a start. I'd take a closer look at them on my computer back home.

I stepped outside. The sun continued to break through the clouds. The chinks of sunlight reflected from puddles and glistening pavements. I put my camera away and thought about taking the bus home to save time. As I headed towards the nearest bus stop, I stopped mid-step.

There in the distance, standing out from the rest of the crowd, stood a woman in a grey dress with her back towards me, staring at something I couldn't see.

I told myself it couldn't possibly be the same woman I had seen on the beach in Tarifa… but I knew it was. The floor-length dress, the pale skin of her arms, her slim frame and long auburn-brown hair, were unmistakable. Here, too, she did not fit in with the rest of her surroundings, like she belonged in another space and time. It didn't seem real. Had she been following me all this time?

I wanted to confront her, to demand to know what the hell she was playing at. I entertained the chilling notion that if I walked towards her, I'd never catch up with her, as if we were playing inside some demented Fun House of mirrors.

But equally I never wanted to lay eyes on her face ever again.

I recalled the incident in the water, the hand reaching out, grabbing me and pulling me under – and suddenly I was back there again. All the familiar feelings of panic, fear of the water and terror of drowning, overwhelmed me. I could feel the blood drain from my face as my skin broke out in sweat and my heart raced faster. Before the panic attack escalated further I turned away from her and began to run.

Chapter Six

I ran all the way home without looking back, the thought that *she* may be right behind me keeping me from slowing down. I was breathing so heavily by the time I made it up to our flat, I felt like throwing up. I had also been caught in a downpour and was now soaked through.

My wet feet squelched as I stepped inside and closed the door behind me. I ran to the bathroom and dry heaved over the toilet. When I was sure I wasn't going to be sick, I stripped off my wet clothes, placed them in the washing machine and set it on a quick wash. I felt chilled, as if I'd swam through arctic waters.

It couldn't possibly be the same woman. She just happened to look familiar, and even if it was some freakish coincidence that I had seen this woman in a beach in Tarifa and then in the streets of Bristol, so what? The only thing it proved was that we lived in a far smaller world than we realised.

Maybe I had just been pulled in by the current that day in the sea, and my mind had conjured up the image of this woman in my distress, because I had seen her on a number of occasions. This idea didn't really convince me, but it was better than believing that the woman was some sort of walking corpse that only I could see. Yet there was something not quite right with her, and for some reason, she unnerved me on a level I couldn't quite explain, an echo of a primeval instinct which signalled danger.

I was still trembling so I took another shower, so hot it scalded my skin, but I welcomed the pain: it grounded me. Once I felt calmer, I turned off the water, dried every inch of my skin and put on navy leggings and a warm sweater. I caught a glimpse of myself in the hallway mirror as I walked past. My eyes looked too wide and my face too pale.

I counted to ten and breathed in and out slowly, as my therapist had told me to do in order to help control my thoughts, rather than allow my thoughts to control me. In the kitchen I opened the fridge, its near emptiness reminding me that doing the shopping had been a top priority for the day. I nabbed a digestive biscuit from the tin to keep me going, and grabbed my car keys and handbag and made my way out of the flat and onto the tree-lined street.

My car was parked just a few metres away, a VW Golf in metallic blue and black leatherette interior. It had been a graduation gift from my father. It was extravagant and I had hesitated in accepting it at the time, but when you are a freelance photographer, being mobile is a must, especially when working outside of the city. It was also my father's way of providing for me and trying to make up for his *absent* years.

I think part of him loved me, and I hoped he knew I loved him. Maybe in another life, one in which my mother was still alive, I may have been able to experience this love, but she was dead – did he blame me for what happened? I had been too young and too afraid to ask.

I drove to ASDA near Cribbs Causeway, and for over an hour allowed myself to wander slowly around the aisles, focusing only on food. I loaded the trolley with plenty of fresh fruit and vegetables, bread, bags of mixed salad, chicken, fish, turkey meatballs, as well as some chocolate treats. After a week away from the office, I knew Nathan would be home late tonight, and I wanted to prepare a nice meal for whatever time he managed to get home.

I played music loudly in the car as I drove back. The holiday and Nathan's proposal had stirred up feelings and memories within me that I had worked very hard to forget, so I made myself focus on driving and nothing else. I needed to banish the shadows that lived in the periphery of my life.

Once I got home, I put all the groceries away and popped out again to pick up Nathan's dry cleaning. It was a short walk away but I decided to take the car, due to the weather and the fact I had at least three suits to pick up. Dry cleaning suits for work was an expensive business, but we shared all our expenses and we were doing OK – plus, I loved how good Nathan looked in a suit.

That thought inevitably led me to think about our wedding day, of Nathan in his suit with a single Calla lily on his lapel. Although we had become engaged, we hadn't actually spoken much about the actual wedding. We had been too engrossed in enjoying the holiday to think of the future. Also, we were both only twenty-five, so there wasn't any rush. In the little we had talked about the subject of kids, I knew

Nathan wanted them, at least two. He had a great relationship with his grandparents, his parents and his sister, so I guessed it was only normal he would want that for himself. He would make a good dad too, I knew that, but not all of us are fortunate enough to have that kind of TV-perfect family life growing up. Some of us know only too well, that behind some closed doors lies a unique hell masquerading as family.

And just like that, just as I had laid the suits out neatly on the back seat, a navy blue one, a black and a grey suit with fine white lines, and began the journey home, the recollection I had tried my hardest to consign to oblivion escaped. It bloomed across my mind's eye like a field of red poppies in spring.

My father is at the wheel; we are driving back home after a long day at the seaside. I had scraped my shin quite badly falling down by the beach groyne, cutting it on a sharp rock. Helena had pushed me. My new yellow sun dress was now dirtied, my white socks tinged with blood that trickled down my leg.

Helena had demanded to bring home the stick she had been playing with, and every once in a while she hit the stick against my open wound.

Thwack, thwack, thwack.

The blood had dried in parts but still glistened in others.

Thwack, thwack, thwack.

I told Helena to cut it out. Mother was having another migraine and had laid her head against the cool glass of the car window —our afternoon had been cut short. The sound of the car radio as Lionel Richie belted out that they *were running with the night*, filled the car. It didn't help Mother with her headache but helped to drown out Helena and me.

Helena was mad. Mad at me. She glared at me, her face a mirror of mine. Strangers often could not tell us apart, but Mother always could. I wonder what the expression on my face had been.

Thwack, thwack, thwack.

"Stop it!" I yelled finally.

The smile she had given me as she replied, nonplussed, "Have I hurt you Beth? I was only playing," still shocked me.

Helena had turned away from me then, smiling out of the window. I could see her reflection in the glass. The green and brown shades of the trees and hedgerows blended together as the car whipped past. I flipped like a metaphorical switch and yanked myself free from the seatbelt and lunged, clawing at her.

"I have had it up to here with you, Beth!" my father bellowed. "You will learn to behave or so help me God!"

"Beth, get back into your seat and leave your sister alone!" my mother said angrily, but with a tinge of weariness. Her hand was clasped to her eye socket as if she could press the pain away.

"I was only playing." Helena repeated softly, with a venom I had never heard before and which I would have thought her incapable of displaying.

Her eyes had been filled with hate and her words continued to fan the flames that had ignited within me. I wanted to simply tear her to pieces. My mother had had enough of us fighting. She undid her seat belt and reached into the back seat, gripping me so forcefully by the arm that it hurt, and a bruise bloomed there the next day. Mother wrenched me back into my seat and managed to slap me hard across the face. I sat stunned as she ordered me to keep still and put my seatbelt back on.

My father turned to face me. "I am tired of having the same talk with you, Beth, over and over again. I will send you away! You hear me? You carry on like this and I will have no choice but to—"

But he never finished that sentence.

In his anger, he had lost focus on the road ahead and veered onto oncoming traffic. It was bad luck, really. It had been an almost empty stretch of road, other than the cargo truck carrying hundreds of pounds of timber that had just turned onto the lane.

The car was written off. My father, Helena and I walked away with a just a few scratches and bruises. Perhaps my mother would have done, too, if she had been wearing her seatbelt. The impact, even at a reduced speed as both vehicles hit the brakes, sent her crashing against the windshield.

And that is how I killed my mother.

I could barely focus on driving; there was more of me in the past than in the present. Thankfully, I was almost home and managed to park the car at the end of our street. I sat, staring but unseeing, as the heavens opened up again and rain pounded onto the roof of the car. I had done such a great job at building walls around the past that when something seeped through the cracks it hit me like a battering ram.

This wasn't my fault. We exist in a culture in which we try

to avoid unpleasant emotions at all costs, in which our social media platforms are filled with happy, fun-filled snapshots of our perfect lives. If we are not happy we are failing – failing at life, falling behind... no one wants to fall behind. And how do people escape from sad thoughts? We drink, we take drugs, we fill up our days with activities in order to be too busy to feel. But in numbing my regret, my past and my pain, I had also numbed my happiness.

Until now. Nathan had shaken me out of the half-life I had been leading, and that threatened to tear down the walls I had so carefully and painstakingly constructed since as far back as I could remember. Nathan had filled me with so much joy, but I wasn't sure I'd survive if my defences turned to dust.

It took me a few moments to compose myself, and I then hurried up to our flat. I placed the suits in Nathan's side of the wardrobe and crawled into bed. The photos I had taken that morning could wait. I was too exhausted, too emotionally raw, to deal with anything at the moment, and I just wanted to close my eyes and bury myself in sleep.

Sleep came quickly but it was not restful.

I am back in Tarifa. The sun is dipping below the horizon and the sky looks as if it has been set ablaze. The wind is howling, the sand peppering my skin with force, the waves bashing against the shoreline.

There was no one around.

I am the only living soul on the beach. In the periphery of

my vision, all I can see is blackness. The world ends here, on the fringes of this space in which I now found myself. To venture any further would be to be lost forever.

Within the roar of the gale comes the sweet voice of a woman singing. It is not the song I had heard before, and this voice seems to belong to a younger woman. As the wind dies down, the melancholy utterances become clearer: she sings in Spanish. I make myself concentrate hard on the words to understand what she is saying.

"Oh where, oh where has my love gone? Lost to faraway fields, to ocean's blue, to valleys deep... He is lost and even if he were to return, he could no longer be mine, because his love was never true—"

From the water, a woman –the same woman I'd been seeing– rises from the surf and heads straight towards me. The long grey dress hangs wet and heavy around her small frame. Her hair is tangled in thick wet tendrils like seaweed around her face, a strong wind blows it back to reveal a face as pale as a moon on a winter's night and eyes as black as coal.

"Who are you? Why are you following me?" I yell at her.

She opens her mouth as if to speak, but only water gushes from her lips. Her dead eyes focus on mine. Her skin continues to rot right in front of me, as if death is ravaging her with accelerated eagerness. The stench of decay stings my nostrils and fills my lungs and I can barely breathe.

"Why won't you just leave me alone?" I cry.

I want to take a step back, but the darkness had spread and there is now only a void behind me. Soon she would be upon me.

"You belong here with me! In the cold! In the dark!" the dead

thing hisses like a venomous snake.

She may have been beautiful once a long time ago, but death and a watery grave have stripped her of all that had made her so. She emanates such hatred that it made me recall emotions I didn't wish to. From somewhere unknown, perhaps from somewhere deep in my subconscious, a single word formed on my lips.

"Isabel…"

And the creature lunged at me, clawing at me with her emaciated hands and long, sharp nails. I screamed and tried to step back, only to fall – and keep falling – into a never ending blackness.

"Honey, Beth, wake up… Beth, just wake up!" Nathan said, his voice reaching me from the abyss.

I opened my eyes, my hands gripping the bed sheets, the ruby ring glinting in the warm light from the bedside lamp. Nathan must have switched it on: I glanced out the window and noticed that the daylight had been replaced by nightfall.

"Nathan," was all I managed to croak.

"Beth, you OK? I'm sorry I'm so late… did you have another bad dream?" he asked tenderly, stroking my arm affectionately.

I nodded.

"The sea again? You had been doing so well," he said.

It was easier to simply agree with this assumption, and so I nodded once more and allowed myself to be enveloped by him. I could feel his heart beat against his chest, strong and reassuring, and I felt calmer.

"Why don't you go have a shower, and I'll whip us up something for dinner?" I suggested, trying to inject some brightness into my voice.

"Are you sure? I could just scrape something together if you want to stay in bed?"

"Nope – I need to get up. I slept for much longer than I had planned to."

"OK, only if you're sure, because I'm actually starving. It's been a crazy first day back – only managed to get a sandwich for lunch," he said, kissing me on the forehead and heading towards the en-suite.

When he'd closed the door behind him, I slipped out of bed and hurried to the kitchen. I needed to keep myself busy. That woman had unravelled something inside me, and I had to stitch it back together before Nathan realised how truly broken I was.

Around thirty minutes later, I served us up some brown rice, oven baked salmon topped with Philadelphia and chives, and green beans sautéed in garlic butter. I set up our little dining table with some candles and our nicest plates, and opened a bottle of chilled white wine. Nathan kissed me deeply, his hair still wet from the shower, and thanked me as he sat down.

"Wow – this all looks and smells amazing, hun. Thanks – I knew you were a keeper," he said, giving me his cheekiest grin.

"You're welcome, and I definitely am a keeper," I replied coyly.

I took a good long gulp of the wine; the alcohol would help dull the experience of the dream. During the meal, Nathan filled me in on his first day back, the draft he was preparing for some corporate agreement, a motion he was drafting and how he had been selected to assist a more senior lawyer on a pro-bono case. I listened, commenting here and there, but I wasn't fully in the conversation.

Instead, I picked at my food, and I drank, as I fought to keep the memories of the woman emerging from the sea and that of my mother's final expression —the fear in her eyes when she realised we were about to crash - at bay.

Chapter Seven

I awoke to sunlight streaming in through the window and heard the water running in the bathroom. I stretched out in bed, thankful for a blissful night's sleep with no dreams. I hopped out, placing an old university T-shirt of Nathan's over my head, and stepped into the kitchen.

I felt energised as I made us some freshly ground coffee in the fancy cafetière Nathan's parents had brought us as a gift, and sliced up some wholegrain and walnut loaf and placed the slices in the toaster. Nathan walked in and kissed me on the cheek, and I breathed in the lime and minty scent of his aftershave.

"Morning babe, how'd you sleep?" Nathan asked.

"Much better, no nightmares," I replied, taking a sip of the hot coffee and savouring it before continuing. "I got some great shots at the cathedral yesterday. Gonna spend the morning reviewing them, but I think I'll give the apartment a quick clean first."

"You sure you'd not rather wait till the weekend when I can help?" he said, munching on toast.

"No, it's fine really – feel like blasting a little music and moving around a bit before I get stuck on my computer for the rest of the day."

"Have you had a chance to look at the photos from the trip?"

"No, not yet, but hopefully later this evening."

"Well, I better dash. Sorry, but it's probably gonna be another late one today," Nathan said, sounding apologetic.

"It's okay, honey. I knew what I was signing up for when I decided to marry a successful lawyer."

He chuckled before replying, "Well, I don't know if I'd go that far, but how's about I pick us up some cronuts from the new Choc place that has opened in Cabot Circus for dessert?"

"A cronut? What the hell is that?" I laughed.

"It's a cross between a croissant and a doughnut – ingenious really."

"I never say no to dessert."

Nathan kissed me on the lips, grabbed his briefcase and headed out the door. As soon as the door clicked shut, I noticed the deafening silence in the apartment. It had never bothered me before – I enjoyed my alone time – but suddenly the stillness felt almost... threatening.

Choosing to ignore the feeling that something wasn't right, I put away the clean plates from the night before and washed up the breakfast dishes. Nathan hadn't noticed my unease at dinner, as we'd cleaned up and watched a little bit of late-night television before getting into bed.

Unsurprisingly, after the very long nap I'd taken that afternoon, I had found it hard to get to sleep. I had tossed and turned while Nathan slept like a log next to me. But after a couple hours of counting sheep, counting to one hundred and anything else I could think of, I had finally succumbed to slumber.

I connected my phone to the Bluetooth speaker in our living room and played a 'best of 2020' playlist on Amazon Music to crush the noiselessness as I set about cleaning the flat. About two hours later, I was done and had managed to work up a bit of a sweat. I had a nice cool shower and changed into some comfy jogging bottoms and a T-shirt. I powered up my laptop on the dining room table and fetched the camera from my camera bag.

I removed the SD card and inserted it into the media card reader on my laptop. I had cleared all previous photos from the card before our trip, so I simply downloaded everything on the file. Once downloaded, I segregated the photos from the trip into our 'Holidays' folder and placed all the others into my Water-Well Media Centre folder.

I made myself another cup of coffee, then sat down to peruse my work. I had taken well over a hundred photos. Firstly, I clicked quickly across all the images. It helped me get a clearer idea of what I had captured and what I had to work with. I was pleased to see that very little re-touching was required on most of the images. At this stage I had just wanted to capture some simple no-frills photographs, which would also look great in black and white. For the next stage I wanted to get a little more creative. A quote from a photographer, who had inspired me to pick up a camera in the first place, sprang to mind: *You don't take a photograph, you make it*. I felt that way about my work and, like Ansel Adams, I considered that I was creating art and I loved it.

I lost myself in the images of the historic cathedral and toyed around with ideas for the exhibition, making notes as I went along. I thought I could contrast this building with other chapels and churches, and with some of the primarily glass constructs that were popping up around town, such as the new office block down at Temple Quay. The relationship with light that these various types of architecture had could be rather interesting to explore, the atmosphere they evoked and the sense of place they created.

Hunger pangs sent me back into the kitchen, where I made myself a tuna and salad sandwich and poured myself a generous glass of peach squash. I had just sat back down at the computer when the phone rang. The internet package we subscribed to included a landline, although I could count on one hand the number of times it had ever rung. Nathan always called me on my mobile, and his parents, knowing the long hours he worked, usually tried his mobile first before ringing the house.

"Hello," I said, picking up the phone with one hand and running my hand through my hair with the other, having caught sight of my errant curls in the hallway mirror.

"Beth," a voice said, so softly it was almost a whisper.

"Yes."

"It's me. It's... Dad."

"Dad, hello. Sorry... I could hardly hear you. I didn't recognise..." I said awkwardly.

"That's OK, it's been a while since we've spoken." There was no trace of remonstration in his tone; he was simply stating a fact.

"Yes, it has. Sorry. Nathan and I just got back from being

abroad and I've just received a new commission for an exhibition. Been a little busy lately, sorry," I rambled on, noting I'd said 'sorry' three times in as many seconds.

I felt as if I had spent my entire adult life apologising, as if I had had to excuse my very existence, but no amount of saying sorry would bring my mother back.

"I'm sorry to bother you," he continued. Great – now he was the one apologising, but what for? For me? For the distance between us?

"You aren't bothering me. I—"

"There's something I need to tell you," he said, interrupting me, then blurted out, "I have cancer, and, well... it's not good."

"Dad, I—" I began, but couldn't form any more words. Upon hearing the dreaded C-word, and fighting a rising panic which compressed my throat, I glanced into the mirror.

The woman in grey, the woman from the beach, was standing right behind me. She was a horrific vision of death which stilled my breath, and when she screamed like something demonic, everything turned to black.

I could hear the dial tone trilling as if from far away, as I slowly regained consciousness to find myself lying on the cool wooden floor. Before I could even think a single thought, I began to cry big, heart-wrenching sobs. All my life I had been haunted by images I had no wish to see. Memories which invaded my thoughts, my dreams, though not my waking life – but this *thing*, this woman I couldn't explain, I couldn't rationalise. *What is happening to me?*

My father's sullen words rang in my mind: *"I have cancer and, well... it's not good."* I mean, cancer is never good, but the way he said it made it sound like if there was no hope, as if he had been given a death sentence with a set number of months to live. I had to call him back, I had to know more, I had to be there for him even though I didn't know how.

I raised myself off the floor, feeling a little unsteady, and peered fearfully into the mirror. I could only see myself and the interior of the flat reflected. I hung up the landline phone and retrieved my mobile from the dining table and called my father. I could remember neither his home phone number or his mobile off by heart, so determined had I been to sever my ties to the past and to my past self.

I allowed the phone to dial for almost a minute before ending the call. I then tried the landline, but again there was no answer. I felt I really should go over to see him; I even picked up my car keys before setting them down again. Yes, I would see him, but first I had to speak to Helena – something I had not done in years. I scanned my contact list, tapped on her name and rang her. She picked up on the sixth ring.

"Helena, it's me, it's Beth."

"Beth."

"I'm calling about Dad. He just called. He told me he had—"

"Cancer," she interjected.

"Yes," was all I could muster.

Of course she knew. Helena and my father were close. She was always the favourite, even Dolores'. Would Nathan prefer her too? I shook myself. Now was not a time for self-pity or petty jealousies.

"I fainted," I explained. "I tried calling him back to find out more, but I couldn't get hold of him. I was going to go see him, but thought I should speak to you first."

"I'm here with him at the house. We'll wait for you," she said simply before hanging up.

I found my hand was shaking as I put my mobile back on the table. Those few words were the most Helena and I had shared in many years. I looked down at the small birthmark on my right arm, just above my wrist, a small brown patch. It looked a little like a map of Australia – at least, that's what my mother used to say to us affectionately. Helena had never liked hers; it was another reminder of how similar we were, at least on the outside.

I thought back to that fateful day, when everything changed, when *I* changed. I had lost so much more than just my mother that day. Talking to my father and Helena just served to remind me of that. Now my father had cancer and I was going to lose him all over again.

I put on my trainers, tied up my mass of curls in a messy ponytail, and grabbed my keys. I darted down the stairs and into my car. The blue sky, as pure as clear water, did nothing to brighten my mood as I floored the accelerator towards *home*.

Home was a stately yet modern detached home on Mariners Drive. It was nestled within its own private gardens and had great views over the nearby park. I pulled onto the drive and parked behind Helena's own white VW Golf, which she had also been gifted by our father when she graduated from the University of Edinburgh as a nurse.

I got out of the car, hurried up to the front door and rang the doorbell. As the door opened I sucked in a deep breath as I caught sight of my father. He looked like he had aged twenty years since the last time I had seen him.

My mind fumbled to remind me of when that had last been – had it been two years ago at Christmas? No, I had spent that Christmas with Nathan and his family at his grandmother's house in the Cotswolds. Giving it some thought, I realised it had been close to three years since I had last seen my father, and even then, it had been the briefest of encounters, accidentally bumping into each other in the Cribbs Causeway mall. We may as well have been living on opposite sides of the world for all the contact we had, and even though we had our reasons, in this moment, it just made me feel guilty and wretched.

"Dad," I croaked.

"Hello, Beth, come in," he said politely, if a little awkwardly.

I stepped inside. The house smelled as it always had, of Dolores' pine floor cleaner and lavender polish. Dolores had long ago retired but my father had instructed the new cleaner to buy the same products. I guess some things in life are easy to keep, to control, whereas others... others are out of our hands all together.

"How... how are you, Dad?" I stuttered.

"I've been better. Come through to the living room and we can catch up." This cordiality was unusual, but these weren't usual circumstances.

I followed him into the light-filled sitting room, which opened onto the terrace and gardens. Helena sat on the single armchair, looking out at the greenness dotted with colourful flowers. My father's gardener had kept my mother's green-fingered legacy alive; even from here I could see the exquisite blooms, their vibrant collage of colours, as radiant as my mother had once been.

I looked at Helena's heart-shaped face and now noticed that her eyes were closed, as if in deep thought. Her eyes flickered open, thick dark lashes over hazel green eyes fixated upon me. Those who are not identical twins will never know how it feels to have your face compared to someone else's every day, as people try and figure out any differences, any flaws. The chances of being an identical twin are very slim, accounting for only 0.3% of pregnancies. We came from one egg, one sperm, but at what point did we become two consciousnesses?

Our personalities differed like fire and ice.

Her hair, like mine, was as black as coal, but she always straightened it and it hung glossily over her shoulders. Our almond shaped eyes, green, with specks of golden brown. Helena was a reflection of me, but to each other we were just as cold and unforgiving as any mirror.

"Hello, Helena. It's been a while," I ventured.

"It has," she agreed flatly.

I sat next to my father on the sofa. This was not the time to focus on my relationship with Helena, or lack thereof, but on my father and what he was going through.

"Dad, why didn't you call me sooner?" I asked, before either of them had a chance to speak.

"I'm sorry, Beth. I had hoped I could beat it and there would be nothing to tell," he admitted, flinching a little as if in pain as he shifted on the couch.

"What have the doctors said, exactly? When did you get diagnosed? What treatment have you had?" I asked.

I knew I was battering him with questions, but I couldn't help myself. I felt as if I had stumbled into a theatre at the end of a play, and was desperately trying to figure out how this had become the closing act.

"Almost a year ago now. I was losing weight, had nausea and loss of appetite, blood tests revealed some abnormalities. After a CT scan and a sample from my liver was taken, it was confirmed I had liver cancer. I have had radiation therapy but the oncologist thinks we caught it too late, and I couldn't be considered for a transplant because..." He seemed unable to finish his sentence.

He didn't need to, though. I may have been young then, but I knew that it was drink that helped my father get by after my mother's death. I guess he became what you would call a high-functioning alcoholic, but I think that term applies more to the outside world. Indoors, I think it could hardly be called functioning. Alcohol turned out to be just one more anchor in a list of compounding factors that prevented him from moving on with his life. There had been only one woman for my father and that had been my mother.

How much responsibility can you take for one action that leads to a whole series of events, like cascading dominoes, one pushing onto the next, until nothing remains standing?

My father had been the one driving that day. I guess he was as unable to forgive himself as I was incapable of letting go of my own guilt. Perhaps my father and I had more in common than we cared to believe.

"Dad, I am so sorry. I should have been here for you. Surely there's something more the doctors can do?" I pleaded, taking his hand in mine. My eyes burned with tears I could not shed.

He flinched slightly at my touch, but this was not unexpected, and I had to will myself to keep it together as I released his hand and placed mine back on my lap.

"It is what it is, Beth. I don't want you to worry about me, but I felt you needed to know. I have lived my life and you are living yours now... I do want you to be happy," he told me, with such an air of finality it hurt, as if he was already gone.

"I don't know what to say," I replied lamely. "I wish this wasn't happening to you. I wish I could do something to help."

Helena, who had barely said a word up to this point, spoke up. "I'll be moving back home to help Dad out, so I will look after him, make sure he's OK. You don't have to worry."

"Of course. Well, I'm here for whatever you need," I offered.

"You're engaged," Helena stated. It wasn't a question.

I looked at my hands clasped tightly on my lap. The diamonds shone on my left hand, the cardinal red of the ruby on my right.

"I am. I was going to call you both this week to let you know. Nathan, my boyfriend, proposed while we were on holiday," I spluttered, feeling like I needed to clarify who Nathan was, seeing as neither of them had ever met him.

"Well, that is good news," my father said.

"Congratulations."

"Thank you," I said lamely.

The silence which ensued was deafening as well as painful. The tick-tock of the grandfather clock in the corner was the only sound, other than my heart, which throbbed and pounded against my chest like a wild animal trying to break out of its cage.

There was so much to say and yet so little. I had built walls in order to survive, to become a brand new Beth, one which moved out to go to university, who made friends, got her degree, got a boyfriend, a flat and a career. I was functioning, but if I took down these walls to try and make amends for the past, I wasn't sure I could build them up again. I had tried to forget about the past but within this room, amongst my roots, the past remembered me.

"Well, I guess I will let you rest now, Dad. Again, I am so sorry. I'm glad you called me and I mean it – I am here for whatever you need. Just call me anytime," I said as I stood up.

Without waiting for them to reply, I strode out of the house and back into my car. I turned the ignition and drove down to the next street where I parked, engine idling, and let the tears fall.

Chapter Eight

I don't know how long I sat there crying, but the afternoon light had turned autumn yellow and the sky to orange embers. I got home on autopilot. I let myself into the apartment and shut the door behind me, leaning against it for support.

I suddenly felt as lost as I had when I was a little girl, in the days after my mother's funeral. Images of that day had grown faint and remote, but now bloomed in my mind in full colour and high definition.

The feel of the black starchy dress my grandmother had pulled over my head. It was making my skin itch and felt too tight on my skinny chest. My grandparents —on my mother's side —had travelled from up north for the funeral. They had had my mother quite late in life and were already ailing by that point. I believed they wanted to do more for Helena and me, but the distance and their health made it hard. My father had also promised them he would hire a nanny to help take care of us, and that made them feel slightly better at having to leave us with this man, who was clearly unravelling just days after his wife's death.

Helena and I trailed behind my mother's gleaming coffin, hand in hand. Helena gripping my fingers so tightly my knuckles ached, but I was too numb to pull my hand away.

The church was full of people. A young tragic death always seems to attract crowds. But once the service was over, they all disappeared back to their own lives, relieved they were not the ones facing tragedy. Their fleeting grief is dispelled quickly, but it is one which those closest to the deceased must endure endlessly.

The faces of so many strangers loom above me, their expressions of sadness and pity making me feel faint as I struggle to breathe through the cloying smell of too many flowers. My father appeared stoic, eyes focused straight ahead, without shedding a single tear as the priest read the funeral rites. He shed his tears afterwards, away from prying eyes. His brother, Steve, sat in the pew on one side of him, Helena and I on the other. I was surrounded by family but I had never felt so alone.

I bounded into the kitchen, took the bottle of white wine chilling in the fridge, got a glass from the cabinet and poured myself a very generous measure. I gulped it down, along with two anti-anxiety pills.

"I should have called him sooner," I said aloud to the empty flat.

My father was dying and it was perhaps too late to mend our relationship. Can you even rebuild something that is based on so little? My family interacted like strangers, a complete antithesis to the relationship Nathan's family shared. I won't lie, the closeness Nathan had with his family, the love and care they shared for each other, attracted me to him, to them. Isn't it natural to yearn for something you've never had?

I could only wonder how different things might have been if my mother hadn't died. Would we have been a normal family? But I knew the answer to that question; I just couldn't dwell on it too closely. I was already too close to the edge.

Now, with Helena back home, I would feel even more like an outsider if I went to visit. I thought of calling Nathan, to let him know about my father, but this wasn't the kind of thing you shared over the phone, even though my father had done just that. I would wait until he got home; my face would give away that something was wrong. I was no longer as good as I had been at keeping my thoughts hidden.

I took another long gulp of wine, which was already helping to settle my nerves. Could I really blame my father for drinking? I didn't remember much following the crash but I did remember my father's face. The way his features contorted in horror and anguish, the way he had screamed and screamed as he looked at my mother's bloodied corpse beside him, was yet another memory I wished to banish into the abyss.

The man in the truck had called an ambulance and the next thing I remembered was the paramedics pulling me out of the vehicle. My father's almost inhuman wails continued to resound across the landscape as twilight stole away the colours of the day. Later, I overhead the nurses talking; they said that he would not let go of my mother's body and that they had had to sedate him to remove him from the car.

I closed my eyes to block the memory. When I opened them, from the corner of my eye I saw someone walk across the doorway. A thump of shock to my chest and I jerked in alarm, spilling wine onto the floor.

"Damn it," I hissed. "Nathan?" I called out hesitantly.

It wasn't Nathan. I knew I was alone. It had been merely a glimpse of movement, a dark silhouette, and I knew I had seen that woman again. Not for the first time, I wondered if I had finally lost my mind. Dreams were one thing, but seeing things whilst you were wide awake was another thing completely.

As a child I had thought I had seen my mother on a couple of occasions after her passing, but now I did not trust those experiences. I was certainly not spiritually gifted in anyway. I had never experienced anything supernatural before, but I believed there were people out there that could – I just didn't believe I was one of them. My soul may have been touched by something, but it wasn't a sixth sense. Yet I couldn't explain what was happening to me, or why it was happening to me now. Didn't I already have enough to deal with?

I listened for footsteps. Could someone have broken into the flat whilst I was out? I couldn't control the tremor in my hands. Silence hung thick in the air, like the moment before the suspended guillotine falls. There was no one else here with me –at least, no one real. Was I simply hallucinating? And what did she want from me? Surely if anyone was going to come back from the grave to haunt me, it would be my mother. I didn't even know who this woman was.

Perhaps I had some sort of mental illness, like schizophrenia or bipolar disorder, which was only now rearing its monstrous head. Perhaps I was simply delirious because I was allowing my past to creep into the present. I would need to reign it in. I would not allow myself to be swallowed up by the past. I had Nathan, and I was not going to lose him or the life we had planned due to introspection.

I also shouldn't have been mixing my anti-anxiety medication with alcohol, but whatever *she* was, I needed to get to the bottom of it. I was no longer a child and, just like with my father's diagnosis, I would have to handle it and keep moving forwards whilst hoping that any cuts and wounds I accumulated along the way would scar but not kill.

All of a sudden, the tangy and distinctive fragrance of oranges overwhelmed me; the air was laced with it. The pleasant aroma took me back to the orange groves of Tarifa and for a moment I forgot all about the woman in grey–as I was starting to think of her –and my father's diagnosis. Instead, I was back amongst the trees, the sunlight caressing my skin and the earth slightly damp beneath my bare feet.

It has always amazed me how a smell can evoke memories so powerfully, perhaps more so than any other sense. I closed my eyes and allowed myself to be transported back.

It was the rapid onslaught of pain which yanked me back to reality. At first it was just my fingertips that began to burn, followed instantly by my hands. Then my eyes flew open, and I was shocked to see dozens upon dozens of ants crawling up my hands and onto my arms. Their tiny but powerful jaws clamped onto my skin, injecting formic acid. My skin began to swell, itch and redden.

I shrieked, shaking and flailing at my hands and arms, trying to dislodge the vicious little creatures. As they fell to the floor and scurried across the rug and under the sofa, more seemed to appear from thin air and rush up my arm. I rushed to the kitchen sink, flipping the tap on and allowing the water to gush onto my forearms. Small whimpers escaped my lips and tears flooded down my cheeks as the tiny black bodies were washed down the drain.

"Beth, what's the matter? Are you crying?"

I hadn't heard Nathan's key in the lock, but suddenly he was behind me. I turned towards him, water dripping onto the kitchen floor and thundering from the open tap. I held my arms out in front of me, expecting Nathan to rush at me and swat the bastard ants away, but he just stared at me, his face filled with worry.

"What's the matter, babe?" he asked again.

I lowered my gaze from his face to my hands, only to find nothing on them. I couldn't understand where the ants had all gone. The skin was clear, there were no angry red welts, and it no longer stung. I peered into the sink but no ants were frantically trying to escape from the torrent of flowing water either. I turned off the tap.

"I... I saw... There were—" But I could not form any more words. "My father has cancer," I finally managed to blubber.

"What? Oh my God, I am so sorry, Beth," Nathan said as he wrapped me up in an embrace. "What did he say? Is he going to be OK?"

"It's liver cancer. Its terminal... There's nothing more that they can do for him."

"Oh honey, how terrible. I don't know what else to say," Nathan whispered, kissing me on the top of my head and holding me closer.

I didn't know what to say either, so I said nothing and continued to weep – for my father, for my mother, for Helena and even for myself. For the future I had dreamed of that seemed to be moving further away, out of reach.

That night we lay in bed after a quiet evening, wrapped in each other's arms. We often slept this way, cocooned in each other's bodies. It was where I felt safest. But tonight I couldn't sleep. When Nathan head's felt heavier on my shoulder and his breathing had deepened, I disentangled myself from him and went to stand at the window.

It was a dark, moonless night. I gazed down onto the tree-lined street, staring at the branches swaying rhythmically in the breeze, at the late night dog walkers and at the occasional car which drove past. It was the beams of car headlights which, just for a moment, illuminated the pane of glass, reflecting not only myself but the woman in grey standing right behind me. I spun around to be confronted by nothing.

The temperature in the room plummeted, and it was now as cold as the night air outside. I couldn't understand how Nathan hadn't woken up. I glanced over at him, his arm draped over his chest as it rose and fell softly. His face, serene yet so sensual. I wanted to climb back into bed and kiss him awake. Touch him so that he would want nothing else but to make love to me, so that I wouldn't feel so alone. But that would have been selfish of me. He was working long hours and needed his sleep. He had also told me he had to be up early for an 8am meeting with a potential new client.

After having seen the woman in grey's face, I knew sleep would not come easily, and so I padded quietly to the kitchen. I popped a couple more anti-anxiety tablets into my mouth, and a sleeping pill for good measure, and gulped them down with a large glass of water from the tap. When I thought I had seen my mother after her death, I longed to catch a glimpse of her again, to know that she still lived in spite of my actions. Now that I was seeing something otherworldly, I wished I could *un-see* it.

As crazy as it sounded, I now realised I had inadvertently stumbled across something on my trip to Tarifa. Something had been triggered; something had attached itself to me somehow, and whatever it was, it scared me, more than my night terrors and more than my fear of the water ever had.

Once the pills started kicking in, I made my way back to bed and settled in next to Nathan, who stirred slightly and mumbled something unintelligible in his sleep as I lay my head on his chest. Part of me wanted to wake him up and tell him what had been happening to me, but the bigger part of me, which erred towards self-preservation, wouldn't allow it.

Nathan loved the Beth with which I had presented him, the Beth I had worked hard to create. I had allowed him in to a greater degree than anyone else, confiding in him about my phobia and my estrangement from my family, but there was a side of me I had never let him see. A side of me I knew he could never love. I listened to the rhythmic throb of his heart as I drifted off into the oblivion of sleep.

The next morning, I awoke again to the sound of water spray from the shower. Nathan was already up and, even though I was exhausted, I made myself get out of bed. I may have been losing my mind but I still had deadlines to meet, and so I would lose myself in my work. Photography had always been my escape; by seeing the world through a lens I detached myself from it, becoming an observer rather than an active participant.

In the kitchen I made us some fresh coffee and heated up some porridge in the microwave, handing a bowl to Nathan as he walked in.

"Morning, babe. Thanks for this," Nathan said as he took the offered bowl and kissed me on the lips. "How are you feeling?"

"Not great. Hasn't quite sunk in yet, I guess," I replied, not wanting to elaborate further.

Nathan knew I didn't like talking about my family, so he wouldn't push me but would allow me to say as much or as little as I wanted to on the subject.

"I could stay home with you if you like?" he continued gently. "I could call the office, explain the situation—"

I cut him off. "No. It's fine, I need to get on with work anyway. It's better if I keep myself busy. Plus Helena is home with him now, so..." I trailed off.

"OK, but you call me if you need me. I better head off to that meeting, but I mean it – you call me if you need me to be here with you."

"I'm sure. Thanks for offering. Now go, or you're going to be late." I nudged him out of the door and kissed him goodbye.

As soon as he shut the door, the silence was once again absolute, and gnawed at my insides. I hurried into the shower and got myself ready. Applying a small amount of make-up and donning some leggings and a light pink sweater, I left the flat hastily and walked out onto the streets of Bristol.

Whilst in the shower I had come up with a new dimension for my project. Recalling my university days, and a history of art module I had taken, which examined 'Seeing and Being Seen in English Art in the 14th Century', I thought of contrasting classic, historical art with some of our more modern artists. I thought of Banksy's work, which highlighted Bristol's underground scene. His satirical street art and subversive epigrams would be a polar opposite to works which depicted the Black Death and the Hundred Years' War, for instance, but would have the common thread that all art does, to evoke feeling and convey a message.

Happy with this train of thought, I made my way to Frogmore Street, thinking that the 'Well Hung Lover' would be a good artwork to include. I decided the best place to capture the piece of art was on the small bridge off Park Street. I took a series of images at different exposures, to capture a range of light to dark, making the most of the hard light of the bright, sunny day. I also included some candid shots of passersby; after all, art is there to be seen. What good is it to hide away such treasures that only a privileged few can enjoy?

As I placed my camera back in my bag, I decided to take a walk through town, which was pretty busy as shops began to open for the day. I popped into Starbucks and got myself a large latte, then strolled through the crowds. I usually avoided people – I had never been one for large groups – but today I welcomed being lost and anonymous amongst the throng of shoppers and those heading to work.

I sipped my coffee slowly, savouring the taste and the much-needed caffeine hit. My thoughts inevitably turned to my father and, before I could talk myself out of it, I sent him a quick text.

Hi just me, just thought I'd text to say I'm thinking of you and to call me if you need anything.

It wasn't much, but it was something.

I soon found myself in the enchanting parkland of Brandon Hill and sat down on an empty bench underneath a weeping willow. The beauty of my surroundings did nothing to mitigate the ugly memories which spread to the forefront of my mind, like mould growing across the surface of the walls I had built.

Nine years old, coming home from my first piano recital, Dolores the only one in attendance, to find my father passed out drunk on the couch.

Silent dinners alone because my father was working late.

Missing out on school field trips because my father had misplaced the permission slips.

Ten years old, my father showing up drunk to parents' evening at school.

I pressed my palms into my eyes to ease the ache of the tears that threatened to pour out from them. I remembered that when my father had dropped me off at the university halls, all I had felt was relief. Relief that that part of my life was over, that I could distance myself from my roots and from my beginnings and be someone, *anyone* else. And that was exactly what I did. Now he was dying. Would he even make it to the wedding? Would I be relieved if he didn't?

I admonished myself. That was the dark side of me talking, the one that dwelled in the shadows, but the new Beth kept to light-filled places. I stood up and walked along the sunlit path, taking shots of Cabot Tower as I made my way back home.

Chapter Nine

The following day, I found myself once more in the city centre, but this time I had come to shop. Nathan's parents had phoned the night before, saying they wanted to take us out for dinner on Friday night to celebrate our engagement. They had booked a table in a posh tapas restaurant that had recently opened on the waterfront, thinking it a very fitting place in which to celebrate. It was very thoughtful of them, and I wanted to find the perfect outfit for the night.

Over the past couple of years I had gotten to know the Walkers pretty well, but I still tried to make a good impression whenever I got the chance. Since the first day I had met them, I had been desperate for them to like me. I knew how close the family were and I wanted to be part of that.

I thought I'd check out Oasis in Cabot Circus first, and I wasn't disappointed. I tried on a gorgeous sky-blue pleated skirt and a white laced bodysuit, which contrasted well against my tanned skin and dark hair.

The girl at the till commented, "Wow, what a striking engagement ring – and gosh, I really like the ruby too. So vintage!"

"Thanks – I'm celebrating my engagement with family tomorrow night, hence the new outfit. The ruby, I actually found on the beach," I replied.

"Lucky find – and congrats, you are going to look stunning!" she said, looking more pleased for me than either my father or Helena had done.

"Thank you," I replied, giving her a genuine smile.

My phone buzzed as I exited the store. After a couple moments of rummaging in my bag, I pulled it out. It was a text from Nathan.

Hey babe, just to let you know I'll probably be home a little later tonight. Looking forward to tomorrow though & the weekend together xx

I replied back instantly.

Yeah I am too, love you & missing you, see you later xx

I rechecked my text-message inbox, but I had no reply from my father. My smile faltered a little. I resolved to visit him this weekend, whether he replied or not. Visiting him and Helena would certainly be awkward and uncomfortable, but it was the right thing to do. The new me tried to do the right thing. I couldn't change the past, but the present was within my hands.

As I walked home, happy that my trip into town had been short, my thoughts inevitably turned to my experiences – or my hallucinations; I wasn't sure I had a word to describe them –and then to the woman in grey and what it all could possibly mean. Perhaps karma had finally caught up with me. Or I was having a severe adverse reaction to my meds. Or I was actually being haunted by something. It felt real, though, and I had to put an end to it before Nathan realised there was something wrong. His love was the only true thing I had ever experienced and I wouldn't let anything jeopardise it. I decided to make an appointment to see my therapist. It wouldn't hurt to talk with someone else about this, and he had already seen glimpses of how messed up I was.

As I let myself into the flat, the stillness within hit me like an invisible wave. Since returning from Spain it no longer felt the same; it had ceased to be my haven from the world. Now, every time I was alone here, I felt like *I* was the intruder. Even the air felt different, weighted somehow in a way that seemed ominous.

But I was an expert at compartmentalising my life, so I kicked off my boots and proceeded to the bedroom to hang up my new skirt and top. I had wanted to treat myself to a new pair of shoes, too, but the holiday had eaten into my savings and I knew I should really wait until my next pay check before spending anymore.

I wondered what would happen to my father's house once he was gone. Would he leave it to Helena? Would he sell it? I hoped it would be sold, so that some other family could inject some love into that place. It was a beautiful property, but it was not my home. If those walls could talk, I wouldn't ever want to listen to what they had to say.

A memory of a night I had so desperately tried to forget, stirred from within the deep chest in which I had stowed it away. It was shortly after the accident. I am holding Millie dead in my hands, her fur wet and her body cold. Helena stands in the doorway, a black silhouette, and even though I can't see her eyes I know they are filled with something akin to satisfaction.

I forced the image away before it had a chance to settle and put down roots. A single memory can act like a pebble thrown in a pond, one recollection leading to another, as the ripples spread... My father's diagnosis, the engagement, the woman in grey, all acted like the elements, wearing away at my defences. I envisaged a calm body of water in my mind's eye, flat and perfect: and pushed the past beneath its surface and out of reach. I hoped it would rot there.

I took off my jewellery and placed them in a little trinket plate shaped like a swan, on my bedside table. The trinket dish had been a gift from Sam. Sam and I had met at university, during our first year in halls, and we lived together in our second and third year. I hadn't made many friends at university; I couldn't afford to let people get too close. Starting anew required determination, patience – practice, even – and I needed to keep my audience to a minimum. Sam was the closest I'd ever been to having a real friend. Sam had a radiant disposition, all warm tones, kind and sweet – everything I longed to be, and like a chameleon I learned those colours by mimicking her.

Sam and I still stayed in touch with the occasional WhatsApp message, but mostly kept tabs on each other's lives via Facebook updates, but not much else. After university life we had gone our separate ways. From her latest Facebook update I knew she was expecting her first child, and I was happy for her.

Now that Nathan had proposed we seemed one step closer to parenthood. That thought filled me with as much dread as it did excitement. Given my experience of family, I wasn't sure if bringing a child into the world was something I wanted to do. What if the child was like me? Would not having kids become a deal breaker between Nathan and me?

I took off my jeans and changed into some jogging bottoms. I knew I should really spend some time on my work, but I thought it would be nice to print out a couple of photos of our trip for Nathan's parents and sister as a little token gift.

I stepped into the living room and powered up the laptop and the photo printer I kept on the large sideboard by the window. The photo printer had been a gift from Nathan – he knew how much I preferred having physical copies of photographs rather than simply keeping them all digitally, where they were more easily forgotten. I endeavoured to print only my favourites, and I could spend hours poring over images, deciding on the best ones. The walls and tables of the apartment were dotted with picture frames and collages, mostly of Nathan and me. Photos from weekends away in the countryside, on night outs, of Nathan and his family. They depicted a life, my life.

I opened up the personal photos folder and clicked on the one named 'Tarifa'. We had only been back a short while but already the sandy beaches and glimmering blue skies seemed so far away. I've always wondered why happy memories always seem more distant and less vivid than moments which have caused you heartache or fear – or maybe that was just me.

I was only a little surprised to see that I had taken close to four hundred photographs in a week; I'd always been trigger happy with my camera. I scanned the various pictures I had taken of the beach, the sea, marine life, our trip to the vineyards, the architecture of the old town, our food, and Nathan.

I picked out my favourite of us both, a selfie we had taken after we had just gotten engaged, me with the ring on my finger and both of us looking exceptionally happy. It would make for a nice keepsake for Nathan's family. I also chose four of my favourite shots of the trip for ourselves and sent them all to the printer.

I padded into the kitchen to make myself a snack for lunch whilst I waited for the photos to print. I decided on a toasted wholegrain pitta bread, with tuna, salad and some mayonnaise. I chewed on my lunch absentmindedly as the printer whirred and buzzed in the background and spat out my photos.

I washed my plate, padded over to the printer and picked up the small stack of pictures. I glanced at the first one, one I had taken of Nathan walking in the vineyards, and at first I couldn't quite identify what was wrong with the image, but then I saw it –or rather I saw *her*, the woman in grey, standing with her back to the camera in the far corner of the image, her dress like a dark smudge on the print.

I couldn't stop the shiver which ran down my spine like a wave. She hadn't been in the image before I had sent it to the printer, of that I was sure. Hesitantly, I turned to the next photo, one of the sand dunes, their tops covered in a blanket of grass. *She* was in this one, too, but her body had turned slightly. As I checked the next two photos, my hands now trembling and the pit of fear in my stomach growing as more of her face became visible. She was turning towards me slowly in every frame.

I did not want to look at her again, but I was unable to stop myself from examining the remaining photographs. In the last one, my engagement ring sparkling as Nathan and I looked lovingly into each other's eyes. She now stood next to me.

Having turned around completely, she was staring right at me, her face a mask of horror, the pallid, mottled skin pulled too tightly across her face, exposing white bone. Her eyes were like two white orbs, glassy, like those of a freakish doll. Her lips were black, pulled back in a vicious snarl.

Suddenly, she rushed at me from the image. I dropped the photographs in alarm, jerking back and crying out as I tumbled over the coffee table to hit the ground with a thud. I sat up quickly, too scared to feel any pain, peeking around the coffee table at the photographs now strewn across the floor. I froze in abject fear as dark blotches began to bleed from the images. The shadow-like substance continued to ooze, and I was assaulted by the buzzing of what sounded like hundreds of flies, although I couldn't see any. The patches of darkness began to flow and melt into one another. The stench of decay hung in the air like a foul cloud. The mass continued to grow, rising and transforming into *her*, and yet I couldn't move. Her hair and dress were soaked through and water pooled at her pale, almost skeletal feet.

It was the look on her face, one of pure venom, which finally sent me scrambling from the floor. My only thought was to put some distance between myself and this hellish creature. *She* was blocking access to the front door, so I bolted down the corridor. I could hear the slow *splat* of her wet footsteps behind me. I ran into the bathroom and slammed the door shut, locking it.

"This can't be happening. This isn't real. This can't be happening," I muttered under my breath, over and over again like a mantra.

My hands were splayed against the door, my heart hammering in my chest so hard I felt sick. I could hear nothing but the blood pounding in my ears. I don't know how long I stood standing like that – a few seconds, minutes – but after a while and with nothing else happening, I stepped away from the door.

As my sense of dread began to ease slightly, I listened out for any noise in the apartment, but I was met by silence. I didn't dare open the door yet, and instead I put my ear against it and tried to make out if she was still there.

More silence.

I couldn't stay in here forever, and whatever she was – ghost or ghoul or hallucination – she couldn't physically hurt me, right?

After a few more moments with my ear pressed up against the door, I told myself I was being ridiculous and a coward. This was my home and I was damned if some ghostly *thing* was going to ruin the life I had worked so hard to build for myself. I reached out to unlock the door just as something slammed against it.

Boom! Boom!

Whatever it was hit the door with such force I thought it would splinter.

"Stop it! Just go away!! Leave me alone!!" I shrieked, my fleeting sense of courage and outrage deserting me. I burst into tears.

Boom! Boom!

The door rattled in its frame.

"Just stay away from me!" I sobbed, falling to a heap on the floor, closing my eyes tight and placing my hands over my ears, as if I were a child hiding from the bogeyman.

"This is all in my head. This is all in my head," I mumbled to myself.

I began to rock backwards and forwards slowly, something I hadn't done since the days following my mother's death, or when my panic attacks were at their worst.

I must have somehow fallen asleep, exhausted by panic and fear, curled up in a ball against the door. The sound of the door handle rattling jerked me awake and cold terror flooded my system once more.

She's trying to get in!

"Why are you doing this to me?" I howled.

"Beth? Honey, what's wrong? Open the door..." I heard Nathan say, he sounded tense.

"Nathan?" I whimpered.

"Yes, honey, it's me. Please open the door."

I rushed to my feet, my sense of relief overwhelming now that Nathan was home. My fingers fumbled as I hurried to unlock the door and then jerk it open, ready to fling myself into Nathan's strong arms and feel the warmth of his body against mine – but I rushed out to an empty corridor.

"Nathan?" I called out uncertainly, but I was met only by silence.

I was alone and, worse than that, I *felt* completely alone. I couldn't stop the tears that spilled down my cheeks. I was losing my mind, and perhaps it was no more than I deserved.

I stood there in the corridor for a full minute, listening, but all I could hear was the distant sound of the city. I drifted into the kitchen, filled a glass of water to the top and took two sleeping pills and two anti-anxiety tablets. It was too much to take together, but in that moment I didn't care; I yearned for oblivion. I tucked myself into bed and allowed myself to be buried in the depths of sleep.

What seemed only a short while later, I felt my body being nudged, but my brain was reluctant to release me from slumber.

Finally, Nathan's familiar voice reached me. "Beth? Honey, I'm worried."

Grudgingly, I opened my eyes. The room was in gloom; night had fallen and the dark now frightened me because I was vulnerable to the things that lurked there.

"Nathan," I croaked.

"I'm sorry, Beth, but I called out and you didn't respond – and it isn't like you to sleep like the dead... and you hadn't replied to my messages. I thought something was wrong."

"No, it's OK. It's best that I get up or I won't sleep a wink tonight. I just... I just had a headache, took some tablets and thought I'd have a quick nap. I better make a start on dinner—" I rose up onto my elbows.

"It's fine, babe. You rest a little while longer and I'll whip up my special spaghetti carbonara. How does that sound?"

"Perfect. Thanks," I replied, mustering a smile.

Nathan kissed me on my forehead before making his way to the kitchen. I could hear him opening and shutting cupboard doors and banging pots and pans. He wasn't a bad cook, though he was a tad messy, but I would clear up after so that he could go have a shower and chill for the rest of the evening. I always found it amazing how even after a hard long day at work he still had the energy for domestic chores, I smiled at this.

My smile faltered as I recalled the woman in grey standing in my living room. If Nathan had experienced something weird he would have told me, so whatever this thing was, it seemed to have set its sights solely on me.

I looked about my bedroom, half-expecting her to appear suddenly and run at me, scratching and tearing at my skin with her bony, claw-like fingers. I slid out of bed hurriedly, placing my cold feet into my fluffy slippers that lay on the rug next to the bed, and moved into the kitchen. I still felt a little groggy from the pills, but I needed to spend some time with Nathan. He always grounded me, and since we had got back from the trip, our evenings together were all we had.

"How's your head?" Nathan asked as soon as I walked into the kitchen.

"Much better, thanks. How was work?"

"Crazy, but good. I'm learning a lot from my senior associate and I find the busier I am, the quicker the work day goes by. How's your project for the centre coming along?"

"So far so good. I'm enjoying it, the angle of it that is. I'm going for architecture and art to explore the theme of old and new, how this may contrast light and the dark, good and evil,"

"Sounds interesting. I'm really looking forward to the exhibition."

We continued chatting happily throughout the rest of the evening, and I relished the normalcy of it. The pasta was delicious, especially heaped with parmesan cheese, and I sipped at the sweet white wine and had two large glasses. I started clearing up the table as Nathan stood up to go take a shower.

"Oh by the way did you spill something in the living room?" Nathan asked.

"Huh?" I replied, caught off guard by the question.

"Just asking if you spilt something earlier. There were a few small puddles by the dining table. Don't worry, I cleaned them up and I picked up the photographs that were on the floor and placed them on the sideboard. Nice pics."

The happiness drained out of me as quickly as water down a plughole.

"Oh right, yeah. I knocked over a glass of water. Thought I'd got it all. Thanks, babe," I managed to say, turning back towards the sink so that he wouldn't see that I was shaken up. He obviously hadn't seen anything weird on the photos.

"No worries. I'm off to take a hot shower. I know it's getting late but fancy watching that new movie on Netflix, the one about the astronaut?" he continued, heading out of the door.

"Yeah, sure," I mumbled, not sure if he'd even heard me. The puddles of water that *she* had left behind proved that this wasn't all in my head, but that it was a physical manifestation of something supernatural. I recalled something Sam had said on one of our drunken nights out. She was an avid believer in all things paranormal, whereas I had never given such things much credence. I thought there was enough evil in us all without having to believe in demons and other such creatures. However, Sam had said that some psychologists believed that certain neurological phenomena could account for certain experiences, such as out of body experiences or poltergeist activity, and that some visions were simply the brain struggling to fill in missing information.

I needed to talk to my therapist about this. I fetched my mobile and called his number before I could change my mind. It was out of office hours so it went straight to voicemail. I left a message for him, asking him to call me back at his earliest convenience.

I felt a little better seeking help, as if I had taken a step towards taking charge of the situation rather than just being a victim to it. It was something my therapist had often said when we spoke about my fear of the water: how I could either let it control me, or I could control it.

Chapter Ten

The following day I awoke before Nathan did, and I snuggled up to him, enjoying the warmth his body always seemed to emit. I decided I would make the most of the day and head out early to take more shots for my project. Recent events had left me unfocused and behind on my work, and I needed this job to be a success. The exposure that this exhibition would give me would be great for my career.

As I stepped outside a short while later, I noted the sky was a rolling blanket of grey cloud and I missed the sapphire blue skies of Spain. However, I welcomed the cool air on my face, which helped clear the cobwebs from my aggravated mind. I needed to focus, plus tonight was our celebratory dinner with Nathan's family and I wanted to enjoy it. It's not every day a girl gets engaged, and I wanted to revel a little in this milestone in life.

As I made my way to Christ Church, which was located close by, I thought of the weekend ahead. I still hadn't heard back from my father; perhaps he wasn't feeling too well and just hadn't got round to sending me a message. Either way, I would visit tomorrow; I could print out an engagement photo for him, too. It would then be up to him whether he chose to frame it, stuff it in a drawer or bin it.

Soon I found myself staring up at Christ Church. The soft, diffused light of the overcast sky would help create some hauntingly beautiful shots. I was just deciding where best to position myself when my mobile rang. I rifled through my handbag, hoping I'd get to it in time before the caller gave up. Finally, I located it and slid the green caller icon upwards.

"Hello," I said quickly.

"Good morning. Beth?"

"Yes, speaking."

"Hi Beth, it's Dr Roberts. I heard your message this morning. How can I help you?"

"Morning, doctor. Thanks for calling me back so quickly. I had just called to ask for an appointment," I explained.

"Of course, Beth. I know it's been a couple of months since our last session. I'm just rechecking your file, and I see that during our last session you decided to take a break from therapy. So how are you? How can I help?"

"Um, yeah, I felt we had made such progress with my phobia that I thought it would be a good idea. I'm doing OK, and the holiday was great and I managed to swim in the ocean, but I have been having some… strange dreams since I've been back and I feel it would be helpful to talk them over with you."

"Sure thing. Well, let's see… I have availability next Tuesday at 11am. Does that work for you?"

"Yes, perfect. I'll see you then," I said, then concluded the conversation and hung up.

I had been seeing Dr Roberts for almost two years, and he had been a great therapist. It was Sam who had suggested him in the first place and with Nathan's encouragement I had decided to give him a go. Sam's older sister had been one of his clients; he had helped her with her crippling arachnophobia, as well as her eating disorder. He was astute, often sensing what I was thinking and feeling before I even spilled it out –well, to the extent that I permitted anyone to really know me. He had a certain warmth and acceptance which I found reassuring, and over the months I felt myself opening up to him, not just about my fear of water, but about my mother's death and my estranged relationship with my father and twin sister. He had inspired in me hope and optimism that I had never thought possible.

I hadn't wanted to go into details as to why I needed to restart therapy over the phone, preferring to mention only the dreams. Strangely, I didn't want him to think that I was cracking up either, perhaps because I thought I had made such strides and I didn't want to feel like I was failing or disappointing him. I had disappointed too many people in the past. Besides, regardless of how open I decided to be with Dr Roberts, I needed *this* to stop. On Tuesday I would recount my experiences as far as I felt I could, and I would hope that he could draw up a reasonable conclusion and course of treatment or action.

The wind had started to pick up, scattering the fallen autumn leaves. I had always envied the wind. I know that sounds a little weird, but I saw the wind as free, flowing to an infinity of possible destinations, flexible and changeable –I needed to believe change was possible, that you could travel far away from where you originated.

I hadn't wished to be tied down – well, not until I met Nathan, who changed how I saw the world and my place in it. The wind tousled my hair, and I reached into my handbag and fished out a hair band I tied my hair up in a loose pony-tail and then, taking out my camera, I took a few steps to my right to capture the spires of Christ Church and the crosses that jutted towards the sky like elevated headstones.

Once I felt I had taken sufficient shots, I made my way inside. I had brought along my macro lens to focus on close-up details, and I switched lenses as I made my way towards a specific painting. It was one of my favourite paintings, one I had included in my dissertation project. The painting was aptly called 'A Vision of Heaven and Hell' and was tucked away in one of the alcoves in the nave of the church.

I glanced around the church's interior, taking in its altar and row upon row of wooden pews and berry-red cushions. It was early and the church was empty of parishioners. The painting took up most of the alcove, encircled by cold grey stone. It was simultaneously awe-inspiring and intimidating.

The landscape of the painting was divided into three parts. The bottom third depicted the depths of Hell, in which nightmarish creatures with horns, tails and sharp teeth roamed. They reached upwards with clawed talons and dwelt in the dark, in-between rivers and pits of fire and blood. The middle part was in some ways worse, as desperate and pained-looking naked people stretched their pale limbs towards the heavens in supplication, whilst others tried to escape from the demons that had sunk their claws into their legs, their blood soaking into the earth beneath them. The top section depicted

Heaven, all light, wispy clouds and angelic creatures with beatific smiles. I guessed most people would find this part reassuring, but I could only think how far away Heaven seemed from ordinary people, how cold the smiles of the angels appeared, and how much closer we all seemed to be to Hell.

I forcibly dispelled my sombre thoughts and got to work, taking shots of the individual hellish creatures, the forsaken people and the winged divine beings. I was just about to leave, happy with what I had got on camera, when I heard the *drip, drip* of water, I took a backwards step right into a puddle.

"What on earth—" I muttered under my breath, shaking the water off my trainer.

The sound of dripping water continued. I looked around but couldn't identify where the leak was coming from. Nevertheless, the puddle grew into a small pool. The sound of flowing water became louder, sounding more forceful, like rushing water, as if the ocean itself was crashing into the church, the smell of salt water now heavy in the air.

When I had first arrived I was glad of the solitude but now I wished for other people. The sound of the sea took me back to Tarifa, when I had stepped in the water and *she* had grabbed me and pulled me under. The look on her face would haunt me for the rest of my life.

I turned around in a circle, scanning the confines of the church, feeling vulnerable, exposed and alone as the temperature plummeted around me. *So this is what it feels like to lose your mind? Dread, panic, doubt...*

I took another step backwards, and the squelching sound of my feet stepping into a much larger and deeper puddle sounded unnaturally loud within the church's stone walls. The light dimmed considerably, as if the ashen, clouded sky outside had turned black and daylight no longer shone through the stained-glass windows. The kind of darkness that seems to eat the light.

Suddenly, I felt a heavy hand on my shoulder, and I could feel someone or something breathing behind me. I felt my body start to turn, when all I really wanted to do was get the hell out of there. My mind prepared itself to see that face again… but it wasn't her. It was an old priest, his kind brown eyes on mine but I was terror-stricken, already braced to run – so I did.

"Are you OK, child?" I heard him call after me, but I didn't stop.

I ran outside into the weak light of day and kept running until a stitch in my side forced me to stop. I panted heavily. A few people walking by stared at me curiously but I ignored them, glad to be out in the fresh air, away from the cloying, ominous atmosphere of the church. I had planned to visit other sites today, but now I only wanted to go home.

I inserted the key in the lock, but felt hesitant before turning it, wondering if *she* was in there waiting for me – but I couldn't stay out wandering the streets for hours until Nathan came home, so I opened the door and stepped inside.

I felt that I was alone. I took off my damp shoes, leaving them by the door, and moved over to my computer. I would lose myself in work until I got dinner ready. I spent the next few hours going over all the photos I had taken, answering emails and applying for other upcoming jobs. I stopped only for lunch, making myself some scrambled eggs on wholemeal toast and cutting up a pink lady apple for dessert, which I munched on while I got back to editing my best photos into a collage for the exhibition.

After a couple more hours I decided I would start getting ready. I put on a face mask, had a long, hot shower, washed my hair, painted my nails and dried my curls poker straight. I spent extra time on my make-up, defining my eyes so that the green in them stood out. I then put on my new top and skirt and appraised myself in the full-length mirror. I felt glamorous and radiant, and I allowed myself a smile. Tonight would be a good night.

I heard Nathan walk in and shut the front door behind him.

"Sorry I'm late! Meeting overran and the new client we're trying to bag just wouldn't stop talking!" he called out. I heard him place his briefcase on the dining-room table and then his footsteps as he made his way to the bedroom. "I just need to have a quick shower—"

I couldn't help but grin when I saw the look on his face.

"Wow, Beth, you look unbelievable!"

"Thanks, babe. Oh, you know, just a few minutes work," I joked.

"Those were some well-spent minutes," he exclaimed goofily, still gaping at me but moving towards me.

"I've missed you."

"I've missed you too," he whispered as his hands roved the length of my body and he kissed me deeply. "Do you think we have time before…" He let the question linger.

"No way," I laughed, slapping him playfully on the arm. "But later." I promised him, kissing him lightly on the lips.

"Now go get ready, we can't be late for our own engagement celebratory dinner thingy."

Ignoring the mock pout on his face, I pushed him towards the shower. Whilst Nathan got ready, which would take a grand total of fifteen minutes at most, I decided to pour myself a glass of red wine. Spending time with Nathan's family always made me feel a tad nervous; they had been welcoming from the start, but I kept worrying they'd figure out I didn't fit in with them, or with Nathan. Like a cheap knock off faking qualities it could never possess.

As I sipped the wine, I savoured the intense, full-bodied taste and inhaled the earthy smell. It was a good wine; it had been a gift from one of Nathan's clients, and we had been saving it for a special occasion.

I smiled inwardly, and then I remembered the photos I was going to gift Nathan's parents and sister, and the happiness flitted away. I could see the little pile of prints resting on the sideboard. They looked innocuous and harmless. I made myself go over and pick them up. I turned them over and…nothing. Well, not nothing –they showed Nathan and I, of course, but s*he* was gone. Even though there was nothing wrong with the photographs now, I didn't want to see them ever again. I placed both copies of our engagement selfie in some pretty envelopes I kept in one of the sideboard drawers, and sealed them in, then I placed the others in another envelope and put them away.

Out of sight, out of mind.

Nathan walked in just as I shut the drawer. He looked handsome in his dark jeans, smart shirt and brown leather shoes. He was beautiful – I knew men didn't like to be described as such, but Nathan was just that. He reminded me of one of the Greek statues that decorated ancient Olympia or the Acropolis. Timelessly beautiful.

"Hey, why you looking at me like that, gorgeous?" Nathan asked with a cheeky grin.

"Just thinking how lucky I am that I'll soon be the new Mrs Walker."

"You know, we haven't actually started talking about the wedding itself. I thought women starting going all crazy the day after the engagement. Setting up binders with info about flowers, wedding venues, wedding favours, guest lists, honeymoon destinations, et cetera, et cetera." Nathan said cheekily.

"You've been watching too many *Friends* re-runs. I probably will go crazy –as you've so nicely put it –but I guess I wanna enjoy the engagement part too, know what I mean? Although now that you've mentioned the honeymoon, I wouldn't mind starting to plan that! Where would you like to go?" I asked excitedly, pouring him a glass of wine.

"Anywhere, really... Mexico, Canada, California, Italy... What about you?"

"I'd love to go to any of those places," I replied eagerly.

Nathan checked his watch, gulping down the wine. "We better get a move on. I thought I'd order an Uber – tonight is a night for drinking too much *tinto* and eating too much *gambas al pillily*."

"*Gambas al pil-pil*," I corrected him, laughing.

"You know prawns are the cockroaches of the sea, don't you?" Nathan declared.

I grimaced. "Ew! Please don't say that – I love prawns as

much as I hate cockroaches!"

We put on our coats and headed out. I was just locking up when I realised I hadn't put on my jewellery after my shower. I couldn't go to my engagement party without my engagement ring!

"Oh shit, I've forgotten the ring – just give me a sec!" I said, re-opening the door and rushing to the bedroom.

"OK – I'll wait downstairs and make sure the Uber doesn't leave without us," Nathan called after me as he headed down the stairs.

I darted straight to my bedside table, picked up my engagement ring from the trinket dish, slipped it on and then slipped the ruby ring on my other hand. I gasped loudly as a sharp pain pierced my finger. I eyed the ruby, which was as red as tulips, reminding me of meadows on spring days – but the red was blooming, spreading, and it took me a moment to realise that it was blood.

My blood.

The blood covered my finger and continued to flow over my hand. I couldn't understand what was happening. I yanked at the ring, trying to take it off. The pain was as piercing as a pair of scissors cutting into me. There was so much blood that my grip kept slipping. The ring felt as if it were welded onto my bone.

My white top was now covered in crimson, as well as the floor and my new skirt. I cried out both in panic and pain.

When my mobile rang, I groped at my clutch bag, struggling to get the catch open.

As soon as I managed to fish out my phone and take the call, Nathan asked quickly, "Beth, what's keeping you? I'm in the Uber already."

"Nathan – Nathan, I need you—" I began to cry, but stopped when I looked at my hand.

It was clean.

There was no blood, no pain. My clothes were unmarked. It was as if nothing at all at happened.

"Is something wrong?" he asked, his tone now a little anxious.

"No, sorry – the ring just wasn't where I thought it was. I'll be right down!" I lied and hung up.

I picked up my clutch bag and rushed out of the door and down the stairs. I jumped into the Uber, apologising to the driver, and gave Nathan a brief kiss on the cheek, trying to appear calm and composed as my racing heart gradually returned to normal. The wine now felt like a pool of acid in my stomach, and I could only hope I could keep it together for the rest of the night. Tonight was about us, about the future Nathan and I had together, and I was not going to let *her* ruin it.

Chapter Eleven

I stared out of the car window, focusing on the darkness, the florescent lights of shops and bars and the flash of headlights, until we made it to the waterfront. We got out of the car and started walking alongside the water. I held Nathan's hand firmly to help stop me shaking. I breathed in the cool night air, filling my lungs and exhaling slowly. My heels clicked on the pavement and I felt a little lightheaded, as if only a little piece of me was here and the rest of me was drifting further and further into my mind, hiding from the world but also avoiding what was kept there under lock and key.

Only a few minutes later, we were standing outside the new tapas bar called *La Cortina* –The Curtain – where we actually had to pull aside an intricate, colourful silk curtain to enter the premises. The venue did not disappoint – if I had to describe it in a single word, it would be *stunning*. The white oak floors, the lighting – bright in places but intimate around the ebony tables and chairs – silk tapestries adorning the walls, a single glass panel so you could watch the chefs working busily in the kitchen.

As we waited to be led to our table, I noted that the

restaurant was already quite busy. I caught sight of Nathan's family sitting in the far corner. His sister and parents were chatting away together, gesticulating, throwing their heads back in laughter. They had a sense of ease about them that I admired, as if being happy and loving towards each other was the easiest and most natural thing in the world.

They soon caught sight of us, standing up instantly, looking happy and excited as they hugged us and offered their congratulations. Nathan's sister, Louise, and mum, Eleanor, *ooh*ed and *aah*ed over the ring, and I allowed myself to be swept up in their joy and excitement.

We took our seats and Alex ordered a bottle of champagne to celebrate. They asked us about our holiday and Nathan told them how great the surf had been, how breathtaking the landscape and, of course, how amazing the food and wine was. We sipped at our champagne; I was not normally a fan, but the more I drank, the better I felt, and before I knew it I had finished the glass and Alex was topping me up. We perused the menu and decided it all sounded delicious and that we would stick to *tapas* so that we could all try a bit of everything.

Nathan said I was great at ordering tapas, so the honour was left to me. I ordered a variety of fish, meat, prawn and potato dishes. Once the champagne was gone, we moved onto red wine, which flowed as easily as the conversation. Nathan's parents asked us if we'd made any plans for the wedding, and we admitted that we hadn't given it much thought yet, and both Louise and Eleanor offered to help me out with anything I needed. I knew Nathan had informed them that my mother had passed away when I was young, and that I was not very close to either my father or my sister. It touched me that they wanted to help me choose a wedding dress and they all loved the photo I'd printed of Nathan and me as a little token gift of our engagement.

The food was rich, tasty and wonderful. For dessert, we ordered some scrumptious cheesecakes and chocolate cake and, even though I felt I couldn't eat another bite, I finished every last morsel. The bill was a little pricey, but Alex refused to let us pay, saying it was their treat.

At the end of the night, as I was putting on my coat, Louise noticed the ruby ring on my other hand.

"Oh wow, Beth, I adore this ring too," she exclaimed, taking my hand in hers. "Very retro and vintage. Where did you get it?"

"Can you believe she found it on the beach?" Nathan declared before I had a chance to reply.

"No way –lucky you!" Louise replied.

"Yeah, can't quite believe I saw it in the surf one night as we walked along the beach," I added.

"Oh, how romantic. Next time you guys go I'd love to come along, bag myself some Spanish *amor*. The ring reminds me of an engagement ring from, like, centuries ago."

I stared at the ring seeing it in a whole new light. Louise's words had hit a nerve. I hadn't thought about it before but I supposed it did look a little like an engagement ring. I wondered who it may have belonged to, if she had had a happy life, and how the ring had ended up lost and washed up on the beach.

"Yeah, I guess you're right," I mumbled, trying to muster a smile, then fastening my coat and stuffing my hands in my pockets.

We said our goodnights, promising to meet up again soon, then getting into an Uber to take us home. Nathan looked happy, having had a great dinner with his family, and was jubilant as we entered the dark apartment. Instantly, I flipped the light switch to banish the shadows and took off my heels, welcoming the coolness of the tiles on my slightly sore feet. I brushed past Nathan and into the bedroom, where I took off my engagement ring and placed it on the trinket dish. I hesitated for just a second before pulling off the antique ring, worried that it wouldn't come off, but it slid off easily. I never slept wearing jewellery. I also removed my silver and rose gold bangle and began to unzip my skirt.

"Hey, not so fast there future Mrs Walker. Let me help you with that," Nathan whispered seductively as he came up behind me and placed his hands on my hips.

He kissed the side of my neck in the way he knew I loved, and which was always certain to turn me to jelly. I turned around to face him and kissed him deeply, running my fingers across his toned stomach.

"You looked so beautiful tonight. I couldn't wait to get you back home..." he murmured, slipping off my skirt, taking off my top, and kissing me in my most sensitive of places.

I sighed deeply, allowing Nathan to pick me up and carry me to bed. I gave in to the effects of the alcohol and Nathan's skills in the bedroom. After we'd made love, sleep came like a blissful spell.

The kitchen smelled of oranges and pancake batter. I shuffled in, wearing my slippers, to find Nathan cooking up a storm, the counter littered with orange husks, cracked egg shells and flour.

"Hey, look who's up!" Nathan teased me.

"Morning, gorgeous. What's all this?" I asked happily.

"Thought my baby could do with a good breakfast. Come sit, it's almost ready. How's your head?"

"A little sore," I admitted. "That wine was too good."

He chuckled good-naturedly. "Yeah, my dad is a bad influence."

I took a sip of the freshly squeezed orange juice and watched Nathan. His face was a cute mask of concentration as he flipped the pancakes and placed a couple on a plate and set it before me.

"Mmm, I could get used to this," I declared, squeezing lemon and sprinkling sugar on my pancakes.

Sugar and lemon had been my favourite topping as a child. Helena, like Nathan, preferred maple syrup. That thought reminded me that I hadn't as yet mentioned to Nathan my plans to visit my father later that day.

"I was thinking I'd pop in to see my father later and see whether he has had any more news from the doctor, or if he needs anything. I'm sure that Helena is looking after him, but still, I should ask..."

"That sounds like a good idea, hun," Nathan said carefully.

I felt a little bad that he thought he needed to tip-toe around anything that involved my family. He knew how much the subject upset me and that I avoided talking about it, yet he was always supportive.

"I can go with you? If that helps?" He added.

"Thanks I appreciate you offering, but I think it's best if I go alone."

"Sure I understand. Please say hello for me and that I'm... well sorry to hear such terrible news and you know I'm always here to talk about anything if you want to."

This would have been the perfect opportunity to open up about a number of things, and I even opened my mouth to try to start explaining, but instead I found myself saying, "Yes, of course – I know that, and thank you for always being so understanding."

"Of course – I love you, Beth. You know that, right?" he said earnestly.

His affection and tenderness made my heart ache a little, but in a good way and tears pricked my eyes. "And I'll love you for always."

He doused his pancakes in maple syrup and began to tuck in. "I hope you realise what a lucky lady you are, Beth. These pancakes are awesome." He grinned.

"The luckiest." I agreed and kissed him.

After breakfast, I hopped into the shower, allowing the water to ease my hangover state, and then dressed in a long-sleeved burgundy fitted dress and black boots. I plaited my hair into a braid. If I left it loose I would look too much like Helena, and neither of us would appreciate that. I applied a little make-up, hoping it would help disguise the grey pallor induced by the thought of spending time in my childhood home. I picked up my car keys and strode back to the living room, where Nathan was playing on his PlayStation: some sort of military game.

"So, what are you going to be up to whilst I'm gone?" I asked him as I picked up my bag. I wrapped a scarf around my neck and gave him a quick peck on the lips.

"Was actually gonna head out to the Wave for a bit, do a little surf – that cool? I didn't know how long you were planning on being away…"

"Of course– have fun. You could do with winding down after the week you've had. Tonight I thought we could order some food in and binge-watch some Netflix?" I suggested.

"Yeah, sure, sounds good," he replied, his fingers moving erratically over the controller, and he bit his lip in concentration. "Hope it goes well today."

"Thanks. Me too."

I took a deep breath, grabbed my jacket and let myself out. I descended the stairs slowly. I was procrastinating and I knew it, but I still didn't move any faster. I strolled to the car and got in, started the engine, then decided I would stop at Sainsbury's on my way over to pick up some groceries for my dad.

I parked at the edge of the car park and made my way inside. It was a nice day: a clear blue-jay-coloured sky, dotted with a few white cotton clouds which shifted slowly in the light breeze. It was busy in Sainsbury's. I grabbed a basket and continued to the fresh fruit and vegetable aisle. I picked up some seedless red grapes, which seemed to be the fruit of choice that people brought others when they were ill or in hospital.

But what do you buy for someone who is terminally ill? If it was me, I guess I'd want a cart full of ice-cream, no longer having to be bothered about calories. What I believed my dad craved was the one thing I couldn't buy him: beer, whiskey, vodka, wine... anything with alcohol, really.

As I stared at the lonely bunch of grapes in my basket I started to think this was a stupid idea, just another excuse to delay the visit, but I was here already so I figured I may as well stick to the plan.

I recalled that my dad used to be a big tea drinker – at least I think he was before my mother died. Even before that fateful day we had never been close, so my recollections of him were hazy at best.

A thought, which I was surprised hadn't come to me sooner, stopped me in my tracks. If my mother hadn't died, my father wouldn't have reverted to drink to survive, and wouldn't have gotten liver cancer – meaning I was now responsible for *his* death too.

"Can I help you?" a young man with freckles, who was stacking shelves, asked me.

I looked at him blankly and finally managed to blurt out, "Yes, I'm looking for tea."

"Aisle six," he replied, looking at me a little uncertainly.

I imagined I looked as if I was about to faint, and I felt like I might, right there amongst the strawberries and blueberries. I progressed, zombie-like, to aisle six and got some tea and some chocolate digestives too. I racked my brain for something else to get as I meandered around the store, eventually picking up a crossword puzzle book from the stationery section and a large bottle of water for myself. I paid and left.

Back in my car, I opened the bottle of water hastily and

took several long gulps. I remembered something Dr Roberts had once told me in one of our sessions: *"You are not responsible for anyone else's happiness."* That was all well and good, but what if you *were* responsible for their misery? *Answer me that, Dr Roberts.*

I switched on the radio. Some upbeat song by Justin Bieber was playing; I turned it up, hoping it would help drown out my inner voice. I drove with the music blaring until I reached what had once been my home. I looked up at it and switched off the engine, the sudden quiet disturbing.

The beautiful sky had begun to darken. In my current mood, it felt like a warning. I made myself get out of the car and ring the doorbell. No one came to the door, so I rang it again. Perhaps they were out. I felt momentarily relieved, but it didn't last long, as I soon heard footsteps approaching. The door didn't open right away, and I assumed I was being peered at through the peephole. I took an involuntary step backwards and then the door opened to reveal Helena. She was dressed immaculately in navy blue dress pants and a mint-green sweater, embroidered with lace along the neckline.

"Beth," she stated simply, sounding more than a little surprised.

"Hi Helena. I messaged Dad the other day but I didn't hear back. I thought I'd pop in and see if he needed anything, or if he had had any more news from the doctor. I brought grapes." I offered up the Sainsbury's bag as proof.

She looked at me warily, as you'd mistrust a wild dog that was getting too close. "Well, I guess you best come in, then," she said finally, and stepped aside, letting me walk ahead of her. "He's sitting in the living room. Hasn't been feeling too well these past few days."

"Hi Dad—" I started as I stepped inside, but then had to stop myself from gasping.

He was lying on the couch, a thick blanket draped over him. In a matter of days he seemed to have deteriorated considerably. He looked thinner and his skin had taken on a sickly, yellowish hue. He turned his eyes away from the muted TV broadcasting the news, and faced me. Helena followed me into the room and took a seat next to him. I sat opposite them on the beige recliner chair.

"Hello Beth —didn't expect to see you," he greeted me softly. There was neither warmth nor coldness in his voice, only acceptance.

"I know. I'm sorry I didn't call first, but when you hadn't replied to my message, I thought I'd pop in to see how you're doing. I got you some grapes and some tea, although I'm sure you probably have tea... and a crossword book. I thought you might be a little bored. Helena mentioned you haven't been feeling too great these past few days…" I rambled on, desperate to fill the thick silence between us which seemed to press against my chest.

"Yeah, I don't think I've charged my phone in a while. Not been feeling up to much lately. I'm sure it's around here somewhere," he said, scanning the room as if expecting his mobile to jump out from wherever it had been hiding. "Thanks for the fruit and tea."

"Don't mention it. Can I make you anything now? A cup of tea? A sandwich?" I offered lamely.

"He just had something to eat," Helena interjected.

"That's good. You need to keep your strength up." I said

awkwardly, thinking it was one of those generic things people tended to say to those who are unwell.

How do terminal patients react to such inane statements? If you tell them not to give up hope, to fight when the battle is already lost, when they are bleeding slowly onto the battlefield waiting for death to claim them?

"Have you had anymore news from the doctor?" I continued.

"They wanted to see me again next week, although I think it's more to just check on how fast I am deteriorating." My father chuckled grimly.

I didn't know what to say in response to that, and the silence stretched on painfully. I gazed out the picture window to the rolling colour-filled garden beyond, and the overcast sky, which continued to blacken. I noticed a large black fly continuously bumping against the glass in a desperate bid to get out –I could relate. Our muteness continued, until all I could hear was the buzzing of the fly and its incessant, desperate knocks on the window.

"Excuse me – I just need to use the bathroom," I blurted out and hurried out of the room and up the stairs.

I closed the bathroom door behind me and let out a breath I hadn't realised I had been holding. I felt a little shaky, as if I'd climbed a thousand steps rather than just a single floor. Being back in this house stirred too many memories, and I wanted to be far away from here. Far away from my dying father, who had really been dying since the day my mother died, and far away from my sister, a mirror image of myself that reflected too much of what I desperately wanted to forget.

I splashed cold water on my face and steadied myself on the sink unit. I counted to ten slowly in my head to help temper my nerves, and was just about to walk out when I heard a voice. At first it was just a soft humming, a few disjointed notes but which morphed into a lullaby: the one from my childhood and the same one I had heard in Spain.

Duermete mi nina, de mi corazon, ya no llores mas,
Duermete ya, que viene el cuco y te comera,
La, la, la... la, la...

"Please, not here," I implored through gritted teeth.

The sound reminded me of when my mother used to sing, her voice angelic and consoling. Before I could even try and block out the flashback from my mind, the room began to transform around me, transporting me back and enclosing me in a memory of another time.

The room is softly lit in the glow from a unicorn night light. I had been sleeping, tucked deep within the thick covers, which were now too warm and felt suffocating, but I dared not stir. It is my mother's voice which has woken me. She is singing one of her favourite songs, Dream A Little Dream Of Me.

I opened my eyes slowly, sluggish from sleep, allowing them to adjust to the faint light. My mother sat on Helena's bed. I could see that Helena had been crying, tears glistening on her cheeks like tiny raindrops. My mother wiped them away, brushing Helena's hair from her face with her fingertips as she sang and whispered soothingly to her.

I must have moved, as my mother suddenly glanced over at me. For a split second, I saw fear in her eyes and in that moment I hated her.

Chapter Twelve

The rest of the weekend passed quickly, as weekends often do. Nathan and I enjoyed a lie in on Sunday morning, and then a trip into town to window shop, enjoying some Häagen-Dazs salted caramel ice-cream as we strolled along, hand in hand. We had even started to discuss the wedding, or more precisely the honeymoon, and had looked briefly at a number of options online, including the Maldives, Riviera Maya and an Alaskan cruise –I wanted to do it all.

I awoke on Tuesday morning equally dreading and looking forward to my session with Dr Roberts. I would feel relieved to discuss my recent experiences with another human being. I didn't think a problem shared is by any means a problem halved, but I would feel less alone. Yet I did also worry about the conclusions he would draw.

The thought of how I had left my father's house on Saturday made me cringe. I had burst out of the bathroom, run down the stairs, darted back into the living room and made a jumbled excuse about not feeling well and needing to get home. Without waiting for a response, I had grabbed my handbag and rushed out of the front door. Once I was in the car I had glanced back up at the house. Helena had stood on the front porch, her arms folded across her chest, an unreadable expression on her face. I had floored the accelerator back home and was relieved when I shut the door behind me, thankful that Nathan had already left to go surfing so he wasn't around to query why I was home so early.

I released a heavy sigh and tried to forget how crazy I must have seemed to them, and instead listened to the water running in the shower as Nathan got ready for work. I got out of bed with renewed determination to get my life back on track. I went to the kitchen and made some coffee, drinking it black as I stared out the kitchen window. A few minutes later, Nathan came in and wrapped his arms around me and kissed me goodbye, taking the pasta salad and cheese roll I had made for him the night before for lunch.

I hadn't mentioned the appointment I'd made with Dr Roberts. Not that it was a secret or anything. Nathan was well aware how Dr Roberts had helped me with my aqua-phobia. My terror of the ocean wasn't something I could explain or justify; it was just there. Fear, I had learned, was not a condition, but rather a response, just like sneezing. Humans need fear as an emergency survival response, a warning of danger.

Now I feared the woman in grey could have been a manifestation to signal impending danger – of what exactly, I didn't know. The reason I hadn't mentioned the appointment to Nathan was simply because I didn't want him to worry.

Nathan had suggested we could speed up our wedding plans, so that my father could attend. I hadn't really known how to answer that, because I wasn't sure if he'd even attend or if I'd want him to. He just didn't fit into my life anymore, and hadn't done for so long... did that make me a monster?

It definitely didn't paint me in a nice light, and I didn't want Nathan to see vestiges of the old Beth, so I'd sidetracked that conversation and started up one about something else completely.

I finished my second cup of coffee and rinsed it under the tap. I wasn't all that hungry but I made myself eat a slice of toasted wholemeal bread with butter. I washed the plate and put it on the dish rack to dry.

I checked the time – it was already gone 9.30am. Had I really just spent an hour daydreaming and looking out of the window? I hurried into the shower, got dressed and applied a little make-up. For some women, make-up was something they used simply to accentuate their beauty; for me, make-up had always been something I used to hide behind. To help create a mask, one which smiled with richly coloured lips, had rosy happy cheeks and thick black eyelashes that accentuated the eyes whilst simultaneously shielding them.

I put on my flat boots and headed out. Dr Robert's clinic was located on the other side of Clifton. The weather was pleasantly sunny, if a little cool, and I wrapped my wool coatigan a little tighter around my body.

I preferred walking to my therapy appointments; the exercise helped me think about how and what I wanted to disclose. My sessions with Dr Roberts had become comfortable over the years. I felt like I was talking to a friend rather than a therapist, but one who I knew would keep our chats confidential. At least, that had become the case when discussing the usual topics. I had no idea how to even begin talking about *her*, and that made me nervous.

I made it to the clinic by 11am on the dot. The clinic was situated in a garden-level apartment in a row of terraced houses in Ferring Ford Street, painted blindingly white. It had been converted into three private offices, a communal bathroom, a small reception area and kitchenette. A group of three therapists of various specialisations had opened up the business together about ten years ago. The clinic itself conveyed both a sense of professionalism and homeliness, with clean lines, minimalist furniture, cotton-white walls with colourful paintings of forests and beaches, comfortable sofas and large, bottle-green potted plants. As I stepped inside, the familiar face of the receptionist greeted me with a warm smile.

"Morning Beth, please take a seat. Dr Roberts will be with you in just a moment. Can I get you a cup of tea? Green, mint or regular?" she asked kindly.

"Thanks, Olivia, but I'm fine," I replied as I took a seat in the graphite-grey armchair and ran my hands nervously over its plushness.

Olivia nodded and returned to typing away at her computer. There was no one else in the waiting area, but the doors to the three clinics were closed and I could hear the soft murmur of voices beyond.

Thankfully, I didn't have to wait long before the door to Dr Roberts' office opened and an elderly woman stepped out. I could tell she had been crying, even though she was trying to hide it, slipping on her sunglasses before leaving the clinic. I knew Dr Roberts offered grief counselling services and I wondered who she had lost. A son? A husband? She wore the pain like a heavy cloak, and I found myself wondering if she was going home to an empty house.

"Beth." Dr Robert's mellifluous voice broke me from my reverie. I turned to face him and got up from the chair. "Please come in, sorry to keep you waiting."

"Oh, I had only just arrived," I told him as I stepped into his office and took my usual seat opposite him.

Dr Roberts looked to be in his early forties. He had a mop of dark hair with a scattering of grey, which made him look distinguished. He was tall and slim, with dark brown eyes in a broad face, which would become virtually expressionless once our session began. He was difficult to read but an underlying sense of kindness and caring permeated through, which is what I believed made him such a good therapist. The fact that I could never be completely honest with him didn't detract from this conclusion.

"It's good to see you. So, how was your trip?" he asked casually as he settled back into his seat and sipped from his glass of water. He poured me a glass and placed it on the oak coffee table between us.

"The trip was great, and I managed to swim in the ocean a few times," I told him, unable to stop grinning, knowing he would be pleased. *How sad am I? Seeking approval and some sort of validation from my therapist.* "Nathan proposed and I said yes," I added, extending my hand to show him the ring.

"That's excellent news on both fronts. I am very happy for you."

I placed my hand back in my lap, looking down at the diamonds, crystal clear, flaw-less, strong, –everything I wasn't. On my other hand, the ruby ring flamed red. After what had happened on Friday night, I thought I would never wear it again, but I found myself inexplicably putting it on every morning.

"Thank you. Nathan makes me very happy."

We had, of course, discussed Nathan in my sessions. Dr Roberts was aware how much of a positive influence Nathan was in my life, although he had hinted at the importance of not using my love for Nathan to put a plaster over my family issues. He was a firm believer that you could not fully love another unless you had first come to love yourself, in order to have a truly healthy relationship. But what if you couldn't love yourself? What if your true self was not worthy of love? I had never dared to ask.

I'd always considered honesty vastly overrated, as was self-awareness, but of course I didn't tell Dr Roberts this. Half-truths have been the basis of my entire life. It was too late to construct anything different now.

"And how do you feel about getting engaged?" Dr Roberts began, his voice mellow and almost hypnotic.

That was an easy topic to start off with, and I was grateful for it. "Great, really great. I was a little surprised, but I had always hoped he would propose someday. I mean, I knew he was the man I wanted to marry after only a couple months of dating."

"Is there anything else on your mind? Anything troubling you?" He was cutting to the chase. His small notepad lay on his lap, his pen in his hand.

During our sessions, Dr Roberts would often scribble down a point or two in his notebook. In this way, he gave me his full attention and would only write a full set of notes afterwards.

It has always amazed me how often people fail to give you their complete attention when you speak to them. They ask you how you are without really listening to your response, asking more out of politeness than genuine concern. At university parties there were always those who would only be half absorbed in what I was saying, whilst they kept an eye out for someone more popular, prettier or more interesting to talk to.

"Beth?" Dr Roberts prompted, tugging me away from my thoughts.

"My father is ill, dying," I replied bluntly.

"I am very sorry to hear that. I know you do not have an easy relationship with him. Shall we talk a little about him? How did you find out? How did you react to the news?"

"He actually called to tell me. I was quite shocked, even though perhaps I shouldn't have been. Still, nowadays, even when you get a cancer diagnosis you still expect to have some hope, but he hasn't been given long to live. It's terminal. Liver cancer, which I guess is almost to be expected given his years of drinking. He drowned himself in the bottle to survive my mother's death and now the bottle has finally destroyed him."

"How do you feel about that?"

"Guilty. I was responsible for my mother's death and now I am responsible for my father's," I replied without even thinking. My tone was unemotional, deadpan, resigned to this fact.

This wasn't how I had expected the session to go, but it would have been unusual for a person not to mention such horrid news, and discussing my father gave me some buffer time before opening up about the woman in grey.

Dr Roberts scribbled something in his notepad and I shifted in my seat. I tore my eyes away from the notebook. I couldn't see what he wrote in it – I had tried to before – so instead I focused on the potted fern in the corner and the large canvas photograph of what I guessed to be Yellowstone National Park.

"Beth, in our sessions we have talked a lot about your guilt with regards to your mother's death. But what is the truth about what happened that day?"

"That my mother's death was ultimately an accident. A series of unfortunate events and bad timing. I also know I was just a child, but it's so hard to not feel responsible. Accidents can so often be cause and effect, and I was the cause..." I trailed off.

"We have discussed the importance of acceptance, of forgiving yourself, even though it was an accident. We have discussed the value of these feelings in order to gradually overcome your sense of guilt, anger, even fear. I believe you have made great strides in this respect. Your father is unwell, and I'd like us to focus on your present-day reality and how I can help you cope with what you are currently going through. It may even help alleviate some of your past hurt," Dr Roberts said softly.

"I feel like an outsider when I'm with them. As if my father and sister stand together in one room, and I'm stuck in another, and no matter what I do, there will always be this wall between us."

"And why is it that you feel like an outsider when you are with them?" he probed.

"I guess I distanced myself from them in order to distance

myself from myself. If that makes any sense? It was the only way to start again. Perhaps I must simply accept that this is how things are."

"I can't stress enough that acceptance is the key to healing and growing, but we must be able to differentiate between acceptance and giving up."

I nodded. "But I feel like I need closure from the past. I want to focus on my future with Nathan."

"That's understandable. You have an opportunity now to get that closure with your father, and perhaps develop a better relationship with your sister."

I nodded again. "I... the reason I called to make another appointment wasn't really to do with my family. Although I know I need to talk about that too," I finally managed to say.

"We can discuss your family at a later time if that works better for you. What else is bothering you at the moment?"

"I don't know how to even begin..."

"Just start at the beginning and we can take it from there," he said soothingly.

"Well, ever since the trip – actually, it started during my time away – I've been seeing things, hearing things," I explained, looking him in the eye.

Dr Roberts expression remained neutral. I could just as well have been talking about the weather.

"Talk to me about your experiences," he continued evenly.

"It's been numerous things: dreams, visions of this woman, hearing a song from the past... I'm worried I'm losing my mind."

"Take me through exactly what you've seen and heard."

So I did, and I didn't tell half-truths as I'd thought I would. I told Dr Roberts everything: the experiences I'd had in Tarifa, and what had occurred within my own home, at the church and at my father's house. I didn't leave anything out, and by the time I'd finished I realised just how much had happened in just a few short weeks and how much I had been trying to ignore.

As I recounted each frightful event I felt my pulse accelerate, and a thin layer of sweat had broken out over my skin. I found myself taking quicker and shallower breaths. It was the beginning of a panic attack, like the ones I'd had when trying to swim for the first time, or when I'd wake up from a nightmarish underwater world.

"Take a deep breath, Beth, nice and slow," Dr Roberts instructed in his almost hypnotic voice.

I took three lungfuls and reached over with a trembling hand to take a sip of cool water.

"I understand how troubling and unsettling this must all be for you. I'm glad you called to talk to me about this."

I nodded for a third time. I often felt like the bulldog mascot of the Churchill advert when in therapy. I made myself stop.

"Is that the ring you found on the beach?" he asked, having glimpsed the crimson stone as I'd put the glass back on the table.

I was about to nod again, but instead said, "Yes... and for some reason I can't quite explain, I find myself putting it on every morning, almost automatically, even after what happened on Friday night."

"What do you think has triggered the change in dreams

and these experiences?"

I thought for a moment, trying to come up with something other than *Clearly, I am insane*. "I don't know, but I'm scared. Whatever this is, I don't think it's going to stop, and I don't want to talk to Nathan about it. I'm worried that this is all in my head. That my mind has conjured up this woman to torture me, or that perhaps I've brought something back from that place, something not of this world, which is equally just as crazy," I blurted out.

To his credit, Dr Roberts didn't even raise an eyebrow. I guess he heard a lot of weird stuff in his consultations.

"What goes through your mind during these experiences?" he asked.

"I feel like I need to get away. There's this sense of impending danger... but at the same time she seems familiar, as if I've met her before – but I know that I haven't."

"The water theme pervades these experiences too," he noted.

"I've noticed that too. It's almost like a message that I can't understand. But I don't want this to keep happening to me. I need to make it stop," I said with finality.

"You mentioned how at home you felt in Tarifa," he reminded me.

"Yes. It was almost like going home, even though I'd never set foot in Spain before."

"*Déjà visité?*" he suggested.

"I'm sorry?"

"*Déjà visité*, like *déjà vu*, but instead of an experience seeming familiar, it's a place – a place we feel we've been before," Dr Roberts explained.

"Yes, exactly that."

"There are many scientists and psychiatrists that insist that there are numerous neurological explanations for the *déjà vu* phenomena. However, there are those that believe that these peculiar feelings are fleeting memories of past lives. Memories of past lives can also manifest themselves as recurring dreams or nightmares."

"Past lives," I repeated softly, sounding out the words.

Even in my current predicament I couldn't help but be fascinated by this. My whole life there had been so many things I wish I could undo, or do differently. The thought of past and possible future lives was oddly comforting.

"Do you believe in past lives?" I asked him.

He didn't often speak of his own beliefs, but I respected him and often wished I knew more about him, since he knew so much about me.

"If there is one thing that I've learned in my career is that nothing is ever black and white. There is so much we still have to learn about the human mind – and who am I to disregard entire beliefs. The idea that people are born and reborn has been around for at least three thousand years. Discussions on this subject are found across ancient traditions in Greece and India, and were held by the Celtic druids. Reincarnation is also a common theme of new-age philosophies."

"Is that what you think I could be experiencing? A fragment of a past life?" I asked hopefully.

Even though this concept was up there alongside UFOs, vampires and werewolves, it sounded better than losing my marbles or being haunted by a dead woman.

"It's not for me to say but in our previous sessions we did find hypnosis useful in helping you cope with your aquaphobia." He paused before continuing. "Past life regression therapy is also a form of hypnosis. It is believed that we carry with us emotional, psychic and occasionally even physical aspects of our past lives into our existing one. By accessing those memories and dealing with them, past life regression has helped some people confront issues they face in their current life."

"So you've done this before?"

"It's not something I've often practised," he admitted, "but I did have one client, many years ago, who had done some research on his experiences and believed in past lives and wished to undertake past life regression therapy. It helped him deal with a lot of what he was going through. Obviously, I can't discuss his case with you, but I can tell you about a particular case study I researched during my training in this particular style of hypnotherapy. In what was called the second life of the Pollock girls in the 1950s, two sisters were killed in a car crash. The following year, their mother became pregnant and gave birth to identical twin girls. The parents immediately noticed strange similarities between their new children and those they had lost, including scars and birthmarks. The girls were also familiar with the town in which their elder sisters had grown up, even though they had never been there, and even correctly named toys that had belonged to their deceased sisters. It was even reported that they feared cars and were afraid that one would crash into them."

"That is extremely freaky and disturbing," I stated, feeling goose-bumps rise on my forearms. I felt as if someone had walked over my grave, but I also wanted to know more.

"Indeed. However, when the twins became a little older, memories of their past life vanished and it became another unsolved mystery," Dr Roberts concluded.

"Oh," I said simply, feeling strangely disappointed.

"Past life regression therapy would be similar to what we have done in our previous hypnosis sessions, and would help us understand if it is the cause of your recent experiences. If it's not helpful we could always explore other avenues."

"OK, let's do it," I replied, sounding more sure than I felt.

"I'll schedule you in for Friday morning, same time? This will give you a few days to think about it. As always, there is no pressure. If you come in on Friday and decide not to go down this route, we can just have a chat instead and discuss other options."

"Thanks. I already feel a little better." I said.

I had options, and with options came solutions, right? Until then, I would rely a little bit more on my meds. Dr Roberts was not a fan of prescription medications, but the anti-anxiety meds and sleeping tablets had helped get me through the worst of my panic attacks and nights when bad dreams threatened to unfold every time I closed my eyes.

"But if you feel you need to speak to me sooner, or if you experience something you cannot handle, do not hesitate to call me," he instructed.

"I will. Thank you again, doctor."

"See you soon, Beth, and remember the calming and visualisation techniques we have discussed. In the past, keeping a journal has helped you deal with your worries – perhaps it is something you can pick up again?" he suggested.

"Yes, I think I will. See you on Friday." I gave him a smile as I got up and left his office.

I waved politely at Olivia and stepped outside into the fresh air, feeling a little lighter. My phone began to vibrate. I assumed it was Nathan, but my smile vanished instantly when I saw it was Helena. My throat constricted and I found it hard to swallow. I had the foreboding notion that she had called to tell me my father had died.

There was a momentary silence before I said, "Hello."

It turned out I was only half right: someone had died, just not my father.

"Beth. It's Helena. Dolores is dead. The care home informed us. The service is tomorrow at midday, at the Church of All Hallows. Dad thought you'd want to know."

She hung up before I could utter a single word in response.

Chapter Thirteen

The day was as grey and foggy as my emotions. As I entered the church, Nathan took my hand and I held onto it tightly, fearing that without it I would simply float away like a helium balloon in the wind.

We took a seat near the front of the church. My father and Helena were sitting in the pew in front, and they turned and gave us a nod in greeting. My father looked a little better than he had on Saturday, but a smart suit could not hide the skeletal frame of someone being eaten from the inside by cancer. My sister held onto his arm; her expression was one of ache and despair. Dolores had been our primary caregiver until we had both left for university.

About fifty people had turned up to the funeral, a congregation of black clothes, red puffy eyes and white, waxy faces, but I didn't recognise anyone other than my father and Helena. I assumed many of them were Dolores' friends from the care home, and it must have been Dolores' sister who sat in the front pew. They had the same round face, olive skin and deep-set eyes.

Since my mother's death I had avoided funerals – even churches, really. It had only been my studies or work that had brought me back into the vast halls of the churches.

In front of me, numerous bouquets of pink roses were dotted around the altar. Roses were Dolores' favourite; I could remember Dolores telling Helena how much she liked them. They had both been pottering around in the garden. Helena was crying and Dolores had been trying to cheer her up. I hadn't been asked to join in; I had simply stared at them through the window, my face pressed so close to the glass that it fogged up, partially obscuring them from view. It made them seem less real and easier to hate.

I hadn't wanted to come today, but I had mentioned Dolores' death to Nathan and he had instantly offered to come with me. I couldn't really tell him I had no intention of going. That would have seemed wrong, and I didn't want Nathan to think I was cold and cruel, not ever.

So here I was, feeling empty and numb, in the confines of the church, the silence broken only by the muffled sobs of those grieving. The organ began to play, a haunting sound which made me shiver. Dolores' coffin was dark stained cherry, and gleamed as if it exuded its own light. A sad hymn began to play as mourners took it in turns to shuffle up to the coffin and say their last goodbyes to the deceased.

The priest said his part and the service was soon over, with Dolores' coffin being taken to be cremated. I was glad to be outside once more, welcoming the fresh air and being away from the pain and loss of others. The sun was beginning to win its battle against the clouds, narrow bands of light shining through.

Nathan gave me a hug and kissed me goodbye. He needed to rush back to the office to finish a brief before a client meeting that afternoon. I thanked him for coming and watched him go, with an inexplicable, sinister premonition that I was going to lose him.

"Beth, it's good that you came," I heard my father say as he came up behind me.

"It was the least I could do," I replied, noticing that he now shuffled along like a much older man.

"Nathan had to leave?" Helena asked.

"Yes, his boss told him to take the day off, but he's so busy at the moment with some new clients that he had to head back."

"Have you set a date for the wedding?" my father asked.

"We haven't actually got around to discussing that yet, – we've just had so much going on at the moment... but hopefully it'll be soon," I assured him. "Have you had any more news from the doctor?"

"Nothing more for the moment, but he's prescribed some additional medication to make me more... comfortable." He sighed, and in that sigh there seemed a lot left unspoken.

"You will let me know if there's anything I can do, won't you?" I pleaded with him; with them both.

"Of course." There was a slight pause before he continued, "I'm not afraid of dying, Beth. My time is coming and I take comfort in knowing that I will be with your mother again soon. There comes a time when we must all take responsibility for our actions," he said desolately.

"Come on, Dad, let's go home," Helena prompted, pulling him away. "Bye, Beth."

"Bye," I croaked, watching them leave.

I caught sight of Dolores' sister and when she met my eyes, a smile began to form on her lips in acknowledgement, but then died. I supposed Dolores had told her all about me. I turned away and began walking home. My full black skirt swished around my knees and I focused on the cobbled street beneath my feet.

As soon as I got home I stripped off my skirt and charcoal-grey jumper, leaving them in a pool on the floor. I felt overcome by a sudden wave of tiredness so fierce that I felt disorientated and unsteady on my feet.

I hadn't taken any meds that morning, had I? That was my last conscious thought as I crawled on top of the bed, where sleep came as swiftly as the fall of a guillotine.

Night fell and stars were glittering like snowflakes in the sky, beautiful yet cold. In the chill silver beam of moonlight I walk barefoot on the damp, fertile soil of the vineyards. The thick, harsh vines are heavy with swollen grapes, which look like dark violet eyes watching my every move.

The hem of my dress brushes the floor and is stained with blood, as are my hands, but I don't feel injured. I taste something delicious and sweet on my lips –grapes – and I realise the stains are not blood.

The snap of a twig, the rustle of feet treading on dead leaves: every sound is magnified by the thick silence of the night. I feel panic rise up in me like the swell of the ocean. In the dark, a set of eyes crawls over my skin, envious, assessing, threatening.

I begin to run.

My stalker follows.

I trip. My knee slams into a rock and my palms sting. I am up again almost instantly, fear driving me forward. Thick clouds drift overhead with unnatural speed and snuff out the light of the stars and the moon as if they never existed.

I am running blind.

The wave of panic is now all-consuming. I can feel that someone is almost upon me – and suddenly I crush right into a stone wall. I had made it to the end of the vineyard but in my haste I had travelled in the wrong direction.

I look up and even in the gloom I can make out the hacienda on the hill. It embodies home and safety but seems far away.

It is now blood that trickles down my head, blurring my vision. I couldn't afford to hesitate; I turned and stumbled towards the beacon of white on the hilltop. I had only taken a few steps when I felt a presence behind me.

I knew I shouldn't look back, that I should only keep moving forward, but I couldn't help it. I turned around slowly to find someone standing right behind me, and I stumbled backwards in fear and shock.

There was hatred in her eyes. It was... she looked... like...

I woke up with a start, my heart beating frantically against my chest like a wild bird in a cage. I was slick with sweat.

I peered at the clock on Nathan's bedside table. The time was 3.33pm. I shuddered.

I recalled one of my conversations with Sam. She believed that numbers had meanings, especially those that repeated themselves. She believed the spiritual world was constantly sending out messages and signs, if we only stopped to notice them. I found the conversation would go much quicker if I just agreed with what she was saying. Apparently 333 symbolised the wheel of life, a circular balance, yin and yang, where one cannot exist without the other. These forces both consumed and supported one another.

Such beliefs only served to reinforce my fear that things would not end well for me if such cosmic retribution actually existed. I was more bewildered by how late it was than the three threes, and as the time progressed to 3.34pm I wondered how I could have been asleep for so long.

I lifted my spent body out of bed, feeling like if I had just run a marathon. Not that I ever *had* run a marathon, but I imagined this was what it would feel like if I ever did: every muscle aching and weary.

I realised I could no longer balk at Sam's beliefs so easily. I was now seriously considering the possibility of past lives, partially because I was desperate to have an explanation as to the woman in grey, no matter how irrational, if it meant I wasn't completely demented.

I had another shower to help me feel less groggy, and put on my favourite leggings and sweater. I wasn't in the mood to work, even though the deadline was looming, so instead I popped out to the local Spar, bought a whole organic chicken, some red potatoes, a butternut squash and some chantenay carrots. I would keep busy for the rest of the afternoon preparing a delicious roast for Nathan.

I covered the chicken in slices of lemon and placed it in the oven. I began par-boiling the potatoes to roast, as well as roasting the butternut squash and carrots. As I cooked, I opened up a bottle of red wine and poured myself a generous glass.

In the past, especially during my university days, it had been easy and tempting to drown my unhappiness and loneliness in alcohol, but I started to recognise my father in me, and I made a constant decision to be different. To be more like Sam, carefree and someone who enjoyed being around other people.

I was aware that since I had got back from Spain, I had been drinking more, but who could blame me? Fear created a predilection for alcohol. It numbed, it soothed, it helped me forget. I was on my second or third glass and the smell of roasting chicken and vegetables filled the flat. My stomach grumbled, reminding me that I had slept through lunch. I was considering munching on some peanuts when I heard Nathan's key in the lock.

"Hey babe, how was work?" I called out to him.

I heard him fumbling with something for a few moments before I heard him close the door behind him.

"It was fine! I have a surprise for you," he called back, sounding childishly excited.

I was instantly on my guard. I knew most women liked surprises, but I wasn't like most women and never had been. Nathan knew I wasn't a fan of surprises, so we always discussed weekends away, family get-togethers, and so on, before committing to anything. I had learned to order my life, to control as much as possible what I let in and what I let out. It was exhausting but necessary.

"Oh," I replied hesitantly.

He walked into the kitchen carrying a large box, grinning broadly. I couldn't help but smile at the eager look on his face, and I tried to erase the uncertainty from my mine.

"Close your eyes," he instructed.

I did as he asked.

After a little rustling and the sound of the box being opened, he said, "Okay, now you can look."

I blinked as the tiny kitten Nathan held in his hand gave out a soft mewl. The wine glass I held in my right hand dropped to the floor, the contents seeming to expand and splash in every direction. A puddle of dark blood on the tiled kitchen floor, the glass sparkling like tiny daggers.

"Surprise," he said, a little less sure of himself. "Sorry, I didn't mean to startle you." He laughed lightly. "I'll help you clear up. Isn't she a beauty?"

"I am such a klutz! No, I'm sorry, you just caught me by surprise that's all. I wasn't expecting—"

"Ah, that's why it's called a surprise," he continued, upbeat once more.

The kitten looked just like Millie. A ginger striped tabby with bright blue eyes, white breast, white-tipped tail and white paws that looked like socks. Except Millie had only looked like she was wearing socks on her front paws, whereas this kitten had the full set. Her fur was slightly darker, too, whereas Millie's shade of orange was closer to yellow. Tears stung my eyes as the image of Millie's cold, lifeless body, forever branded in my mind, came to the forefront. I choked a sob as I turned away to grab a dishcloth to wipe up the mess.

Nathan placed the kitten back into the box and went to

fetch the mop from the flat's small utility room. I could hear the kitten meowing and pacing inside the cardboard box, unhappy at having been placed back inside, as I wiped the floor with more force than was necessary.

I had buried Millie in the backyard, beneath the bed of pink roses. She had followed me everywhere and slept in the gap next to my pillow. Thinking of Millie led me down a dark path, one which led to Coco-Pop the hamster... but Nathan was soon back with the mop and I shut down that recollection before it had a chance to grow and fester.

"Dinner smells amazing, by the way," Nathan said as I sprayed the floor with cleaner and he wiped it up with the mop.

"Thanks. A full roast to say thanks for all you've done for me lately," I said, trying to keep my voice from trembling.

"I haven't done anything out of the ordinary – well, not until picking up this little dude! Besides, I'd do anything for you, Beth. You know how much I love you, right?" His eyes were earnest, searching mine.

"Of course I do."

"I'd been thinking about surprising you with a pet for a few weeks now, and the rescue centre called me just a few days ago to say they had a number of very young kittens for adoption. And when you told me about Dolores... I thought it would cheer you up. I think you once mentioned you used to have a kitten when you were a child."

"I am definitely surprised, and it is a lovely gesture. She's beautiful. And I did – her name was Millie," I said softly.

"That's a cute name. So what are you thinking of calling the new addition to our family?"

Our family. I cherished those words.

I thought for a few moments before replying, "Mittens, because of her paws."

"Sounds appropriate. Come on, let's get her out of the box. Sounds like she's gonna be a feisty one. Let me show you the stuff I got for her." Nathan picked Mittens out and handed her over, then hurried back to the front door before returning laden with bags.

I held Mittens carefully against my chest and she instantly snuggled up against my neck. I kissed her softly and she purred. Tears trickled down my cheeks and I closed my eyes to smell the earthy scent of her fur.

"You OK?" Nathan asked.

"I'm good."

And I was. I had Nathan and now I had Millie back.

Chapter Fourteen

Even though Nathan had brought Mittens a cat-bed shaped like a clam, I felt she was too little to sleep on her own, and she soon settled on the edge of my pillow, much like Millie used to do. Nathan had also brought her some kitten food, a couple of food bowls, a small bag of litter and a litter tray, which we placed in a corner of the bathroom.

We had a great evening together, savouring the meal, polishing off another bottle of red wine and happily watching Mittens' antics as she explored her new home. I couldn't remember the last time I had laughed so hard. It was one of those moments in life that you just know you need to treasure, because when you look back upon your life you'll realise they were the happiest moments of your existence.

We had started a new series on Netflix called *Medici*, and had promptly added Florence to our list of places to visit. Nathan also told me his sister had emailed him a list of possible venues for the reception party, and I promised him I would have a look at them tomorrow.

As I lay in bed staring at the ceiling, listening to the soft sounds of Nathan's snoring and Mittens probing the pillow with her tiny paws, I felt my thoughts slow, and then sleep pulled me under.

I awoke to the feel of something damp on my cheek. I assumed it was Mittens rousing me from sleep because she was hungry. I opened my eyes to find myself face to face with the decomposed visage of the woman in grey. Drops of saltwater landed on my face as I gripped the sheets in abject terror. The sickly sweet smell of death filled my nostrils and I felt my stomach heave.

In the light of dawn I could see her face had been feasted on by sea creatures and she stared at me as if she wished to suck the life right out of me. Mere moments stretched out into eternity and I felt I could lose much more than just my sanity if I continued to stare into the black, bottomless pits that had once been her eyes. She opened her mouth into a silent scream, and that movement sent me moving.

I rolled to Nathan's side of the bed and then onto the floor. Above the sound of blood roaring in my ears, I could hear Nathan moving around in the kitchen. My instinct was to cry out for him, but I opened my mouth and then closed it. If this was in fact some sort of phenomenon or an echo from a past life, then whatever the hell it was trying to say was a message for me and me alone.

"What do you want from me? Who are you?" I demanded, still in my crouched position next to the bed.

This must be what descending into madness felt like, but I no longer cared, as long as I could put an end to it. I was no stranger to traumatic experiences, and as long as I had breath left in my body, I would not back down or give up without a fight.

What remained of this woman – a hollowed-out corpse – stayed hovering above the space I had just vacated, turning her head a full ninety degrees to stare at me.

"Isabel..." she said without moving her black, lipless mouth, in a voice that had no place on this earth.

"Isabel?" I repeated and recalled the dream I'd had. I was dumbfounded, unable to believe I was now communicating with this... with this *thing*. "Why are you doing this Isabel?"

She ignored me and turned to stare at Mittens instead, who had miraculously remained asleep curled up on my pillow. This woman may have been human once, but she could scarcely be called that now. She reached out with her fleshless fingers as if to grab Mittens.

"Stay away from her," I said, rising up, my voice now commanding.

This seemed to amuse her. She faced me again with a monstrous grin on her face.

"Hey, you're up. Thought I heard you," Nathan said as he walked back into the bedroom. "I've put some more food out for Mittens – I bet she's hungry... What's wrong?"

He couldn't have missed the horrified look on my face as I glanced back at him and then back towards the space above the bed, which was now empty.

Mittens stretched out her small, furry body and mewled softly at us as she began clambering over the discarded sheets towards us.

"I just had a very vivid bad dream... Guess I'm still just shaking it off," I lied.

"Oh, honey. Was it one of the ones about the ocean?" Nathan asked, coming towards me and giving me a light kiss on my lips.

"No, it was about Dolores," I blurted out without thinking.

"Oh, of course. You know I'm always here to listen if you want to talk, right? I may not be as good as Dr Roberts," he joked, trying to lighten the mood, "but I ain't a bad listener. Why don't you come to the kitchen, I'll make you a mug of hot chocolate with extra marshmallows before I head off to the office."

"I know you are a great listener. Chocolate sounds good," I said, trying to inject some enthusiasm into my voice even as my insides curdled at the thought.

I grabbed Mittens lightly around her belly and held her against my chest. She felt warm and soft and helped to ground me in the moment. As horrible as my experience had been, I had learned something. I now had a name: Isabel. I had never met an Isabel before in my life, yet the name did resonate; I just couldn't figure out why.

Still, if this was all in my head then it could simply be my mind conjuring up random words, and it may not necessarily mean anything – but my gut instinct was that this wasn't the case. A name gave me something to work on. Didn't that give me some sort of power over this thing, or did that only work when exorcising demons in horror movies?

A short while later, Nathan left for work and I sat at the dining table with my hands wrapped around a cooling mug of hot chocolate, the marshmallows already melted to form a congealed mass on the top. Looking at it made me feel sick, and I dumped it down the drain and had a glass of water instead.

I watched Mittens as she devoured her wet food of salmon and sole. I told myself I had to be smart about this, I had to be... *cold,* but the word only served to burn me like a hot poker, as I recalled my mother telling my father that I was cold, the coldest child she had ever met. The memory was so vivid I could almost hear her voice as if it was coming from the next room, rather than being something that had been uttered almost twenty years ago.

Another whispered conversation.

A cut like a knife.

A flash of something black and white.

Coco-Pop.

"Arrgh!" I cried aloud, startling Mittens, who ran off into the next room.

I had to get a hold of myself, and quickly. In my head I began to list what I knew. This had all started in Tarifa, a place that felt all too familiar, even though I had never been there before. Visions of a dead woman, who said she was called Isabel, who appeared to have drowned. A ruby ring and a haunting lullaby. Yet what did this all mean and what did it have to do with me? Any misgivings I may have had about regression therapy were wiped out. I needed answers and I needed them now.

I spent the rest of the day engrossed in my work. Things may not have been normal, but I still had bills to pay. I went through my emails and was happy to have received a couple requests for some small jobs. I didn't have much lined up after the Water-Well exhibition, so I needed to find more work. I often did photography for events such as birthdays, amateur theatre productions and corporate events. I accepted Ruth's request to photograph her husband's sixtieth birthday bash, and the book launch event of a local aspiring author.

As promised, I also looked at the list of possible wedding reception venues Nathan's sister Louise had compiled. The list included a number of hotels, a couple of which were located on the waterfront, beautiful country manor houses dotted around the outskirts of the city, boutique hotels, sprawling estates, posh restaurants and even a castle.

I was touched that Louise had gone to the trouble of putting this list together, and I clicked on all the links which directed me to the web-pages of each venue. I found myself liking most, if not all, of them and began feeling more excited about the wedding. Perhaps subconsciously I had not been giving it much thought because I feared that if I let myself experience too much happiness it would all be taken away from me – that someone would realise I didn't deserve it.

When I clicked on the Old Manor House, I knew it was the place. It was an impressive Victorian country house with panoramic views over the River Severn, and a scenic backdrop. I was sold, although I wondered if we could afford it. Nathan's dad had offered to help pay for the wedding, and my father had always been generous with money, trying to make up for his lack of love and affection.

Nathan and I had to go see this place. Perhaps we could view it next week. I'd ask him when he got home. Mittens, who had been happily sleeping away on my lap as I worked and surfed the net, began to stir. I picked her up and placed her on the living-room floor, where she rolled around playfully. I needed to get her some cat toys, but in the meantime a piece of string would have to do. I popped into the utility room and managed to find some string from an old cross-stitch set I had from years back. It had been a Christmas gift from Sam; I had managed to make a pattern for one small cushion before giving up.

As I made my way back to the living room I called out, "Hey, Mittens, look what I found." But she was no longer on the living-room rug. "Hey, you ball of fluff, where'd you get to?"

I searched behind the sofa and under the dining table. She couldn't have gone too far. I had only been gone a minute. I checked by her food bowl, in her litter tray in the bathroom, and her bed by my bedside table, but there was still no sign of her. I began to feel the first stirrings of unease, which would be undoubtedly followed by an unwelcome rush of anxiety, but I forced myself to keep calm. She was tiny; perhaps she had found a little nook in which to hide.

I took her kitten food from the bottom shelf of the larder and shook the packet, hoping this would entice her out of her hiding place.

"Mittens, here girl. Psst, psst."

After a few more minutes of searching – behind the large sideboard, under the bed, along all the windows sills – I felt tears prick my eyes. I noted a perceptible hush throughout the flat, the type that precedes something bad happening. The sense of *déjà vu* was powerful, the scene all too familiar, and I found myself flung back into the past.

I am young. My pale blue night dress brushes against my

legs as I walk up the stairs. It is night-time, the staircase cloaked in darkness, the only light, that which spills from the living room where Dad is watching TV.

I have sneaked downstairs to get Millie a treat. I was meant to be asleep, but I wasn't tired and Millie wanted to play. I go back to my room but Millie is gone. This is strange, because she always waits for me on my bed to come and get her. I look over at Helena's bed. It is empty, the covers thrown onto the ground.

"Millie," I whisper, but I am met with silence.

Millie knows her name and always mewls back when I call her. It is then that I hear the water running in the bathroom next door. That is also strange, as Helena and I had already had a bath. I tip-toe into the unlit bathroom. Water continues to swoosh into the large bathtub, but there is no one there. The shower curtain is drawn. I pull on the string to light up the little bulb on the cabinet over the sink.

The light dispels some of the shadows but creates others.

I feel someone behind me but I do not turn. Instead, I gravitate towards the tub and reach out, ready to pull the curtain back. But I hesitate. I know what I will find and I don't want to see it.

Perhaps I should have been surprised, but I wasn't, because that's how the world works – an eye for an eye– and so I pull back the curtain, but can't stop myself from gasping when I see her.

Her fur has been darkened by the water. She floats motionless, her little eyes open but unseeing.

The water continues to thunder down, so loud in my ears that it could have been a waterfall. Without taking my eyes off

Millie, I turn off the tap. The ensuing silence is now deafening; all I can hear is the pounding of my heart against my ribcage and the screaming in my mind.

I pick Millie up by her belly, just as she liked me to, and wrapped her in a hand towel. Only then do I turn to face the doorway. I stare at Helena with such hate that the look of satisfaction on her face is soon replaced by fear, and she runs away.

I spend the rest of the night holding Millie, rocking her gently against my chest, until I fall asleep on the bathroom mat. It was Dolores who finds me the next morning. My father had never made it upstairs the night before, having drunk himself to sleep on the sofa and then rushing off to work as the sun came up.

I shook my head, forcefully bringing myself back to the present. I had buried the memory of that night so deep that I hadn't thought about it since leaving home. That night had been imprinted on my mind so vividly that I could still hear the rush and splash of the water.

Wait.

I was still hearing the water running.

I bounded towards the bathroom, sending the door slamming against the wall as I barged in. The water gushed into the bathtub and I fell to my knees, looking within, my heart jammed in my throat, expecting to find Mitten's tiny body drowned within.

But it was empty.

I moaned loudly with relief, brushing the tears from my eyes, as I switched off the tap. I pressed on the lever to release the plug and watched as the clear water swirled away. I was once again surrounded by a blanket of silence, which was suddenly interrupted by the sound of child-like whispering and giggling. The sound held none of the innocence of children, but was instead insidious and full of malice. At first it seemed to be emanating from the bedroom but then it became louder, until it seemed to be coming from everywhere at once: the walls, the ceilings, the air itself.

Still on the floor, I crouched into a ball, covering my ears with my hands and placing my head between my legs, hoping it would shut out the incessant noise.

"Just stop! Just stop and leave me the fuck alone!" I shouted.

Just as suddenly as it had started, it stopped.

I raised my head slightly, fearing what would happen next, fearing that the woman in grey would make another appearance, but instead it was Mittens who cantered in gracefully from the bedroom and mewled softly at me. Tears of relief flooded down my cheeks as I grabbed her quickly and kissed the top of her head. I resolved never to let her out of my sight again.

What does this woman want from me? I couldn't help but ask myself again and again. If she wanted to unnerve me, frighten me or destabilise the life I had created for myself, she was definitely succeeding.

But why was she targeting me? Another thought popped into my head: could she perhaps be trying to tell me something? I couldn't help but recall a horror movie Nathan had made me watch after we'd been dating for a few months. It was an old one, but one of his favourites. I had never been one to watch much TV, but he had suggested a cosy night in with wine, pizza and chocolate-covered strawberries —which he had prepared himself —and I was sold.

The movie was called *The Sixth Sense* and starred Bruce Willis and this little kid who could see ghosts. The ghosts used to torment and terrify him, until he learned that they wanted his help. Some had a message they wanted to pass on to a loved one, others didn't realise they were even dead. By helping them, they moved on into the light or whatever.

If this woman, Isabel, was trying to give me a message, I had no idea what it was, but what had just happened with Mittens couldn't have been a coincidence. It was like she knew what had happened to Millie and how much I would suffer if something happened to Mittens. So either she could read my mind, which I thought was unlikely —not that I thought anything that had been happening lately to be likely – or all this was in fact something to do with a past life. So were we in essence the same person, or the same soul? Wasn't that what reincarnation was all about?

I had never given much thought to what happens to us after we die, because I didn't want to know. In some morbid way it was easier to think that nothing happened. That we simply ceased to exist and therefore we couldn't be held accountable for our actions. I took comfort in that.

Whatever Isabel had gone through, it was clear she had come to a bad end and it seemed that whether I wanted to or not, I was going to come to understand what exactly had happened to her.

Chapter Fifteen

The next forty-eight hours passed without incident, and I was grateful for the reprieve. Tania, who was leading the Water-Well Media Centre exhibition, had requested to see my work by next week. She needed an insight on what the finished product would look like and how it would fit in with the submissions from other artists.

So I focused on editing the best photos for the exhibition, as well as venturing out to take some more shots to complement and complete the theme of *The Old and the New*. I found myself actually looking forward to the opening night. Having your work showcased and having people appraise your work is equal parts unnerving and exciting.

I was also considering starting a book on photography for beginners; it would be good to branch out and expand my portfolio further. I began brainstorming what exactly I could include in such a book.

I hadn't let Mittens out of my sight since the incident in the bathroom. Whilst I worked on my computer she slept peacefully on my lap, and when I had to leave the flat, I took her with me in a small bag which would allow her to pop her head out. She wasn't exactly thrilled about this, but she had an easy-going personality for a kitten, and I think she preferred it to being left on her own.

Nathan seemed pleased at how happy Mittens made me. For me, it was as if I had gained something of the old Beth back, a reminder of one of the few happy moments of my childhood. Nevertheless, I knew it was dangerous to even glimpse into the past; I was no longer that Beth. That Beth had been snuffed out a long time ago, and dead was where she belonged. Perhaps I was living in denial, but don't we all, a little?

I stopped myself from treading that dark path. There was nothing good at the bottom of that road. I needed to believe I could escape my past.

I was trying to focus my energies on being proactive, so I did some research on the whole past-life phenomenon, hoping it would help shed some light on what I was currently going through. One of the first cases I came across was the example Dr Roberts had shared with me, that of the Pollock Sisters, but there were dozens, if not hundreds, of others.

I read about a child in India who had been born with boneless stubs for fingers and who remembered the life of a farm boy who had lost his fingers in an accident when cutting grass.

A three-year-old boy in Thailand, stated he had been shot and killed in a past life whilst riding a bicycle to school. The child could remember the name of the local teacher, as well as where he used to live. The boy who had died, had been shot in the back of the head. The three-year-old had a small birthmark on the back of his head and a larger one on his forehead, where the exit wound had been.

A girl in the USA remembered being abducted in the back of a truck in a past life, her strangled body dumped in the middle of nowhere. With the help of her parents, she managed to lead the police to the body, which was finally laid to rest.

I read case after case, and every one of them caused goose-bumps to rise across my arms. I had to admit the whole concept was both eerie and intriguing. Could it be possible that we had led past lives and that some of these memories, especially the traumatic ones, could transfer into this lifetime, lying in the pit of our sub-consciousness?

It seemed there was plenty of evidence and plenty of accounts of past lives; the debate lay in what these 'memories' actually were. Yet what was happening with Isabel seemed more than just memories: I felt like I was being haunted.

I had shown Nathan the Old Manor Farm online and he had loved it too. We had sent the owners a message, asking if it would be possible to visit and view the grounds. I allowed myself to enjoy these snippets of happiness in which the future was bright and full of possibilities.

It was now Friday, and I was getting ready for my appointment with Dr Roberts. Nathan had left early for a breakfast meeting and I was eating some porridge with honey. I was struggling with each mouthful, the oats seeming to congeal and get stuck in the back of my throat. My nerves were tightening my stomach into a knot.

For someone who had spent her entire adult life turning the page on her past, it seemed ironic that I was now choosing to undergo past life regression therapy. But what choice did I have?

I had a quick shower and changed into a flattering navy blue dress and my brown leather boots with small heels. I let my hair hang loosely around my shoulders and applied a little foundation, blusher and mascara. I completed the outfit with a long silver necklace that Nathan had bought from Pandora, and my rings. I grabbed my woolly shawl from the hook by the door and wrapped it around me.

I also grabbed a deep wicker basket, lined it with a small blanket, and placed Mittens inside. I had bought her a couple of toys from the pet store in town, a feathered ball and a squeaky mouse, and I placed these inside too, and packed a few treats for her in my handbag.

Nothing may have happened during these past couple of days but I wasn't taking any chances. I just hoped Dr Roberts wouldn't mind me bringing Mittens along to the clinic.

I stepped out into the hallway, closed the front door behind me and looked both ways along the landing. It was empty, but I didn't feel alone. I felt like I was being watched. Suddenly, the temperature dropped, as if I had been encased in ice.

I tugged the wrap more closely around me and took a step towards the stairs. I heard a child-like giggle echo throughout the stairwell, followed by the fast pitter-patter of tiny feet directly behind me.

I jerked round, but the corridor was still empty.

The cruel sounding giggles again. Instinct urged me to

flee, so I took the stairs as fast as I could whilst trying to keep the basket steady. I burst through the foyer doors into the open. There was no sky today, just an unbroken blanket of grey that strived to block out the sun.

As I hurried to the clinic, weaving in and out of crowds towards Ferring Ford Street, my phone rang, startling me out of my near-trance. I fished it out of my bag, knocking the basket, eliciting a small whine of protest from Mittens.

"Hello," I said a little breathlessly, once I managed to accept the call.

Silence.

"Hello," I said again, a little louder.

A crackle of static was followed by furtive, rasping whispers, too indistinct to be able to make out any words.

"Betthhh," a hellish voice spoke out from amongst the murmurs, dragging out my name.

I hung up immediately, feeling almost tainted. Instantly, the phone began to ring again, and I answered before I could stop myself.

"What do you want?!" I yelled down the phone, eliciting a startled look from a young woman passing by pushing a pram.

"Beth, it's me, Nathan," Nathan said, seeming only slightly irked at having been shouted at. "What's going on? You sound a little—"

"Oh God, Nathan, I am so sorry. Nothing – I've just been receiving some prank calls recently. Kids with nothing better to do, I guess," I lied, and tried to laugh it off weakly.

I didn't think Nathan had ever heard me raise my voice before like that. I was always so calm, so collected around him

– other than during my night terrors. It was one of the things he said he liked about me: that I seemed comfortable within my own skin. If only he knew the truth. What Nathan didn't realise was that my level of control required a constant and conscious effort.

"Brats. You know you can block them, right?" he told me. "Anyway, I was just calling to see how you were. I've just finished one meeting and I'm about to head into another one, but I was just checking up. You were talking in your sleep last night."

"Was I?" I asked a little hesitantly. "What did I say?"

"Nothing I could make out. A lot of gibberish and maybe something in Spanish," Nathan replied. "Anyway, I just wanted to make sure you were OK. I fancied having some Indian food tonight. Should I pick some up on my way home? Lamb tikka masala?"

"Yep, sure. That would be great."

"OK. Well, gotta go. See you later, gorgeous."

"See you later, and I'm—" I began, but he had already hung up.

I put the phone back in my bag and made it to the clinic with five minutes to spare. Olivia once again greeted me, her expression one of warmth, and asked if I wanted any tea or coffee; I declined but asked for a glass of water. I took a seat in the waiting area and sipped the water gratefully. My throat was parched and I needed to calm my racing heart. Mittens, in turn, mewled loudly.

"Oh my gosh– is that a kitten? How lovely," Olivia gushed as she came over to peep inside the basket. "She's so little! And what cute paws. It's looks like she's wearing socks!"

"I know." I laughed. "We've called her Mittens. Yeah, she is tiny. I've only had her a few days. She was a gift."

"That's a great name. I'd love a cat, but the boyfriend's allergic," she said wistfully, stroking Mittens, who was loving the sudden attention.

"If it's not too much to ask, would you mind looking after her during my appointment? I know I shouldn't have really brought her with me, but I just didn't want to leave her home alone so soon."

Olivia looked a little surprised, but then beamed instantly, "Sure, no problem. I'd love to."

The phone rang and Olivia headed back to her desk, taking the wicker basket with Mittens inside. I looked at the clock on the opposite wall and watched the seconds tick by. I was a little nervous about what this session might unearth. I had undergone hypnosis before, and it had helped with my aqua-phobia, but past life regression…that was something else.

Dr Roberts had come to know me pretty well – at least, he had come to know the Beth I had grown into. What if this therapy exposed something more than a past life? Like my deepest secrets? That could prove to be dangerous but what could I do? Who else could I turn to for help? I reassured myself that all my sessions with Dr Roberts were confidential – and I needed answers.

So, when he opened his office door a couple of minutes later, I stood up instantly, determined to face whatever this was. He greeted me with a smile and ushered me inside.

"Morning, Dr Roberts."

"Hi Beth. It's good to see you again. Please settle in and

make yourself comfortable. Have you had a chance to think about what we discussed in our last session?" he said, taking a seat himself.

"I have, and I did a little research on past lives and past life regression therapy, and even though I'm not sure if the answer lies there, I'm willing to try," I replied honestly.

"I understand, and I'd never want you to undertake anything with which you're not completely comfortable. We've tried hypnosis before and this is relatively similar. Past life regression therapy helps explore a person's deepest, most innermost thoughts. This insight into past lives has offered some individuals a greater spiritual understanding, which has helped them understand themselves better in this life."

I mulled over what Dr Roberts had said for a moment, trying to shut off the alarm bells his words, *'a person's deepest, most innermost thoughts,'* had set off. I had spent a lifetime trying to change who I was at my core – could I risk exposure, even here? No, but I couldn't live in fear of Isabel either. What if she never went away? What if she hounded me for the rest of my life? How long could I keep up the pretence until Nathan found out just how messed up I was and walked away from me?

I could feel a cloud of wretchedness and despair begin to form around me and so I simply nodded, trying to keep my eyes from welling up.

"Well, let's make a start, then. As in the past, I will be acting as your meditative guide. You will be completely safe at all times, and I will bring you back if at any point I feel the experience is becoming too much for you."

I simply nodded again, not trusting myself to speak.

"So lie down, make yourself comfortable and close your eyes. Let any tension you have been carrying leave your body. Shrug your shoulders, move your head to ease out any tension in your neck. Tense your legs and then just let them relax. Take a deep breath and let it out slowly. Now take another deep breath and, as you let it out, allow yourself to unwind even more. With each breath, you are feeling yourself relax a little more."

I surrendered myself to his voice and did as he asked. I allowed the fear and tension of all I had experienced recently to flow out of my body. I imagined recent events as bars of lead which had been pressing down on me, but which were now nothing more than helium balloons no longer tethered to me.

"Now become aware of your breathing and how your breath moves in and out of your body. You are becoming aware of how, with every gentle exhalation, you feel yourself relax deeper and deeper. Take your time... lose yourself completely. Becoming even more comfortable as you go deeper and deeper into yourself. Allow yourself to simply float away."

I felt myself being simultaneously pulled under and upwards. A little voice in my head urged me to stop, but I was too tired, my body too heavy to resist, and I wanted the relief of oblivion...

Suddenly, I felt like I was floating in a dark pool.

There was no light. No air. No sound. It was as if I was drifting in a black void. I could no longer feel my body, and Dr Robert's voice seemed to be coming from very far away.

"Think of a recent moment of happiness and tranquillity.

Can you see it?" his voice reached me.

"Yes," I answered into the nothingness

"Where are you?"

I thought back to our recent trip: just Nathan and me, away from the rest of the world and its complications.

"I am on the beach. Nathan has just gone surfing and I am watching the ocean," I said slowly, each word like thick treacle.

"That's good. You are sitting in a quiet, peaceful spot. You can feel the warm sand on your toes as you wriggle them. You can feel the wind blowing in your face, the smell of the salty sea air, you can hear the seagulls squawking overhead. You feel calm and peaceful. Now feel your mind drift away further. You are beginning to feel tired and heavy, but it doesn't matter because you are totally relaxed as you begin to sail away." A slight pause before he continued, "Now imagine you are in an empty room and there is a single door which leads to a flight of stairs. Do you see the door?"

"Yes," I said, but I wasn't sure if I said it out loud or just in my head.

"Good. You are doing great, Beth. Now move towards the door, open it and go through. Remember you are safe and secure, warm and comfortable. With each step, your body and mind relaxes even further. At the top of the staircase you will see that there are ten steps going down. You can now go down these steps, moving deeper and deeper into your subconscious. Ten... nine... eight... You feel more relaxed with each step. Seven... six... five... Further and further... Four... three... two... Sinking further. You are weightless and open to all experiences. What do you see?"

"I'm in a long, dark hallway," I replied, my voice deadpan even to my own ears.

"Take a look around. What else is there?" Dr Roberts coaxed me.

"Doors – many doors." Even in the gloom I could make out a line of doors on either side of me. I couldn't see the end of the corridor: it seemed to go on forever, into an eternal darkness and I'm scared to walk too far along it.

"That's good. One door in particular is calling to you, one which stands out from the others."

I looked at each door in turn. They were made of dark wood, the same colour as my mother's coffin, and I shivered involuntarily. Some of the doors looked older than others, some were shinier, others damaged as if they had been exposed to the elements. I noticed one door which almost seemed to be glowing, thrumming with energy. I saw a blue light radiating from the gap along the bottom, whereas all the others were completely dark. The handle was golden. I found myself reaching out towards it.

"I see it," I tell him.

"You are completely safe. Step through that door. Remember, nothing here can hurt you," he reassured me.

But I was no longer afraid. I no longer felt anything. I was like an empty vessel, stepping into another plane of existence. I clasped the handle, which felt almost warm to the touch, and turned it. I stepped through without a second thought.

After a few moments, Dr Roberts asked me, "What do you see?"

I shielded my eyes against the brilliant blue sky. In the distance I could see the hacienda standing on the hilltop, gleaming white and looking new. I felt the earth beneath my feet as I took in the rows upon rows of vineyards surrounding me. I heard men working in the distance, harvesting the grapes, tearing stems, and I smelled the sweet scent of the ripe grapes as they were picked. I felt the warm sun beating down upon my skin, the breeze moving through my hair. The whole scene was like a daydream, pristine, the colours too vivid, too bright, then fading into the distance.

I felt... like I was home.

I described all I could see to Dr Roberts and I now knew why I felt so at home in Tarifa. I had been there before, lived there before... in another time.

I heard someone approaching, but I did not feel afraid. I was here but at the same time I was not here. There was a dreamlike quality to the experience that made me feel as if I was no longer me. Beth didn't exist here.

A short woman came hurrying up the path. She looked exasperated, her brown eyes kind but searching. She holds up her long, old-fashioned dress in one hand, keeping it from touching the earth. A white apron was tied around her waist and her long, dark hair was tied in a thick plait. She was middle-aged and shapely, not overtly beautiful, but pretty.

She paused a few metres from me and cried out, "Isabel, Isabel! Where are you, girl? Come back and finish your lesson!"

Chapter Sixteen

"Isabel." The word echoed in my mind like a cry in a pitch-black tunnel. The woman had been speaking in Spanish, and I was only a little surprised to realise that I knew exactly what she was saying. After a moment she had turned sharply and seemed to be staring right at me. I felt panic flutter inside my chest and I took a step backwards – or rather, it felt as though I glided backwards, away from her.

"How did - you shouldn't be here! Go back," she whispered. There was an edge to her voice but also kindness.

She turned her back to me and continued to move through the fruitful vines, calling out for Isabel. I looked behind me and saw a glimpse of movement, but couldn't make anyone out. Just like the location, the woman felt familiar, and so I ignored what she had just said and followed her. She couldn't possibly have seen me, anyway.

The woman wiped the sweat from her forehead with a handkerchief. The sun beat down upon her mercilessly, her tanned skin glistening in the sunlight. She cried in alarm when a little girl of maybe five or six jumped out at her.

"Isabel!" the woman cried. "You really have to stop doing that! One of these days you are going to give me a heart attack!" But now she was laughing.

Isabel was a beautiful child: angelic features, tanned skin from playing outside, emerald green eyes and thick, long auburn-brown hair.

"Sorry, Rosa," Isabel said sheepishly, but with a grin. "But you always get scared, not like Papa."

"Well, that's because your father is much braver than I," she retorted.

"Do we have to keep reading?" Isabel asked with a pout.

"Yes you do – we spent most of the afternoon yesterday playing hide and seek, and today we have to catch up."

"Fine. Then maybe I can draw a picture for Papa. He loves my drawings, doesn't he?" Isabel asked hopefully.

"Of course he does. Papa is just very busy running the farms and the fishing ships – you know that. This whole town depends on him and what we provide."

"I know. I know. I'd just like to see him more," Isabel said glumly.

"You have me, don't you?"

"Yes, I do," Isabel said, instantly all smiles again. "Can you tell me another story about Mama? Please, please, please – I love your stories about Mama."

Rosa relented. "OK, but just one story. But then back to work yes?"

"Yes!" Isabel agreed excitedly. She took Rosa's hand and they walked back towards the hacienda.

I followed just a few steps behind them, intrigued.

"Your Mama Lucia was one of the most beautiful women I had ever seen in my life. As you know, we grew up near Barcelona, and I was but a child myself when I was fortunate enough to be given a job working as your mother's maid. Your mother had eyes as blue as a summer's sky and hair the colour of the sun. She was tall, with pale skin and a voice like an angel when she sang. At night when I brushed her hair, she would sing and it was the most wonderful thing I had ever heard. We too used to play hide and seek when we were younger, in the wonderful green gardens of her home. She was my employer but also my friend. Your grandfather arranged Lucia's marriage to your Papa. The day she was going to meet him for the first time, she was so nervous she couldn't sit still, just kept twirling her hair and asking me loads of questions about Francisco – which of course I didn't have the answers too. Just like when you get nervous or excited, you too are full of questions!" Rosa gave Isabel a warm smile. "They would spend hours walking amongst the gardens. It was love at first sight for both of them. I have never known two people more in love than your mama and papa. Your Papa would ask her to sing to him, I would sneak out to watch them as she sang, as the sun set in the sky. Your mother told me that Francisco told her stories of all the places he had been to, promising to take her there also. Like you, Lucia yearned for adventure.

Isabel sighed contently. "I wish I had known Mama," she said wistfully, her eyes glistening.

"I know, child. She loved you very, very much. She wanted nothing more in the world than to have a daughter."

I stared after Isabel and Rosa as they moved away. There was something special about Isabel, something that made her shine, an aura of goodness that I couldn't quite explain. I was warming to the idea that we had a connection between us –

yet it was difficult to reconcile this child with the woman in grey. It only made me more certain that something really terrible must have happened to her.

"Beth? Beth?" Dr Roberts voice seemed to ring out from the heavens. "What do you see?"

I explained what I had seen and having met Isabel as a child – recounting my most recent experience when the woman in grey called herself Isabel. As I spoke, the scene began to change around me, like an 8mm movie that has jumped and is replaced by another recording.

I am now inside the hacienda. From my spot in the corner I could see Rosa cooking and Isabel helping her dice vegetables. They were laughing together amiably, and I experienced an intense desire to stay here and form part of this homely scene. The image jumped again and I saw Isabel, her face a mask of concentration, leaning over a textbook, pencil gripped tightly in her hand as she scribbled away.

I shared my experiences to Dr Roberts, although I struggled to put these flashes into words, simply because they seemed so real that I was too much in awe to say much. Never in my wildest dreams would I have thought it possible to glimpse past lives in this way. Hell, I had never even really believed in them until this moment.

When researching past life regression, I had found it was generally discredited and deemed unscientific by many medical practitioners, so I was unsure what to think – but now I couldn't deny what I was experiencing, or how true this all felt to me. In my heart I knew these were not false memories or a fantastical delusion. This was real.

The landscape changed around me once more. Isabel was

now a little older, playing in the courtyard of the hacienda with a litter of kittens. She picked them up gently for cuddles, and kisses each one in turn, giggling happily before placing them back down next to their mother who was busy licking her brood clean.

Another jump. Isabel was now a teenage girl, chatting with someone who I assumed was her father, Francisco. They shared the same emerald-green eyes and olive skin. I wasn't close enough to make out what they were saying, but they seemed to be at ease in each other's presence.

Another jump, and I found myself alone in a cold, damp room. This scene felt very different to everything I had experienced until this point, and I didn't like it. In fact, I wanted to get the hell out of there. The emotions that this place stirred were ones of pain and desperation. It was dark, with little moonlight filtering through the only single window, high above me.

A sense of sadness overwhelmed me, so deep I felt I could lose myself in it, and tears streamed down my cheeks. I felt utterly isolated, the loneliness like a slow poison to the soul. There was a cold, calculating fire burning inside of me, morphing the pain into flames of anger and hate, so powerful I couldn't even breathe.

I needed to get out of here, but there was nowhere to go: the window was too high and the large wooden door was locked. The only sounds were the howling wind outside and my shallow breaths. There wasn't enough air. I was suffocating...

"Beth." A voice I couldn't quite place reached me through the cloud of panic. "Beth, you are OK. Nothing can hurt you here." I now recognised the calm voice of Dr Roberts. "Beth, it's now time to return to the present. I am going to count from five down to one, and when I get to one, you will be back in the present, calm and feeling safe, yet remembering all you have seen."

"Five," he began.

I could feel the horrible emotions start to lessen and fade.

"Four."

I was yanked back into the darkened hallway.

"Three."

The door I had previously opened slammed shut before me. But I couldn't leave, not yet – I needed to know more. I tried to reach out, to go back through the door, but I was no longer able to act of my own free will.

"Two."

I was back in the empty room.

"One." Dr Roberts' voice was soft yet authoritative.

I opened my eyes slowly and blinked, squinting at the sudden brightness within the office until my eyes adjusted. Dr Roberts was leaning forwards in his chair, studying me intently.

"How are you feeling, Beth?"

"I'm... I'm feeling a little overwhelmed, if I'm honest. I wasn't expecting... I didn't know what I was expecting, but what I saw was so real..." I trailed off, taking a couple of deep breaths to settle myself back in this moment, in this time and place.

"That is to be expected, but remember, you were only a spectator – nothing can harm you."

But I was not afraid. In fact, I felt almost... invigorated. I had learnt something – admittedly not much, but I had glimpsed into Isabel's life.

"I saw Isabel as a child," I told him once more. "That has to be significant?"

"Beth, as you know, my job here is to listen to your concerns, guide you as best I can, but ultimately to help you find answers for yourself. I have undertaken this kind of therapy with a few patients, but I have never seen anyone take it to as fast as you have, in only the first session. You have a strong connection with this Isabel. Your current experiences and the way that your regression centred around her would suggest you were connected in a past life. There are perhaps experiences from your past that need resolving. I have noticed your reluctance to open up about your childhood, and I can't help but think that this is all related."

"I understand, and I do feel a strange sort of connection to Isabel and her home, but I still don't understand why all this is happening to me. I need to go back... I need to know more," I said firmly.

I tried to ignore his comment about my unwillingness to talk about my childhood. I hoped he wouldn't notice, but of course he would.

"I agree that further sessions may be beneficial, but it is very important to take this slowly. Too much information, too soon, can be extremely overwhelming. Whatever you learn or experience, we then have to piece together – its meaning, its significance – so that we can put these memories into perspective."

"I'm running out of time," I blurted out before I could stop myself.

"I understand how frightful these dreams and experiences must have been, Beth, but what makes you think that?"

"I'm not sure," I replied honestly. "It's just that whenever I see her, I sense this undercurrent of threat. If I'm meant to be learning something from her, I haven't the faintest clue what it is. Could we really share a soul?"

"I always tell my clients that they should reach their own conclusions about certain beliefs and practices. I only offer different perspectives as a way to help people find their own path. Now, the concept of reincarnation is based on the notion that a soul is given the choice to come back to Earth if there is anything left unresolved or incomplete at the end of their life. Buddhists believe that life and death are the same thing, that death is simply the beginning of another chapter, a mirror in which the entire meaning of life is reflected."

"I guess that philosophy sounds more comforting that burning in Hell for all eternity, or suffering in Purgatory," I added thoughtfully.

The idea that we could get another chance to do things all over again gave me hope. Hope that under different circumstances my life could have turned out differently, that I could be different.

"Indeed, reincarnation and karma are also interlinked. A spiritualist once said that each suffering is rewarded, each sacrifice is made up and every debt is paid."

Dr Roberts' replies unnerved and terrified me, each word driven into my mind like nails, but I hid my discomfort behind a weak smile.

"I think we have covered some good ground today. Would you like to have another session soon?" he asked me.

"Yes, I think that would be a good idea."

Dr Roberts got up from his chair and went to his desk by the window. As he checked his schedule on his computer, I stared at the floor, my mind now blank as if it needed a moment to recover.

"Would Friday work? Same time?"

"Yes. Thank you," I replied. I stood up and collected my bag, feeling a little unsteady on my feet, as if I was still partly in a trance.

"Beth, get some rest. Regression therapy can really take it out of you. If you need to talk before Friday, you can always call me," he reminded me, his voice warm and sympathetic.

"Thank you, doctor. See you then."

I walked out his office and into the main reception area, which was empty of clients. Olivia gave me another genuine smile and handed over the basket with Mittens inside. She always seemed so happy; I had often wanted to ask her what her secret was, and if she could share it with the rest of us. She reminded me of Sam; I guessed that was why I had warmed to her, even though we only tended to share the briefest of interactions.

"Thank you so much for looking after Mittens, Olivia. I hope she wasn't too much trouble."

"It was my pleasure. The clinic has been pretty quiet this morning so she's kept me company. I'm sure I'd be the same, not wanting to leave her on her own when she's still so little. I can only imagine what I'll be like when the baby arrives." She placed her perfectly manicured hand on her stomach.

"Congratulations," I said, trying not to sound too surprised.

"Early days, but I'm very excited." Her expression one of pure joy.

I would never have guessed Olivia was pregnant. She had a very womanly physique, what I guessed most guys would describe as having curves in all the right places, and she was so young too – I guessed she was around twenty-two or twenty-three.

"I recently got engaged myself," I found myself telling her. I wonder if anyone else feels the need to do that, to share your own good news when others tell you theirs? For some people, life is a competition. I'm just trying to fit in.

"Congrats to you too. What a lovely engagement ring," she said, glancing at my ring finger.

"Thank you. Well, I best get going. Have a good weekend and see you soon," I said, not really knowing what else to say to her.

"You too. Take care."

I stepped outside. The sky was overwhelmed with dark grey clouds, threatening to unleash themselves upon me. I stroked Mittens affectionately and gave her a few treats from my bag, which she hungrily devoured.

I descended the steps and began to make the journey home at a fast pace. I felt I had taken a small step towards getting my life back on track, and I couldn't help but allow myself a small smile as I held tightly onto the wicker basket.

I was almost halfway home when my mobile rang. Assuming it was Nathan again, I fished the phone out of the bag and accepted the call without bothering to register the caller.

"Hello," I said brightly.

"Beth." Helena's voice stopped me in my tracks.

"Oh, hi Helena, how are you? Everything OK?" I asked hesitantly. If Helena was calling me then nothing was OK. I looked up at the sky, thinking of the impending downpour, but I was rooted to the spot.

After a pause she said simply, "No."

"Helena, what's happened?"

Another pause, before I was hit by a torrent of words which left me feeling cold, although perhaps not as cold as they should have.

"Dad took a turn for the worse early this morning. I called for an ambulance and he was taken to the intensive care unit at Bristol Royal Hospital. They tried to stabilise him but his condition continued to deteriorate. He... he just passed away. We're in room 308."

There were many things I could have said in that moment, things that I wanted to say, such as *Why didn't you call me sooner? I should have been there.* Or *I thought he had been given months to live.* But none of that really mattered now. Many conflicting emotions swirled inside me like a hurricane: pain, relief, guilt, anger, loss. Some of these feelings were darker than others, but there is no light without darkness, so I wouldn't allow myself to feel any shame or self-reproach.

All I said before I hung up was, "I'll meet you at the hospital – I'm on my way."

I began to run back home; it would be quicker to pick up the car and drive to the hospital. I didn't know why I was running – after all, he was already dead. There was no rush, no need to barrel down the streets, but running helped stop me from thinking any further or deeper. I couldn't afford to process my emotions or feelings now. I just focused on moving, putting one foot in front of the other. All I could hear was the mewls of protestations from Mittens at being bumped about.

I was out of breath by the time I made it home. I let myself in and let Mittens out of the basket. Instantly, she scurried into the living room. I would have no choice but to leave her behind – I couldn't possibly take her to the hospital. I could only hope she'd be OK. I'd call Nathan and tell him to come home and stay with her. I drank a glass of water quickly and picked up my car keys from the bowl in the entrance, where Nathan and I would dump our wallets, keys, tissues and other knick-knacks.

"I'll be back later, Millie – I mean Mittens," I called out as I shut the door behind me.

Once behind the wheel, I made myself focus on the journey I'd have to take to the hospital, and nothing else. Running on autopilot made it easier to keep it together.

A short while later, I was swallowed up by the hospital's automatic sliding glass doors. I had just phoned Nathan from the car to tell him that my father had died. Understandably, he wanted to rush to my side, but less understandably I told him I needed him to go home and look after Mittens. It took a while to convince Nathan that that was what I needed, but he finally relented after I reassured him that I wasn't going to be here alone; Helena was here.

Helena and I had never really spent much time alone together – my father had always ensured this. There had always been either him or my mother, grandparents or Dolores, and she and I were always in different classes at school. Helena and I were like similar poles of two magnets, destined to repel and push each other away, and that was something I had come to accept many years ago, on the day my mother died. It was safer that way.

I made my way to the elevator, pushed the button for the third floor, and then headed down the long corridor. The light was too bright, too artificial, and the undertone smell of bleach making me feel lightheaded. The magnolia walls, with their framed pictures of indistinct landscapes, seemed to be closing in on me. The sounds of the medical staff moving around in a purposeful thrum, like bees in a hive, made me feel out of place as I continued reluctantly to room 308.

Through the glass I could see Helena standing by the window, her back to me as she gazed at the world outside. For just the length of a breath, her figure shifted and she resembled the woman in grey, but I made myself grab and turn the door handle regardless.

The room was cold and, as I shut the door, I muted the sound from the other patients' rooms, their various TV sets, chatter, and the muffled sobs of strained relatives. Helena turned to face me. Her eyes were red and she looked as though she had aged overnight. She too carried guilt on her shoulders like an invisible weight, but she was a better person than I, and so she could not bury it as effectively as I had.

"He's gone," Helena said simply, as if she needed to repeat this fact.

I nodded and glanced at the bed. The white sheet had been pulled over my dad's face.

"I thought you'd want to say goodbye before he gets taken down to the morgue. I'll leave you alone with him."

Again, I felt there were half a dozen responses I could give her, but I held my tongue –it was the least I could do – and simply nodded.

When I heard the door close I took a couple of steps closer to the bed. There was an armchair next to it, but I didn't want to get that close. I stood hovering an equal distance between the bed and the door.

I cleared my throat, which sounded too loud in the confines of the silent room. I knew my father was gone, that what lay in the bed was just his corpse, a mass of bone, muscle, flesh and blood, but I felt I needed to say something –anything –because this was the end of us.

This meant one less person tied to the old Beth. One side of me couldn't help but feel relieved, as if the death of people who knew the old Beth meant that she too was fading into oblivion. You may think me cold, but my father died a long time ago.

"Dad..." I began, but then faltered. "I know you blamed me for Mum's death, that part of you wished you had died with her, or that I had died instead, and that's OK. You can't change who you love or don't love... it's either there or it isn't." I paused, almost expecting a comeback, but of course only silence ensued.

I stared at the sheet that covered his face. I supposed that most people would peel the sheet back and kiss their loved ones goodbye for the last time, but I wasn't most people.

"I cannot change the past, but I am letting the past die with you, once and for all. I don't know for certain what comes next, but I hope you are at peace and with Mum, like you've always wished to be."

I turned to leave; there was no more to say. A relationship as broken as ours had no hope of ever being reconciled. I had only taken a single step towards the door when I heard a dry exhalation behind me. My whole body froze as I listened to the thick silence which enveloped me and held me captive.

Another raspy breath.

No, this isn't possible, my mind screamed at me. *He's dead.* Dead.

I whirled around. I could see the soft rise and fall of the sheet over his mouth as he breathed.

This isn't *happening.*

I found myself struggling to breathe. My heart and pulse quickened, and I broke out in sweat and even my hands began to feel numb. The panic attack was coming on strong and fast. With deadened fingers, I fumbled in my bag. I needed to take my anti-anxiety meds. This was all becoming too much and I couldn't think straight.

I needed to get out.

I turned back to see that my father was now standing right behind me.

His body almost skeletal, having been consumed by cancer. His yellowish skin, tinged blue by death, dry and crackling. But it was his eyes that were the worst, opaque like a dead fish. They were wide open as if he could still see through the blue-white haze, as if he could see straight into my soul.

"You cannot outrun your past forever, Beth. We must all pay for our sins," He warned me, his voice like a death rattle.

Suddenly, he charged at me, his mouth open in a snarl of rage. I screamed before I could stop myself. Helena came rushing back into the room to find me cowering on the floor.

"What on earth are you doing, Beth?" she said in exasperation, as if I was a young child misbehaving.

All I could do was stare at her with wide, unblinking eyes. She had enough to deal with, without having to deal with me too. I considered just for a moment telling her everything, everything I had held on to since we were children, but I stopped myself. To show that would be to show too much.

Chapter Seventeen

"Do you believe in reincarnation?" I asked Nathan, holding a mug of hot chocolate in my hands.

I felt numb with cold. A hot shower had helped, but this chill ran deep and wasn't so easily thawed. It was my soul that was cold, but then hadn't it always been? Perhaps no matter how much you try, you can't change who you really are.

We were sitting on the sofa. It was late, but I didn't want to go to bed. Even if I took two or three sleeping pills, I didn't think they would keep the dreams at bay tonight.

I had left the hospital a short while after Helena had walked back into the room. My father had been wheeled down to the morgue and Helena said she would sort out all the paperwork. She informed me that our father had already made his funeral arrangements when he had found out his condition was terminal. I wasn't needed, and Helena didn't want me around either, so it was easier to simply come home.

To come home to my family, to Nathan and to Mittens, who lay curled up on my lap and who had already forgiven me for the time she had spent in the basket that morning. It's a shame people can't forgive each other or themselves as easily and as quickly as animals seem to do.

"Reincarnation? As in past lives and stuff? Not really – I was raised Catholic. So basically when we die, we go to Heaven. It's what I've been taught growing up, and I guess I have never really given it any real thought. Is this about your dad? Did he believe in reincarnation?" Nathan asked.

"To be honest, I'm not sure what he believed in, at the end. I vaguely remember going to church as a young child, but that all stopped once my mother died. My father never forgave anyone, not even God, for losing her." I didn't elaborate further.

Nathan only knew that my mother had died in a car crash when I was eight, but not that I had been responsible for her death. I wondered if he viewed me as a sort of wounded bird that needed his protection.

"I am so sorry you are going through this, Beth," he said gently. "To lose your mother and then your dad, I can't even begin to—"

I interrupted him. "I actually feel like I lost my father a long time ago. He didn't want to live. His drinking was like a slow suicide. One I had to watch every day as I grew up. He wanted to be with my mother, and I hope he is, in some way or other."

But what if there wasn't a Heaven? What if he came back as something that was no longer human, like Isabel? I shuddered involuntarily. I didn't want Nathan to feel sad for me, because I wasn't as sad as I ought to be. What I wanted now, more than ever, was to put this behind me and focus on my future – on our future together.

"And Helena?" he asked tentatively.

"Taking charge of all that needs doing, and I'm grateful for that. I guess she knew for months this day was coming, and soon." *Longer than I knew,* I wanted to add, but I left it unsaid.

"Well, if there is absolutely anything I can do to help, you know you only need to ask," Nathan said, taking my hand and kissing it.

"I know, and thanks. I don't know what I'd do without you. I really mean that."

"I don't know what I'd do without you either."

We kissed, and I wanted him to take me to bed and make love to me till morning came, but I knew he wouldn't understand. Yet I needed to feel alive in the midst of all this death.

The thought of Isabel resurfaced involuntarily in my mind. If she was indeed me in a past life, she had died very young, younger than I was now, and I couldn't help but wonder how much heartache and misery one soul could take before it fractures beyond repair.

"You've had a really tough day, honey – why don't we try and get some sleep?" Nathan said, after we had sat embracing each other for a few minutes in silence.

"Yeah, we should rest," I agreed, simply because I wanted this day to be over.

Nathan took my mug and rinsed it out whilst I went to brush my teeth. We got into bed and Mittens snuggled into a nook between our pillows. As I closed my eyes, I couldn't stop the snapshots of my life that played in my head, so much loss, so much sadness and I also couldn't help but be envious of all those people who weren't perpetually surrounded by darkness.

It was the sound of someone knocking that stirred me from sleep. A persistent *tap, tap, tap* against glass.

I could feel the warmth of Nathan's body next to mine. I had fallen asleep in his arms, and the sound of his breathing was comforting in the previously undisturbed silence. I glanced over at the window, thinking that a tree branch must be blowing against it, but the night outside seemed calm, the leaves suspended and unmoving.

I was still drowsy, my eyelids heavy with exhaustion and the effects of the sleeping pills I had taken, and I didn't want to wake fully. I wanted to return to my cocoon of oblivion – but the tapping continued.

TAP, TAP, TAP.

The noise didn't seem to bother Nathan, but then again he could sleep through almost anything, whereas I wouldn't be able to go back to sleep until I discovered what was causing it. Reluctantly, I got up and tip-toed over to the window. The floor was cold, the heating having automatically switched off hours earlier. I peered out at the street below, but it only confirmed what I had seen from the bed: the night was still and no branches were rapping against the window.

The noise had now ceased, but I felt uneasy. I searched the bedroom, half-expecting something to attack me from the shadows. I decided it was better to ignore whatever it had been and to try and go back to sleep. I knew from experience that sleep deprivation would leave me more anxious and less able to handle all that was going on at the moment. I pulled the quilt over me and had just settled my head on my pillow when the noise rang out again, a little louder this time.

TAP, TAP, TAP.

"What the hell?" I murmured under my breath.

I scanned the bedroom once more. Could it be coming from inside the wardrobe? I shuddered at the thought. But no, it sounded like someone knocking on glass.

I padded out into the hall, and that's when I realised the noise was coming from the family bathroom. Reluctantly, I went in. If Isabel was me, or rather I was her, then surely she couldn't mean me any real harm, right?

The noise ceased as soon as I stepped inside, but the bathroom didn't feel empty. Something was in here with me, something that made the air feel weighted and dense. I listened, but all I could hear was the sound of my own breathing. I realised Isabel was toying with me. I didn't have the energy for this crap, not tonight.

TAP, TAP, TAP.

I spun round.

It was then that I realised the noise was coming from inside the mirror.

I felt my insides grow cold. I was scared to look, but I had to. The dead are unlikely to give up and go back to wherever they came from just because we ignore them.

I approached slowly and looked squarely into the mirror.

I saw... me.

Hair dishevelled from sleep, eyes a little too wide... but there was nothing else.

My relief didn't last long: my reflection then grinned

malevolently at me.

I stumbled back in horror, but my reflection didn't move. It just continued to stare at me like a spider examining prey caught in its web.

I felt weak, my strength ebbing away and taking my sanity with it. I needed to get away from whatever that thing was on the other side of the mirror – but I couldn't move. My eyes were transfixed on the eyes of the other me.

It was only when the other me began to climb out of the mirror that I shrieked, my body finally responding as I bolted out of the room only to crash into something which grabbed me and held me tight. I didn't dare open my eyes, fearing the other me could somehow get inside me if I looked upon her countenance once more. I thrashed, trying to free myself from her clutches.

"Beth!" Nathan exclaimed. "It's only me, honey. It's OK. Calm down, I have you."

I stopped resisting and forced my eyes open. Nathan's blue eyes were fixed intently on me.

"I..." I began, but couldn't say anything else as tears began to fall silently down my cheeks.

"Honey, it's OK," Nathan said tenderly, wiping the tears away with the tips of his fingers. "Did you have a bad dream?"

"I think I may have been sleepwalking," I lied.

"Have you ever done that before? I guess it's no wonder, with all you've been through lately. Let's get you back to bed. Do you want me to get you anything?"

"Just a glass of water, please."

"Coming right up," he said.

He guided me back to the bedroom before heading to the kitchen. A minute later, he was back. I sipped the water, then took several deep breaths and two anti-anxiety tablets. A short while later, I felt them kicking in, and my heartbeat slowed and my racing mind began to quieten.

Back in bed, Nathan held me in his arms once more, and soon he was fast asleep. I stared up at the ceiling for a few more minutes, watching the pale beams of light from the outside world dance overhead, until I too closed my eyes. The darkness came for me again that night, as I knew it would and I allowed myself to drift into the shadows of dreams.

I am a child, sitting in the car as we drive home. I can hear my mother and father whispering to each other in the front seat. I want to make out what it is they are saying, but the sound of the wind, the radio and Helena humming to herself, mean I can only grasp snippets of their conversation.

"Well, we need to do something," my father hisses, and I can sense the anger behind his words. "You can't... well, we can't keep living like this."

"Don't you think I know that? I've tried. I don't know... what do you want me to do?" my mother asks. She too sounds angry, but also tired and exasperated.

Helena continues to hum to herself. It's a tune I have never heard before, but I find I don't like. It scares me. I want to tell her to shut up, but I want to hear what mother and father are saying and they may stop if I speak.

"We need... she needs help," my father mutters. There is a note of finality is his voice that I detest.

Only a few heartbeats later, the car collides into the truck and I see the look on my mother's eyes before she dies. There is such a range of emotions - shock, panic, fear, and pain - it is hard to witness and I have spent years trying to forget that look.

I'm relieved when the memory is replaced by another, but a moment later I recoil when I realise what it is.

I am home, in my old bedroom. Pale sunlight is filtering in through the ballerina-patterned curtains. Coco-Pop, Helena's hamster, is lying unmoving on the ground, but I make myself turn my back on it.

The setting changes once more. Dolores is singing softly in the living room, the TV is on in the background, twilight fills the room. Dolores is brushing Helena's hair, and Helena's face is slightly red from crying. I take a step closer. Dolores hears me; she turns, and when she sees it is me, she forces a smile but I catch a glimpse of something else, something like reproach. I turn and leave, the room darkening behind me.

Now the backdrop is the garden. I am outside, looking for my father. It is late, the blue haze of the day vanishing to reveal the stars above. An empty bottle of whiskey is at his feet, and I can smell the alcohol in the air like a toxic fog. Even to this day, the smell of whiskey turns my stomach. He is mumbling in the dark as if conversing with the shadows themselves.

"Dad?" I say, but he is lost to a world in which I do not exist.

I make out some of his words to my dead mother. "I can't do this —I don't want to do this without you... it's not fair... I can't love her... Helena is all that is left."

Perhaps he hears her replies from the grave, but I do not. I do not need to hear anymore of this, so I turn around, but suddenly all three of them are right behind me.

All dead.

My mother. My father. Dolores.

The life that once dwelt within them is gone, and their skin is dotted with holes where maggots have worked their way through. Their eyes are as black as the earth in which they are buried. They reach out suddenly and savagely towards me. My nostrils fill with the putrid smell of decay as I am enveloped in the cold embrace of the dead.

I jerked upright in bed. I was alone, haunted by the echoes of old memories, like a song I wish I'd never heard but could never forget.

I reached out to Nathan's side of the bed, but it was cold. My hands touched a piece of paper. Nathan had left me a note, and even though the dream had stayed with me, I still managed a smile. We didn't leave each other notes as often anymore, and I couldn't help but wonder why even in the happiest of relationships, couples stop doing those tiny little things that made them fall in love with each other in the first place.

I was still a little groggy, which wasn't surprising seeing I had taken a double dose of my anti-anxiety medication. I wiped the back of my hand across my eyes and began to read the note out loud.

"Morning honey. You looked so beautiful I didn't want to wake you. I had an early morning meeting but if you need me just call me and I'll come home. Love you to the moon and back" Which was followed by numerous kisses.

I folded the piece of paper carefully and placed it inside the top drawer of my bedside table. As I did so, the morning

The Lost Ring

light caught the gem on the antique ring momentarily, blinding me with a flash of red, and suddenly I felt myself plunging backwards, free-falling through the air so fast I had to close my eyes.

All of a sudden, it stopped.

Hesitantly, I open my eyes to discover that it is no longer morning and I am no longer in my bed. I am back in Spain, in the orange groves of the hacienda. The oranges are ripe and full, dark orbs in the moonlight, and I can smell their sweet scent pervading the air. The full moon is high in the sky, making everything it touches glow almost magically. The edges of my vision are distorted and blurred, like if I were gazing upon a fractured mirror.

I am not alone.

I can see Isabel – not as a child or as the woman in grey, but alive, blossoming into womanhood and radiant. Even in the midst of twilight I can see how beautiful she is: tall, slim, large almond-shaped eyes, a mass of silky hair cascading down her back. She is with a young man; he too has dark hair and olive skin, and he is slight but muscular.

They look so happy, whispering and giggling to each other in the dark. They embrace and kiss passionately. I feel slightly uncomfortable watching what is clearly an intimate moment, but I am also curious. I want to know more about her, and about this man who has clearly won her heart.

After a moment they part again, and from his trouser pocket he pulls something out. Isabel clasps her hand to her mouth in shock, but her expression is one of pure joy. He whispers something to her and she nods furiously. They kiss, and when they pull away, he slips a ruby ring onto her finger.

The Lost Ring

The gem sparkles in the luminescent light like a scarlet rose.

Chapter Eighteen

When I blink I am once more in my bedroom. The smell of oranges still laces the air but this, too, fades away quickly. I look at the ring on the bedside table – something so small and innocuous, yet charged and tied to the past in a way I could have never thought possible.

I now knew that finding the ring was no coincidence. Isabel ensured I would find it. Her ruby engagement ring was a physical connection to the past – perhaps even a gateway, which I had pushed open even further by undergoing past life regression therapy.

Mittens, who had taken ownership of Nathan's side of the bed, scrambled over to me and mewled for food, so, reluctantly, I got out of bed, pulling an old sweater over my head to stay warm, and made my way to the kitchen. Mittens followed and wolfed down the food I put down for her. I was surprised that I, too, had an appetite. I poured myself a large mug of coffee and placed two thick slices of wholemeal bread in the toaster, then lathered them with butter and honey.

My phone, which I had left on the dining table, buzzed. It was a message from Helena.

Dad will be buried tomorrow at All Souls Church 11am.

I replied instantly.

Thanks for letting me know. I will see you there. I know you've got it handled but if you need me to do anything just let me know.

She didn't send another message and for a moment I wondered if there was any chance we could try and mend our relationship. Now, when we had no other family but each other – but you cannot rebuild something where foundations never really existed. Helena and I were too broken for that, each in our different ways. Besides, Helena belonged to Beth's old life. As I moved through the dark labyrinth of my mind, I couldn't help but wonder if all sins were in fact forgivable.

I messaged Nathan to let him know about the funeral and I also called Dr Roberts to let him know I wouldn't be able to make tomorrow's session. Thankfully, he had a free slot on Tuesday afternoon, so we managed to reschedule.

I powered up my computer. I had already sent all my files for the Water-Well Media Centre project to Tania a few days ago, and she had been really pleased with my submission. The exhibition launch was only a couple days away now, on Saturday night. Nathan was proud that my work was forming part of such a large event and had invited his family to come along.

After the launch, we had arranged to go for a late dinner at an Italian restaurant called Mangiamoci Su –*Let's eat*. It was known for its very generous portions of pasta and rice dishes, a carbohydrate load which generally left you in a food coma.

Nathan had asked me if I wanted to cancel our plans, but I had assured him I didn't. This project was one of the most high-profile ones I'd been involved in, and the launch party would be an amazing opportunity to network – one I couldn't afford to pass up. Besides, I could compartmentalise and I was very adept at hiding my emotions. Tomorrow I would bury my father and I would spend Saturday with my new family.

I was so engrossed in my thoughts that I jumped when the doorbell rang, breaking the silence. I peeked through the peephole but all I could see was a mass of colours; it took me a moment to realise it was a bunch of flowers. I opened the door to find a young delivery man holding up a bouquet. He handed them over and I signed for them.

I carried them back into the kitchen. The bouquet, wrapped in pink cellophane, was a dazzling mix of carnations, freesias, irises, violets and roses. They were beautiful. I retrieved the card from between the stems and read it out loud.

"To our dear Beth, our sincerest condolences on the loss of your father. We are always here for you. Love Eleanor, Alex and Louise."

It was very thoughtful of them. I un-wrapped the cellophane, held the flowers by their stems, placed them in a glass vase half-filled with water, and set it on the dining table. The vase was one I had picked out from the Bristol Glass Factory in the city centre, with intricate ribbons of blue swirling along its base. I was glad Mittens was still too little to climb onto the furniture.

I wondered if Nathan and I would still live here once we were married. I had always loved this flat. It had felt like my first real home, but recently it had no longer felt like the haven it always had done. Starting somewhere fresh once we were married now sounded quite appealing. Perhaps somewhere a little further out from the city, where we could perhaps afford a place with a small garden, so I could plant my own flowers and maybe even have a couple of apple trees.

Noticing the time, I got up and had a quick shower and got dressed in a casual but smart navy dress with a delicate blush-pink flower print. I applied a little make-up and tied up my hair in a messy bun. A couple of months ago I had been hired to take photos for a baptism, and had almost forgotten all about it, but I always set reminders on my phone for these odd jobs. Word of mouth was essential in my line of work, so not showing up for a job was career suicide, not to mention the fact that people were counting on me to capture lasting memories of their special moments.

Nowadays, however, with everyone owning a smart phone, bookings for such events were becoming rarer. In the past I had considered offering video-graphy, but there was just something about capturing a single moment in time in a photograph that appealed to me much more than film ever had.

I donned my tan brown boots and dusty-pink trench coat. I was loathe to leave Mittens behind, but I didn't really have a choice. I grabbed my camera bag and handbag and moved towards the door when something dark in the corner of my eye made me stop.

"What the hell..."

The vase was still on the tabletop but the once multi-coloured blooms had turned brown, and petals littered the table and floor like rotten confetti. The sight of the dead flowers repulsed me. They were now a reflection of death, their petals curled and stiff, lifeless, joyless and ugly.

I checked on Mittens, who was napping in her clam-shaped bed. I couldn't leave her behind, not now, and so I placed her in the wicker basket. I didn't have time to clean up the mess in the kitchen; it would have to wait until after the baptism. If I didn't leave right now I would be late.

I hurried out, down the stairs and into the car, and drove down to the church a little faster than I should have. I parked under the huge oak tree by the old stone wall and climbed out. I reached back inside to grab the camera bag and handbag from the back seat. Thankfully, Mittens had fallen asleep in the basket. I left the window open just a little.

I shrieked as I stood up again.

Something large and black darted past my face. It was a crow, larger than any I had ever seen before, and it was now perched on the roof of my car, its gaze fixed on me as if preparing to gouge out my eyes.

I took a step backwards and it beat the air with its wings, feathers as black as tar, and cawed loudly. The sound was replicated and magnified ten-fold above me, startling me once more. I looked up to find a dozen crows peering down at me from the branches. A voice in my head whispered, *It's called a murder of crows*, and I shivered. They clicked their ebony beaks in unison as if they were discussing when to attack and rip my body to shreds.

But they were just a bunch of birds. I felt foolish for allowing them to unsettle me.

"*Shoo!* Get away!" I cried out to the crow on the roof, flapping at it with my free arm.

It seemed to find my fretful state amusing; it cocked its head to one side as if to assess me through a single black eye.

"Fine, just stay there, see if I care," I muttered, turning my back on it.

Instantly, I heard the swift movement of wings and then felt pain as talons clawed at my scalp and hair. I cried out in shock and dropped to the floor. I swung my arms at the space above me desperately, to free myself from the evil bird's clutches.

"Lady, are you OK?" I heard someone ask.

I peeked up to see a young man looking down at me, a mixture of concern and amusement on his pale freckled face. I dared look up at the tree. Its branches were now empty of birds.

"Yes, I'm OK, thanks. It was just a crow that flew right at me," I told him, gathering my bags from the ground and praying my camera hadn't been damaged.

"Ah, right," he said, not sounding entirely convinced. "You're the photographer, right? Beth? I just came out to see if you were about. The ceremony is about to start and my wife is freaking out a little," he said with a laugh.

"Yes, I am. Mr Allen? I'm so sorry I'm late… Traffic – you know how it is…" I trailed off lamely.

He simply nodded, still with a slight grin on his face. Clearly he was not as stressed as his wife was about the baptism. He turned around and began walking back towards the church, and I followed closely on his heels, glancing up to the sky only once before setting foot inside All Souls Church.

It took a moment for my eyes to adjust to the relative gloom of the church's interior, compared to the bright sunlit day outside. I greeted Leanne, the lady who had hired me to do the job, with a gracious expression and apologised once more for running a little late. She smiled back, clearly relieved I was here and she could now get the show on the road. She had a young baby girl in her arms, dressed in a beautiful pink and white lace gown, who was loving the attention she was getting from all those invited.

I took my place near the baptismal bowl and began to take pictures of the ceremony and the guests, moving silently and fluidly amongst the group to capture the event from every possible angle.

I wanted to keep my mind fully focused on the job at hand, trying not to think that I would be back here tomorrow for my father's funeral, but it was impossible. This was the way of life and of death. A new soul in an innocent child, whilst another was gone and entrusted into God's hand. But not all souls go to Heaven and not all souls stay there – apparently, some come back.

Whatever enlightenment I was meant to gain from Isabel, I was still no closer to discovering. Perhaps she was being deliberately obtuse. Perhaps she simply wanted me to suffer – but why? I recalled the dead flowers on the counter. I had had enough of all this.

I stopped taking photos for a minute to watch the young family surrounded by relatives and friends, cooing over their new and completely innocent baby. Would that be Nathan and I in a couple of years' time?

As soon as the thought occurred to me, the already weak light grew darker and I turned to find wisps of grey smoke rolling slowly upwards from a set of candles that looked as if they had all just been snuffed out by a burst of wind.

The votive candles had been lit to pay homage to the statue of the Virgin Mary. Her hands were delicately encircled around a crimson heart at her chest; in the darkness the heart now appeared to beat and ooze blood, which trickled down her blue gown and plopped sickeningly on the floor. I watched in horror as the blood began to pool and ooze slowly towards me, I looked back up to the statue, but her face was no longer the serene, saintly face of the Virgin Mary.

It had been replaced by my mother's.

She was glaring at me, and I wanted to tell her I was sorry, that I wished Helena and I hadn't fought that day and that I was better now, that I wasn't who I was then... but I felt as fragile as a piece of glass. I would shatter if I spoke a single word.

Leanne's voice reached me. "Beth, please come over here and take a picture of Ella with her godparents and the priest by the altar."

I tore my eyes away from the hideous vision and hurried back towards the group. I spent the next few minutes taking group shots as directed by Leanne, and was happy when it was all over. I quickly said my goodbyes as the family thanked me, and was glad to be back outside in the crisp, fresh air.

I got back into my car swiftly, keeping an eye out for any vicious black winged creatures. Thankfully, the sky was clear apart from some puffs of white cloud, which looked as if they had been painted on the otherwise perfectly blue sky.

Mittens mewled at me reproachfully and I fished out some treats from my handbag and caressed her reassuringly. I started the engine and drove home, happy to put some distance between me and the church.

Once I got home I changed into some comfy clothes and downloaded all the photos I had just taken and began working on them, trying to erase the image of my mother's face from my mind. I deleted ones that were too similar, arranging them and retouching as necessary, changing the colour temperature slightly in my raw files to rid the images of the nasty yellow colour certain lighting conditions can cast.

It was my rumbling stomach that made me realise I had been working well past lunch time. Happy with the progress I had made, I saved all my changes and prepared myself a cheese omelette. As it cooked I chopped up a large tomato and an avocado to accompany it.

I sat down and read on my Kindle whilst I ate, savouring the melted cheese. It had been a while since I'd had a chance to read, probably not since holidaying in Tarifa. This was unlike me. I found reading a little like photography, in that it let me escape to another place, to see the world through someone else's eyes and point of view. For a while, I didn't have to be Beth; I could be the main character of whichever novel I was reading. Dr Roberts would accuse me of escapism, but I couldn't be the only one wishing to be someone else.

I tried to lose myself in a new book which had begun with the disappearance of a five-year-old girl after a kids' birthday party, and the search had just began in earnest. It was the author's debut novel and although it was fast-paced, well-written and intriguing, I just couldn't get into it. I guess there are days when a book simply cannot tear us away from reality.

As I tapped the screen once more, a new chapter began,

but I had only read a line or two when, despite my distracted state, I realised that something was very wrong. I reread the lines over and out loud, as if somehow I was simply misreading the words.

"The car was driving along an empty deserted stretch of road, not typical for this time of year when beachgoers flock to the coast. The sun was beginning to dip, the warmth of the day dissipating with the setting sun. The young family had spent the day at the beach. The parents were tired from the sun and of having to deal with their twin girls, or more accurately of having to deal with one of their daughters. Throughout the girls' childhoods the mother had often thought how different and how much easier it would have been if she had only had the one child. If it was only Helena that had been born—"

I wanted to stop reading. Each sentence was like a toxin, dripping into an open wound, spreading and contaminating every inch of me, but stopping would be like ceasing to breathe. I could do neither. Instead, my eyes devoured the words and my mouth spat out each one like venom, my voice echoing off the walls.

"Would she have been happy then? What was she to do? How could they continue living like this? It wasn't safe and she knew it, and something had to be done. Something had to be done about Beth."

I paused to take a deep breath and to wipe away a single tear which had trickled down my cheek. Mittens seemed to notice my distress and I felt her nip at my ankles, but I ignored her and pressed on.

"The mother closed her eyes against the pounding headache, hoping it would help drown out the girls' bickering in the back seat. It was constant, like the buzzing of a mosquito. She didn't even notice the truck coming towards them. When realisation dawned on her, it was too late to

even cry out. She could only watch the truck barrel into them, as if she were viewing it all in slow motion. The sickening crunch of metal on metal bellowed in her ears, followed by pain – indescribable pain."

I tapped the screen again, but when I began to read I realised that the text was now back to the original storyline, with the little girl's mother calling the detective in charge of her daughter's disappearance. I tapped the left side of the screen to go back, but it just continued to the next page in the novel. With a little more force than necessary, I rapped at the screen on the left a couple more times, but as the pages finally flipped back, I realised that what I had just read was no longer there. Yet I could still see each painful sentence in my mind's eye. Angry, hurt and more than just a little freaked out, I threw the Kindle on the sofa as if it had burned me.

Chapter Nineteen

I was here, yet at the same time I wasn't. I was simply disassociating myself from what was going on around me, something I had often done as a child. It is a dangerous thing to do; you can almost fool yourself into thinking your actions are not your own... almost.

The coffin had been carried into the church by four pall-bearers, who had then placed the casket on the catafalque by the altar and partly covered it with a red cloth. The old priest, his expression solemn, sprinkled holy water onto my father's coffin. The coffin appeared to gleam in the light that streamed in through the expanse of the windows of All Souls Church. The faux-gold handles shone with a polished sheen, as did the rosewood veneer of the coffin. Such extravagance for something that would be buried deep into the earth in just a few moments. Such pretence, to help distract you from the fact that what remains of your loved one is nothing more than dead and decaying flesh and bone.

When I had first arrived at the church, Father Peters had mistaken me for Helena, and started discussing all they had agreed on previously, but I had just stared blankly at him until

Helena had shown up moments later.

Having passed all the identical rows of tired-looking benches, I was standing by the front pew, feeling numb. Nathan had guided me to my seat as if it were some sort of morbid theatre production. He now stood between Helena and I. I was wearing a dark charcoal dress. It had reminded me of Isabel when I saw myself in the full-length mirror, but it was the only thing I could think to wear, so I had allowed the image of Isabel to fade to black.

We had awoken to another brilliantly sunny day, the bluest of skies, the air wonderfully crisp and clear. The birds chirped happily to each other and I felt like yelling at them to shut up, because I didn't want to do this today. Death brought back too many memories, and I wondered how much more I could take.

Everyone's heads were bowed and, as Father Peters began the funeral liturgy, I felt the past tugging at me, pulling me backwards. I stiffened slightly and Nathan reached out and held my hand. I couldn't look at him. I didn't want him to see into my eyes; he wouldn't like what he saw there.

"Dear friends." Father Peters' voice was deep and flat. "We are gathered here today in sorrow at the death of Mark Ellis. The reality of death, with all its sense of loss and pain, hits us today, but we are united not only in our sense of sorrow but also in our faith. Our faith comforts us with regards to what happens after we die. We speak about Heaven and the resurrection not because it gives us consolation and strength, but because they are true. They are the words of God. It is life that has the last word, not death. There is another chapter to come. Jesus himself said, blessed are they that mourn, for they shall be comforted. Death cannot rob us of the treasured memories left behind by our loved one. It cannot remove the legacy and wisdom they imparted into our lives."

Father Peters read a psalm and a passage from one of the gospels but I was no longer paying attention to his words. His voice had become a murmuring hum to my ears, and instead what I heard was my father's voice, his words like a disease which ate at my insides.

"It's all your fault! You hear me? What the hell is wrong with you? You are like a plague destroying everything you touch! Now your mother is dead because of you! Are you happy now?! Are you?!"

We had been at the hospital, my father, Helena and I, getting patched up for minor scratches and bruises, whilst my mother lay dead and cold on a mortuary slab. The nurses had been horrified to hear my father say these words to me. They had tried to calm him down but he was furious. I had never seen him this mad; it scared me more than the accident had. I thought he was going to kill me.

That's when everything changed.

When I changed.

The nurses had no choice but to sedate him. Helena was in shock and was just staring at a spot on the wall, her eyes vacant and unfocused. But I could recall my father's expression as vividly as if he were standing right in front of me, and I never wanted anyone to look at me that way again. Now he too was in the past.

I leaned forward ever so slightly and cast a sideways glance at Helena. Her eyes were red from crying, although she had done a good job covering it up with make-up. She too had been staring at the coffin, as if she couldn't quite believe our father was dead. I suppose he had been more of a father to her than to me. Perhaps she now felt truly alone... I had Nathan.

Perhaps she did have someone special in her life – it wasn't as if I would have known if she did. If there was someone, he hadn't come to the funeral with her. I wonder if Helena also felt free of the past like I did. I hoped she found peace and happiness in her life. The new Beth wanted that for her very much.

Father Peters' voice pulled me from my thoughts. "Today is but a temporary farewell to our brother, Mark Ellis, and one day we shall all be together in the kingdom of Heaven. Death can never change the fact that Mark made a great difference to the lives of countless people. Mark suffered great tragedy when he lost his wife many years ago, but he leaves behind two wonderful daughters, Helena and Beth." He sprinkled the casket with holy water once more. "It is now time for friends and family to say their goodbyes to Mark."

I stayed rooted to the spot, watching people as they shuffled slowly towards the coffin. I couldn't say I recognised any of them. Since I had left for university, I had had very little contact with my father and had no idea what he did with his free time, other than drink. Did he have some sort of social life after Helena and I had left home? Did he have friends? I assumed that many of the people here today were his co-workers. My father had spent his entire life at the same firm; it would only be common courtesy for his colleagues to attend his funeral. The mourners gave Helena and I polite, sad nods as they trailed back to their seats.

Finally, the trickle of people who had murmured a few words at his side or placed a hand reverently on the coffin dissipated, and it was time for me to say my own goodbyes. I let go of Nathan's hand and took a few steps closer to the coffin, the sense of despair washing over me. I didn't want to be here. There was so much to say, yet at the same time nothing at all. Besides, it was too late, and if there were other lives for us to lead, then perhaps it would be better if our paths never crossed again.

Father Peters offered me a friendly smile. I imitated one in return, but beneath it there were only screams.

The sun was now high in the sky, and there was no wind or cloud. Like a photograph, this still moment would remain etched in my mind, as the first shovel of cold earth was laid upon my father's grave. I took another glimpse at Helena; tears were now silently falling down her cheeks but her expression remained almost neutral.

I did not look at the grave again. Instead, I focused on the nearby headstones. No two appeared to be the same shape or size, like snowflakes, and they were just as cold but nowhere near as beautiful. These stones were meant to represent permanence; they would not melt away at a mere touch. They meant to say that the dead would not be forgotten but, inevitably, we *would* all be forgotten and it would be like we never existed at all and perhaps that was a good thing.

I focused on the ivy creeping across the ground, over the twisted roots of trees; the roots looked to me like contorted bones reaching from their graves. I shivered. The morning dew had long since evaporated and the trees in their autumnal blush only served to remind me of the transient nature of life.

I heard Father Peters say something about the dead being laid to rest, and I felt like speaking up, telling him that not all who were dead were at rest. That there were some souls, like Isabel, like mine even, that had no peace and perhaps never would. *What about those who have committed deadly sins, Father? They are not resting in Hell, surely? So, no, Father, not all who die are resting.*

I closed my eyes.

I was now standing in the corner of a garden, staring at a stream, the water clear and cool. A few ducks waded in and allowed their plump bodies to be carried away downstream. Nathan was standing next to me, having just brought me a glass of apple juice which I sipped slowly, savouring its sweetness.

We were at my father's wake, which Helena had organised. A picturesque pub close to my father's house, a renovated old watermill. I had escaped to the garden as soon as I could, after I had smiled politely at strangers' words of condolences. I wondered if my father was a stranger to them too.

I wondered what Nathan really thought about the peculiarity of my family's dynamics. Would he look at me differently now that I had been unable to shed a tear at my father's grave? Now that I was unable to comfort Helena, even if she had allowed me to?

If our roles were reversed, if it was Alex's or Eleanor's funeral, Nathan would be inconsolable. He and Louise would cling to each other for support as their foundations crumbled from underneath them.

I had made sure Nathan had never seen how broken I was inside. It was a mask I had worn for many years, one that altered and re-made itself as needed, my second skin.

I turned to face Nathan and said, "Nathan, I think I'd like to go home now. Some people have already left and I'm sure Helena can handle it from here."

"You sure, babe?" he asked, taking the empty glass from my hand.

"Yeah, I'm just feeling really drained. I just wanna go home and lie down and watch some mindless TV."

"Of course. Some rest will do you good," he said kindly, giving me a quick kiss on the cheek.

"I'll just go say my goodbyes to Helena, and I'll meet you in the car," I told him.

I watched him as he set the glasses down on a nearby table and headed back towards the car park. I walked slowly back up the slope to the pub, the kitten heels of my black shoes sinking into the grass with each step. As I stepped inside I allowed myself to take in the space, something which I hadn't been able to do earlier. It was an upscale modern pub, its light grey walls adorned with pastel, abstract paintings, and it had polished dark wood flooring, comfortable-looking blue cushioned seats and tall ceilings with exposed wooden beams. It was a bright and airy place, with green potted plants everywhere. A few men were at the bar nursing beers, their dark suits already looking a little crumpled, their almost empty pint glasses lined up next to them, waiting to be cleaned and refilled. It seemed ironic to me for people to drink at a funeral of a man killed by alcohol, but I no longer cared. I just wanted to get home and shut myself away from everything.

I spotted Helena chatting to an elderly couple who, if memory served me correctly, were Dad's neighbours. I didn't want to interrupt, but I didn't want to leave without saying…*What exactly was I going to say to her?* Something, at least. The Beth I had become would not think it right to leave without a word, and so I made myself move towards them. They noticed me approach and stopped mid-sentence. I opened my mouth to speak but nothing came out, but luckily for me, the old lady spoke first.

"Hello Beth, it has been such a long time since we last saw you. Shame that we should meet again in such circumstances. Fred and I are so sorry for your loss. We were just telling your sister how saddened we were to see Mark deteriorate so quickly," she told me, her voice so soft it was almost a whisper, as she wiped a tear from her eye.

"Thank you so much, and thank you for coming," I replied, my voice sounding too high even to my own ears, as if I was thanking them for attending a kids' birthday party.

They nodded politely and joined another couple who were helping themselves to a selection of hors d'oeuvres. I turned back to face Helena, who was now peering out of the window, her brow furrowed. With a chilling sense of disquiet, I followed her gaze. Even though the glass was slightly frosted, I could make out a woman standing on the hill.

Can I not have a single moment's peace? I felt like screaming, but instead I looked at Helena, who still seemed fixated on the spot where Isabel stood. But how was that possible?

Could Helena see her too?

I glanced outside again, but the hilltop was now empty. I hoped Isabel would vanish for good, but I knew that was just wishful thinking; she'd be back soon, no doubt. Helena still looked a little confused, as if she had stepped into a room and forgotten what she was there for. After a moment she looked at me and we stared at each other. She was close enough to touch but an ocean lay between us. You can see in your twin something that other people don't get to see, but I didn't want her looking at me, because she could see what I had spent so many years trying to hide.

"Thank you Helena, for organising all of this. I'm happy to split the costs of everything and if there is anything you need, you can call me. I know we're not exactly... but I am here," I said quickly.

"Dad made all the provisions necessary, and his lawyer will be contacting me in a few days about the reading of the will. I'll let you know."

"Oh, OK, I guess I'll see you soon, then. I am sorry about Dad. I know you two were close."

"I didn't want him to suffer any longer," Helena said softly.

There was a world of meaning in that statement. It wasn't the cancer that had made him suffer –although that was a terrible way to die –it was having to live without my mother. It was knowing that even though I had been responsible for her death, he had been the one behind the wheel.

I nodded, not trusting myself to speak. There was no kiss goodbye, no heartfelt hug, no tears of sadness at our shared loss. I simply turned and walked away. In an odd way, I felt lighter, because more connections to the old Beth were being severed, and as I stepped outside into the sunlight and headed towards the car, I reminded myself that to survive you did what you had to do. Even if that meant shutting the door on your past.

I was glad to get home. Nathan made us some toast which I nibbled at with no real enthusiasm, as we sat on the sofa and watched *Ozark* on Netflix. We cuddled under the bright turquoise blanket Nathan's grandmother had knitted for us, as Mittens ran and jumped back and forth playfully across our laps.

I wanted this day to be over, to put some distance between myself and the day I had to bury my father. I also had to put an end to Isabel. Even now, she was tainting this quiet moment with Nathan and Mittens, because I was wondering what she was going to do next.

As the sun began to lower in the sky and the day bled into the night, I felt my eyelids become heavy. The TV was still on, but I hadn't been keeping up with the Byrde's latest unfolding disaster, and so I let myself drift off to sleep, unable to stop the shadows from creeping in.

Chapter 20

The shadows swallowed me whole, banishing me into an inky darkness that seemed to blot out the entire world. Suddenly, a dim light appeared in the distance and I found myself moving towards it, the proverbial light in a tunnel. As I got closer, I realised it was not a light but a full moon. Then I noticed the cool, damp sand beneath my feet. I was back on the beach, amongst the ancient but forever changing sand dunes.

I felt drawn to the sea, and I stepped closer to the dark expanse which seemed to stretch into eternity. I looked down at my feet, noting that I was leaving no footprints. I raised my gaze once more to the ocean, and that's when I saw her.

Isabel was standing knee-deep in the ocean, but she looked different. It took me a second to realise that was because she was now a living, breathing person.

She was mesmerizingly beautiful. Her skin was bathed in the light of the full moon and she shone brighter than the stars in the sky. But there was also something profoundly tragic emanating from her, and as I inched closer, I realised she was crying. Tears slid slowly but steadily down her cheeks, as the water rushed around her legs. I wanted to speak out, to ask her what had happened, what she wanted from me, but I found I could not speak. I was here only to observe, but it still felt wrong to witness what was clearly such a raw, heartbreaking moment in her life. I tried to take a step back but a force held me in place, and so I watched her.

I watched her as she glanced at her hand. I now noticed the ruby ring glinting in the half-light. She clenched her fist as if in anger, tears continuing to spill down her cheeks. She glanced up at the sky, as if beseeching to the heavens. I could see her lips move but couldn't hear what she was saying.

Then she took a step forward.

And another.

Followed by another.

The water now swirled around her waist, her long dress billowing around her, seeming to pull her in all directions at once. I wanted to scream at her to stop; I wanted to go in after her and pull her out. But I couldn't do either.

The sea was ablaze in the silvery light of the moon and she seemed to be following this light deeper and further out. The waters had reached her neck, but she continued to swim farther away into that endless expanse of sea.

Just come back, Isabel. Just swim right back and get out of the sea, for God's sake! My mind bellowed.

After a few moments I couldn't see her anymore. I scanned the water, hoping to catch sight of her once more, but she was gone.

I felt myself plummet, as if the earth had suddenly given way beneath me and I too was now sinking into the ocean. My lungs burned for air, my arms flailing uselessly around me, the warmth of my flesh leaching out into the cold water.

I realised in dismay that Isabel wanted me to experience

her final moments.

I was so desperate for air that I took an involuntary breath. Water followed into my mouth and down my windpipe and my throat constricted in response. I was suffocating and could do nothing to stop it, and in that final sepia-coloured moment, I witnessed the last thing Isabel ever saw and felt. The ruby ring, the stone as dark as blood, slipped off her finger and disappeared into the black, frigid waters.

Beneath the unbearable sadness that weighed so heavily on Isabel's heart, there also lay a dark anger, an anger which I feared not even death could placate.

I woke with a start, taking deep breaths that felt glorious to me. I was damp with sweat and looked around me in panic. It took me a moment to realise I was still on the sofa. I was covered in a blanket. Nathan must have decided to let me sleep here rather than wake me. I pulled the blanket off me, welcoming the cool air on my hot skin. I picked up my phone from the coffee table and checked the time: it was 3am.

I laid back down and stared up at the ceiling, now feeling wide awake. The dream, the vision, my glimpse into a past life –or whatever you wanted to call it –was an experience too awful for words.

But it had revealed how and where Isabel had died, and I also finally understood where my unfounded fear of the ocean had come from. What I still didn't know was why. Why had Isabel committed suicide? I had a harrowing feeling that I would soon come to understand her reasons and that I wasn't going to like what I found.

Mittens mewled loudly, shattering the quiet of the night. I

followed the sound to my right, where the single reclining armchair was situated. There, partly obscured by the night, sat Isabel, staring at me with eyes that mirrored the darkness that lay within her. Her once beautiful olive skin was now mottled by death. Water dripped off her lank hair and her damp clothes as if she had just stepped out of her watery grave.

I gave a small, involuntary cry of alarm. *Has she been sitting there the whole time? Projecting those horrible memories into my mind?* It was then that I noticed Mittens playing by Isabel's bare, rotten feet. She turned her gaze to the kitten and then back up to me, a sardonic smirk on her blue lips, but she made no other move.

"Isabel," I began, my voice little more than a croak.

She cocked her head to one side, a mannerism more akin to animals than humans. She reminded me of the crow on the roof of my car.

"I don't know what happened to you that made you… that made you decide to take your own life or what it is you want from me. Is it the ring? Is that it? You want it back, I understand, and I'm sorry I picked it up." I pulled the ruby ring off my finger and placed it on the coffee table between us. "I don't understand what it is you are trying to tell me. Can't you just speak and tell me what it is you want? Please just let me be," I pleaded with her.

She had been sitting completely still, but in a split second she threw herself at me, her body contorting at impossible, sickening angles. She moved so fast I barely had time to react before I felt her body connect with my flesh.

Light suddenly flooded the room and she disappeared in an instant. My scream was cut short as she was banished into the nothingness from which she came.

"Beth," Nathan called out from the doorway. "I heard you cry out – I think you were talking in your sleep again. Were you having a nightmare?" He moved over to me and enveloped me in a hug. "God, you're shaking, and your skin is on fire." He paused, his eyes scanning my face. "Maybe you're coming down with something? The flu?"

"Maybe," I replied, unable to say anything more.

I made myself focus on the feel of his strong arms around me, the sound of his heartbeat as I laid my head against his chest. Perhaps I shouldn't have tried speaking to Isabel. I thought back to some of the horror movies Nathan had made me watch in our first year of dating. There was always a priest or a wizened old woman, who warned people against interacting with the evil spirit, as this *invites* them in.

But Isabel wasn't a demon; she had been human once. If I believed in past lives, then we shared a soul and she was reaching out to me for some reason. I just had to figure out why, and that would be the end of it. Over Nathan's shoulder, I studied the ring lying harmlessly on the coffee table, and wondered what other secrets it held.

We sat like that for a few more minutes, until I suggested we go to bed and try and get a few more hours of sleep. The next evening would be a big night for my career: hundreds of people would attend the latest Water-Well Media Centre exhibition and I had to be at my best in order to try and line up future work. A steady stream of money would be welcome, especially now, when I had warmed to the thought of buying a home when we got married.

I let my mind fill with happier thoughts, of lace wedding

gowns, three-tier cakes, vows of forever, champagne toasts and exotic honeymoon locations, as I closed my eyes once more and prayed for a dreamless sleep.

I could hear the rain lashing on the window panes; it was this sound of running water which woke me, and for an instant I was flooded with the horrible recollection of how it felt to drown, but I pushed the memory away forcibly and turned in bed to face Nathan.

The light of early dawn had started to dispel the black of night to dove-grey but had yet to rise fully. Nathan was still asleep and snoring lightly, his sandy blonde hair ruffled, his lips slightly parted. Before I could stop myself, I trailed a fingertip lovingly across his cheek. He smiled before opening his eyes.

"Morning, gorgeous," he whispered, his voice husky from sleep.

"Morning, sexy," I murmured.

I kissed his cheek lightly, and then his lips, softly at first and then with more urgency. I began stroking him over his shorts, slowly and teasingly, and he groaned in pleasure. All vestiges of sleep had left him, I tugged his boxer shorts down from his hips and held him in my hand, playing with him just as I knew he liked. I stopped only to remove my own pyjama shorts and T-shirt, then continued kissing him. My lips caressed his neck and his chest as he lay down on top of me, and for a while I forgot the whole world existed. In that moment, it was just Nathan and me in our own world, making love to each other as if we had spent months apart. After we came, we held each other closely and I dozed off into a satisfying post-coital slumber.

A little while later, sunlight filled the room, waking me once more. The rain had stopped and I opened my eyes to what seemed another beautiful day. I got up, wrapped my gown around my naked body and padded over to the window.

The street below was now bathed in sunlight. The puddles and dew-laden grass gave the scene a slivery sheen, like a high-gloss photograph, making everything look fresh and new. I allowed myself a small smile. Today was a new day, a fresh page, and this evening promised an event full of possibilities.

Inevitably, thoughts of my father, Helena, Isabel and even Dolores, tried to worm themselves into my mind, but I visualised a wall in my head and placed them firmly behind it. I knew I had a lot still to process, but not today. Today, I needed to focus on the exhibition.

"Hey, you up, sleepyhead? I've made pancakes!" Nathan hollered from the kitchen.

"Be there in a sec," I called back.

I picked up Mittens, who was rolling around on the rug with the toy mouse, and kissed the top of her soft head and left the bedroom.

"Knocked you out cold, didn't I?" Nathan asked cheekily as I entered the kitchen.

"Shut up, you," I replied affectionately, and kissed him passionately again.

"Watch it lady, you're gonna make me burn breakfast."

He laughed and placed a couple of fluffy, golden pancakes on a plate.

I put Mittens down and poured some kitten food into her bowl, then I took the plate Nathan offered, sat and tucked in.

"Delicious, babe –thanks." I said between mouthfuls.

"You're welcome." He took a seat opposite me and smeared chocolate spread on his pancakes. "My folks are excited to see the exhibition tonight. Are you feeling up to it?"

"Honestly, I'm emotionally drained, but it's an important night for me. One I cannot afford to miss."

"You've had to deal with so much recently, in such a short period of time. I don't want you to bottle it up... You're going to have to let me in sometime," he said, staring at me so solemnly I felt uncomfortable beneath his gaze, as if he could somehow sense everything I had been keeping from him.

I took his hand across the table and squeezed it, then dropped my gaze to our interlocking hands. Nathan loved me, probably more than any other person ever had, and I craved and needed his love as much as I needed air to breathe.

A part of me, albeit a very small part, was tempted to let it all out, to try and explain the relationship I had with my father and Helena. To put into words how much my mother's death had impacted my life – but to do that, I would have to go back, back to before, to the old Beth. In that moment, I saw Coco-Pop as clearly as if he were scuttling across the table in front of me, and I knew I never would reveal my past.

I would keep my buried secrets and my suffocating lies, because that's the thing about lies: they can start out small, but they multiply, each new one giving credence to the first.

Like a game of Jenga, if you pull at the foundations, you risk the carefully built structure tumbling down and crushing you.

It wasn't only that; I was also ashamed. Ashamed of who I had been.

Instead, all I said was, "I'm sorry. I know it must not be easy to understand why I avoid talking about my family. And yes, it has been awful recently, with Dad and Dolores – but I'm OK really. I just need a little time to process it all."

"I can't even imagine. Are you sure there isn't anything else on your mind? I've noticed you've been a little distracted since we got back from Tarifa. Are you worried about the wedding? About us?" he asked a little hesitantly.

So he *had* noticed – but if I started telling him all about Isabel, he'd think I'd lost my mind. I also felt terrible that he had been worried about us, but my feelings towards him was the one thing I could be honest about.

"Nathan, you proposing was the most wonderful thing that has ever happened to me, and there is nothing I want more than to spend my life with you," I said, feeling tears prick at my eyes.

"Phew, that's a relief," he said, pretending to wipe sweat of his brow "and I want to spend my life making you as happy as you make me."

We finished our breakfast and I did the washing up, whilst Nathan checked and replied to a few emails from work. It was now a beautiful day outside, so I suggested we go for a walk. We went into the shower together and made love again as the warm water caressed our skin. I dressed in leggings, a thin jumper and jacket. I grabbed the wicker basket to take Mittens along with us.

We strolled hand in hand to the nearest park, just a twenty-minute walk from our flat. It was good to get outside and enjoy the day and pretend, even if just for a few hours, that everything was as it should be. We scouted out a secluded bench and sat down to enjoy the autumn sunshine, as Mittens happily explored around us.

Nathan and I chatted for a long while, keeping an eye on Mittens as she occasionally chewed on the grass or tried to run after a bumblebee or butterfly. It felt wonderful; I had been in my head so much lately that I had barely noticed the weeks tick by without us having spent much quality time together.

I guess that was normal. Nowadays, everyone seemed to live life on a speeding train. One which never stopped. We are all so busy getting an education, working, trying to get on the housing ladder, running a household, raising kids, constantly striving to be happy... does it ever get any easier? Does life ever slow down? Or will we wake up one day and look at ourselves in the mirror, barely able to recognise the wrinkled face staring back at us?

Do people believe in reincarnation because it gives them comfort to think they can have another chance at life? That there will be other opportunities to do all the things they wanted to do in this life but never did?

Shielding my eyes from the sun, I marvelled at the bluest of skies above me. Perhaps life was simply about treasuring the moments that made you feel alive. The moments that made you feel truly grateful to exist, to love fully, so that when death did come, you could go quietly into the night.

After a couple of hours, Nathan was starting to get

hungry —his appetite always astounded me, and I couldn't help but laugh. We decided to stop at a cafe on the way home, agreeing it was too beautiful a day to spend it cooped up indoors. We took the last outside table available. Nathan ordered a club sandwich with fries and onion rings, and I opted for the Caesar salad. I sipped my iced tea and watched the world pass by, but felt as if I were no longer truly a part of it.

Chapter Twenty-One

The cloudless day had given way to a cold night. No hint of the sun's warmth remained, only a matt-black canvas of a night sky. The stars were indistinguishable due to the glow of the city lights. I wrapped my coat closer around my body, my breath misting in front of me in the frosty air, as Nathan and I hurried up the stone steps of the Water-Well Media Centre.

As we stepped inside, we were hit by a welcome blast of warm air, and I felt myself relax a little. I was still nervous, even though I had taken an anti-anxiety tablet with a bite of toast and a glass of wine whilst I was getting ready.

Showcasing my work always made me anxious, even though I had mostly received praise for all my projects thus far. I had discussed this with Dr Roberts, who said this was a classic case of imposter syndrome. It was a term I had heard before: you doubt your own accomplishments and have an internalised fear of being exposed as a fraud. He was right, of course, but what he didn't realise was that this fear related to much more than simply my work: it pertained to me as a person.

The night my mother died, I had broken in two. I had become two people: what I refer to as the old Beth and the new Beth. But unlike a split personality disorder, where someone may not even know that other personalities are lurking in their mind, I was fully aware of the old Beth. Her thoughts and emotions were like an undercurrent which flowed through me. A river of poison, which threatened to taint every aspect of my being if I let it.

As I handed my coat to the cloak room attendant, I was hit by a flashback so real that it was as if I was once again eight years old and standing in my old house, just outside the living room, hearing my father and mother yelling at each other.

Yelling about me.

"Sarah, you know we have to do something!" my father's gruff voice exclaims, sounding both tired and stressed. That was never a good combination.

"What do you want me to do, Mark, send her away?" my mother cries back.

"Yes, that's exactly what we have to do. She needs help, Sarah! Help we can't provide!"

"There must be something we can do..." my mother's voice cracks. I know she is crying now.

"A leopard can't change its spots!" his loud voice booms in my ears.

I step into the living room then. I don't know why –to stop the conversation? To face them? I am angry. How dare they suggest sending me away? I am their child!

My mother sits as still as a statue on the sofa as tear after tear rushes down the porcelain skin of her cheeks. My father paces back and forth on the rug. I hated that rug, as he never let me play on it. He didn't want me to ruin it, but there he was trampling it with his work shoes.

When they realise they are no longer alone, they both turn in unison to face me. My mother looks sad and broken, my father a little embarrassed, but he recovers soon enough and looks at me like if I am a dangerous spider that he didn't want getting any closer to him.

"Beth, it is not polite to eavesdrop on adult conversations," he says stiffly, but in a calmer tone.

The next day my mother was dead.

"You look amazing tonight, Beth," Nathan's whispered as he wrapped an arm around my waist and gave me a quick peck on the lips.

His words and his touch jolted me back to the present. I looked down at the figure-hugging black dress I had chosen for the occasion. It was elegant yet sexy. Sleeveless, with a low, boat-neck cut, and a flowing skirt with a mid-thigh split. The outfit accentuated the curves of my body. I was advertising my skills tonight as a photographer, but I wasn't naive; I knew a pretty package helped you get ahead in this superficial world.

"Thank you, and you don't look so bad yourself, Mr Walker," I replied with a grin.

He was wearing his dark navy-blue suit, which he knew was my favourite. His tie was light blue, which matched his eyes. Even in his suit, I could make out his perfectly toned torso, and I noticed the girl at the cloak room subtly checking him out. It didn't bother me – Nathan was an attractive guy – but it wasn't just that. He had this aura about him, this goodness, that people gravitated towards, much like I had. Nathan had this effect on both women and men, and this made me feel less nervous. Meeting new people, and, potentially, new clients was a much easier endeavour when I had him next to me. He knew how important this night was for me. He looked at me encouragingly as he took my hand and we walked into the main hall.

It was early, so I was surprised to see so many people here already. The hall was dimly but expertly lit, the spotlights focused primarily on the exhibition pieces set up across the vast hall.

The exhibits were of various shapes, sizes and colours. Not only photographs, but sculptures, paintings and even short video-clips playing on a loop on large screens. The works of various artists had been brought together skilfully and effectively to take the viewer on a superb visual journey, experiencing and engaging with both history and the present almost simultaneously, making the contrast all the more evident.

People dressed in suits and elegant dresses paused at each exhibit for a few moments before moving onto the next. Their whispered discussions were a pleasant accompaniment to the soft, slightly haunting music emitted by the surround speakers.

Nathan and I stopped at the first sculpture. The artist had created a replica of Bristol Cathedral in pennies. It was utterly beautiful, and must have taken him a long time. The lighting made the copper hues gleam, which made gazing on the art seem an almost spiritual experience.

We began to move towards the next piece when I caught sight of Tania heading straight towards us. She looked a little wired, as if she had had one too many cups of coffee, but also pleased. I was happy for her – it must have been a lot of work putting this exhibition together. She looked fantastic in a smart navy blue jumpsuit and scarlet kitten heels. Her red hair was tied up in an elegant bun, and her lips were the colour of rubies, in vivid contrast to her pale skin.

"Beth, I was hoping I'd run into you sooner rather than later! I've already had a number of people asking about your work – they absolutely love the photographs and would love to meet you!" Tania exclaimed as she embraced me in a quick hug.

"That's so great – and congratulations! The place looks absolutely fantastic! You must be so proud. This is my fiancé, Nathan," I said, introducing her to him.

"Pleased to meet you, Nathan," Tania said. "So, what's your opinion on Beth's art?"

"Pleasure is mine. Well, Beth, likes to keep her work pretty much top secret until it's finished, so I'm very keen to see it."

"Is that right?" Tania grinned at me. "Well, come with me, let's see if we can find Mr Lambert. He's from the Art and Culture Foundation and is currently working on a new project, and we both think you'd be a perfect fit for it!"

I couldn't help but smile, feeling elated and proud, and for a split second I felt a sharp pang of regret that neither Helena nor either of my parents were here to witness this milestone in my career. My smile faltered a little but not by much.

I remembered that my mum used to like to paint. I wondered what she would think of my chosen profession, whether she would have been proud. Dad had never had much of an opinion about it. I guessed he was just happy I was moving out the house and further away from Helena. What I studied at university wasn't all that important.

Nathan caught my eye and seemed to notice the change in me but before he could ask if I was OK, I smiled at him reassuringly and took his hand, as we followed Tania through the throng of people. She guided me to where they had displayed my photograph of Banksy's 'Well Hung Lover'. As I had requested it had been printed on a large canvas, four metres by two metres. The window scene was brightly lit, but the lover hanging from the window was partly in shadow. Highlighting the darkness that lies in all people and how we are all capable of committing immoral acts.

We then moved onto the photographs I had taken of the Cathedral and of a new office block constructed primarily of glass. As instructed the colossal prints had been framed in matt black aluminium and arranged to form a full 360 degree circle, one half depicted the church the other the new structure. As I had hoped, the images of the glass building created a sense of light, airiness and modernity, which contrasted against the gloomier, colder, sense of permanence that the stone building of the Cathedral evoked.

A handsome older man, who looked to be in his early fifties, was gazing up at it. He was wearing a black suit and white shirt. Before Tania had a chance to introduce us, he turned and spoke.

"So this must be Beth," he said, giving me an appraising look. "I have had a look at your previous work and your submissions for this exhibition, and I must say I am impressed."

"Thank you very much, Mr Lambert. I was honoured to be chosen to form part of it."

"Please, call me Paul," he told me.

I introduced him to Nathan, and Tania repeated that Paul was interested in speaking to me about an upcoming project.

"At the Art and Culture Foundation, one of our main goals is to make the arts, in all its various shapes and forms, more accessible to children – especially those from more impoverished backgrounds," Paul explained. "We believe art is not a luxury and that it shouldn't be viewed as something for only the privileged few to enjoy. Instead, we want to alter people's perception about how they think about art, and make it available to everyone. We believe it is a necessity which serves to brighten our lives. For myself, art can remind me of what it means to be human. It inspires us and connects us."

"I completely agree," I declared. Paul's obvious passion for the arts was inspiring. "I also find that art is a great form of escapism."

"Precisely, Beth. We collaborate with a number of centres who work with underprivileged children and those who have suffered hardships such as abuse or neglect. Art is a great form of therapy. One of the projects in the pipeline involves exploring street art across the country, and demonstrating that it is much more than just graffiti or vandalism, and showing how this type of art can form an important part of a community and provide an outlet of creativity for children who may not have much else. If you'd be interested in forming part of the team, we'd love to have you."

"That sounds like a wonderful opportunity – and yes, I'd love to be part of it. I can't thank you enough," I said, handing him one of my business cards and having to restrain myself from jumping excitedly on the spot.

"Wonderful. I shall be in touch soon," Mr Lambert said as he pocketed my card. "I shall let you all enjoy the rest of the exhibition. Pleasure to meet you both."

"Thank you so, so much, Tania," I said to her once Mr Lambert had left.

"No need to thank me – your work speaks for itself, and you deserve it Beth," she replied. "Now go, you two, enjoy the rest of your night! I must mingle!" She grinned and strolled away.

We spent the next twenty minutes viewing the other pieces, and Nathan wanted to see the other photographs I had submitted. He especially liked the photography of 'A Vision of Heaven and Hell' I had taken in Christ Church – as I knew he would be, considering his predilection for horror movies.

Here as instructed, the lighting to the bottom and middle part of the printed canvas had a subtle red tinge to it, making the fires of hell look as if they were aflame. The expressions on the faces of the individuals being dragged down towards Hell looked so real and horrific I couldn't suppress a shudder.

"Would be better if Louise didn't see this one," Nathan commented at last. "We watched *The Exorcist* together as kids and she didn't sleep for two weeks."

"Beth!" I heard Louise cry out. I turned round to find her and Nathan's parents heading towards us.

"Don't look!" Nathan cried comically, trying to block the four-metre canvas with his body.

"Ha ha, very funny, you!" Louise retorted when she'd

caught a glimpse of the art, poking him playfully in the ribs. "I'm not ten anymore. I can handle a little horror."

I couldn't help but stifle a giggle. Louise was such a lovely, bubbly girl that I didn't think she could handle it, actually. If she took just one look at Isabel, she would probably never sleep properly again.

As if merely by thinking about Isabel, I conjured her. She stood a few metres from where we were, beside a six foot wood carving of Cabot Tower.

"What a wonderful exhibition! It's been years since we had attended one at the centre," Eleanor told us. "Beth, we just wanted to say again how sorry we all are for your loss," she continued softly, embracing me in a hug.

"Thank you for coming tonight. It means a lot – and thank you for the flowers. It was very thoughtful," I said as we parted.

I ignored Isabel. Perhaps if I didn't give her the satisfaction of a reaction, she would leave me alone, at least just for tonight.

"It was the least we could do. I hope you know that you can come to us if you ever need anything – anything at all," Eleanor said kindly.

I nodded, touched by her words. Is this what it felt like to be part of a family?

"Louise was just pointing out to us some of your works. Some great stuff, Beth," Alex said. "I'm sure your father would have been very proud."

All I could say was, "Thank you."

Perhaps my father would have been proud, but I doubted he would have told me. Forgiveness was not something that came easily to him, but I had accepted that long ago.

"And that's not all – she's just had an offer to take part in a new project by the Art and Culture Foundation," Nathan informed them proudly.

"No way – that's amazing news, Beth! We must celebrate!" Louise exclaimed.

I cast a furtive glance at Isabel, who still hadn't moved. People seemed to skirt around her. It wasn't that they could see her, of course, but it was as if they could sense something was wrong in that spot, and stayed clear of it.

I couldn't help but examine the vintage ring on my hand. I had never given much thought to how perfectly it fit and how I couldn't seem to stop wearing it. I wondered what would happen if I simply threw the ring away. I could simply go down to the waterfront and throw it back into the sea. Would Isabel vanish too? But I knew that wouldn't be the case. Severing this connection with her, with my past self, wouldn't be quite so easy.

I felt her eyes on me, and when I looked back up, she was staring at me as if she knew what I had been thinking. It was almost as if she could stare right into my soul and take it from me.

The voices of Nathan and his family catching up with one another buzzed around me, but I couldn't make out what they were saying. It was as if I was trapped underwater. Familiar feelings of trepidation and fear washed over me. I knew that something lurked in the gloom. I fought against the rising tide of anxiety and gazed defiantly at Isabel.

A wicked smirk spread across her thin lips, exposing black, rotten gums, as if she were amused by my attempt to face her. She wanted me to cower from her, to be afraid. What could I have done in a past life to warrant this? I already had enough to answer for in this life. But if a fight was what she wanted, a fight she would get. After all, I had spent my entire life battling my inner demons. I could handle one more.

    I felt the old Beth stir within me, like a wild animal that had been caged for too long and which was now hungry. I mirrored Isabel's devilish smile with my own, but this only made her grin broaden to something that wasn't even remotely human. Something passed between us then. Something that had been set in motion the moment I saw her on the beach but which now was shifting and morphing into something else. I feared the real game was just beginning.

Chapter Twenty-Two

We continued to stare at each other in a sort of standoff. Whatever game Isabel was playing, it suddenly dawned on me that I didn't know the rules. I felt a pang of anxiety in my chest but strived to quash it, whilst trying to maintain a look of composure.

Louise and Nathan were talking about our wedding plans, and it wasn't until Nathan repeated my name that I realised they were waiting for me to respond.

"I'm sorry," I began. "I was in my own world for a moment. What was that?"

"Louise was just asking about the venue we're seeing next week... You sure you're OK, hun?" Nathan asked.

"I'm fine really, just a little tired," I reassured him. "And thanks again, Louise, for the list of venues. They were all so beautiful. I fell in love with the Old Manor House as soon as I saw it."

"Oh yeah, I remember that one. It was definitely one of my favourites too," Louise said. "It's the kind of place I'd want to get married one day. Just need to find someone worthwhile," she added, laughing brightly.

I tore my eyes away and back to Isabel, expecting her to

have either vanished or to be still piercing me with her gaze – but it was much worse. To my horror, I saw she had now directed her attention to Nathan.

I felt a cold sickening sensation in my guts as I watched her watch him. Other than Mittens, I had never seen Isabel respond to anything or anyone other than me. She no longer wore a sadistic expression on her face, but rather appeared to be appraising Nathan. When she finally looked back at me I had the overwhelming and terrible sensation that in these few seconds something had changed.

I didn't know what it was, but when Isabel observed me once more, I saw it in the depths of her black eyes.

"You stay away from him!" I screamed at her in my mind, just before she vanished.

"We have about an hour before we need to leave to make our reservation at Mangiamoci Su," Alex informed us, checking his watch.

"Right, I guess I should go network a little," I said, even though I didn't really feel up to it anymore. "Nathan why don't you continue with your parents and Louise, and I'll meet you all by the exit in an hour?" I suggested.

"Sure I can do that." Nathan replied giving me an encouraging nod before heading off with his parents and sister to the next piece over.

I decided to explore the far end of the exhibition, admiring the work other artists had submitted and around five minutes later I bumped into Tania again. I spent the next half an hour with her, as she introduced me to numerous other artists and guests, some of whom were interested in my work and I managed to hand out quite a few of my business cards.

I was starting to enjoy myself once more when I saw Isabel again. She had appeared from thin air and was clearly set on ruining this night for me. She was but a few metres away - heading straight towards me. Her expression one of open hostility and maliciousness. I couldn't cause a scene in front of all these people.

"Tania," I began quickly, "I just wanted to say thank for everything and please keep me in mind for any future projects. I'm sorry but I really have to dash." I said apologetically, giving her a quick kiss on the cheek and hurrying away.

"Of course, I'll be in touch." I heard her call out after me.

The exhibition was open until midnight, and people were still arriving. I had to weave in and out of them as they moved between the exhibits. I felt exposed somehow; my nerves raw and I quickened my step until I burst through the bathroom doors, startling the two older women who were just about to exit.

I headed straight to a sink, gripping its sides to hold myself up. A panelled mirror covered the whole top half of the wall. I stared at my reflection. I was alone. The only sound was the *drip-drop* of a leaky tap. The smell of roses permeated the air and made me feel nauseous. I was tired of trying to find a plausible explanation or justification for what I was going through. Maybe there just wasn't any.

"Isabel," I called out.

The soft lighting of the bathroom flickered, plunging me briefly into darkness before illuminating the space once more.

"Isabel, just quit it OK? Enough with the smoke and

mirrors. Just tell me what it is you want? What are you trying to tell me?"

I heard a scuttling sound behind me, I swung around, but there was nothing there. I turned back to the mirror to find Isabel watching me from within the glass. Fear overwhelmed me.

"You took something from me." I heard her voice in my head, a sound like wind through a dry husk, papery and thin but with an underlying edge to it.

Even though she spoke in Spanish, I could understand her, just as surely as she could understand me.

"Is this all about a ring, Isabel?" I cried. "I've already told you to just take it!" I tore the ring from my finger and flung it at the mirror.

I wasn't sure what I was expecting exactly: for the ring to magically pass through the mirror and reunite with its rightful owner, who had been dead for centuries? I kind of wished it would, but it just rebounded and clattered to the floor. Isabel didn't even react; she just continued to glare at me.

I was tired of this. Isabel had lived her life and this one was mine. If she regretted having taken her own life, that was her problem, and had nothing to do with me. I had had my fair share of death already.

"You took... everything from me! Everything!" Her voice boomed in my mind, sounding even angrier, and a sharp pain tore through my mind.

I clutched my head and closed my eyes, as if I could somehow block it all out. A few moments later, when the pain had subsided to a dull ache, I opened my eyes to find that Isabel had gone.

The bathroom door opened and a couple of young women tottering in high heels stepped inside, chatting away to each other, champagne glasses in hand.

"Are you OK?" the blonder of the two women asked when she saw my pale face.

"Yes, I'm fine," I managed to croak. "Just a migraine."

"Aren't they the worst? I get one every other week. Only thing that cures it is two ibuprofens and bed," she told me. "I actually have some if you'd like? I always carry them around with me."

"No, thank you. That's very kind of you to offer, but I've just taken some," I lied.

"No problem. Oh, I think you've dropped your ring," she said, bending down to pick it up and offering it to me. "It's so unique."

Reluctantly, I took it from her outstretched palm, feigning an expression of gratitude. Discarding the ring on a bathroom floor was not the solution, of that at least, I could be sure.

"Thank you again. Well, I better get back. Enjoy the exhibition," I told them both.

"You too," they replied in unison.

I hurried back the way I had come, heading towards the exit, where I found Nathan and his family waiting for me.

"Sorry, there was a line in the lady's bathroom," I offered by way of explanation.

"Isn't that always the case!" Louise exclaimed. "I went to a friend's wedding last year. Over two hundred guests and the venue only had two female toilets! I spent half the night queuing for the loo!"

"That's because you probably spent the other half of the

night drinking your body weight in wine!" Nathan teased her.

Louise giggled. "Probably."

"My daughter, ladies and gentleman," Alex said in mock disapproval. "I don't know about you lot, but I'm starving."

"You feeling OK, Beth? You do look a little pale," Eleanor enquired.

"Just a headache. Perhaps some food will help," I replied quickly.

"Well, it's no wonder, after all you've been through. The exhibition has been wonderful. I can't wait to see more of your work," Eleanor added, then gave me another quick hug.

I welcomed the cold night air as we left the centre, but the myriad of artificial lights from passing cars, street lamps and bars was dizzying, the sound of Bristol's Saturday nightlife too loud.

Inside the restaurant, which was decorated in an elegant white and black theme, we took our seats around a circular table. I scanned the menu with more concentration than I normally would have, the throbbing in my mind insistent.

What did Isabel mean, I took *everything* from her? Obviously this was more than just about a ring. I remembered the old woman's words from the market, something along the lines that the ring doesn't belong to me. I reasoned it belonged to me more than most antique jewellery belonged to anyone.

The waitress appeared after a couple of minutes to take our order. I asked for a large glass of white wine and the prawn and courgette risotto. I tried to engage in the conversation which flowed freely. Such a simple thing, but it was so different to the stilted, agonising discussions I had with Helena and my father when I was growing up. At the beginning I could talk to Dolores, but I was younger then and not as good at keeping the old Beth sealed away, and so even that relationship was soon tainted.

I smiled, laughed and nodded at all the right moments. I uttered a word here and there, but I was like a mannequin putting on a good show. The essence of me was in a dark place, wondering if I was simply losing my mind or if I was answering for my past sins. If it was the latter, then I feared the price I would have to pay would be much too dear.

I gulped down my wine and ordered another. It helped dull the pain, and when the food arrived, I munched and chewed on the garlic bread and risotto almost mechanically, not even tasting them. When I swallowed the food it became a leaden weight in my stomach.

Thankfully, the others were all stuffed after their main meal and we decided against desserts, so I was soon home, slipping beneath the covers and closing my eyes. The migraine tablets and sleeping tablet I had taken as soon as I got home, combined with the three large glasses of wine, meant I soon slipped into a deep sleep.

I awoke before dawn. The room was still cloaked in twilight. I was about to try and drift off to sleep again when I saw something scuttle across the floor. It was too small to be Mittens, and I could feel the kitten's weight on the pillow above my head.

A mouse? I didn't want Mittens getting hold of it and

killing it. The thought grossed me out, so I got up, closed the bedroom door behind me and padded down the hall. I caught a glimpse of it again before it ran into the living room. It seemed a little big to be a mouse, but it was most certainly not a rat. I flipped the light switch and, as my eyes adjusted to the sudden brightness, I caught a glimpse of something black and white dash under the dining table. On my hands and knees, I looked under the table.

And there he was.

Coco-Pop.

"*No, no, no.*"

I closed my eyes and counted to three slowly, hoping this hallucination would cease once I reopened my eyes – but he was still there.

Coco-Pop sat back on his hind legs, resembling a little ball of fluff, his little nose twitching, his eyes the colour of onyx, observing me. I pushed a chair aside and reached out slowly to grab him. He didn't scarper or protest as I picked him up carefully.

I sat down on my bottom, the coldness of the tiles seeping into my skin and chilling my body, but not as much as the sight of Coco-Pop had done. He felt warm and solid in my hands, so real, but I knew he couldn't possibly be.

Coco-Pop had been dead for years. Helena and Dolores had buried him in the yard.

He was dead.

He was dead because I had killed him.

I stroked his fur softly and, it acted like a tactile transfer to the past, I was once again just eight years old sitting on my bedroom floor.

Helena and Dolores are having a tea party in the lounge, I'm not invited. Father has punished me again. He is always punishing me, for any slight misdemeanour or mistake: for spilling a glass of milk, for not placing my dirty clothes in the laundry basket, for not saying please or thank you, the moment such politeness is expected.

It is worse than walking on eggshells, because the shells are already broken. Me existing when Mother did not was a crime in itself. Most days, I take my punishment without complaint. My mother's death has changed me; I am trying to be better. A better child, a better sister, a better daughter, a better everything.

But today I wanted to play. I too wanted cake. I too yearned for some of Dolores' affection.

Their laughter reaches me upstairs and I am overcome with hate for every single one of them. Perhaps it was just bad timing that Coco-Pop chose that moment to wake from his nap and run around and around in his hamster wheel. The noise drew me to him and I reached into his cage and held him in my lap.

He had never liked me, perhaps because I smelled of Millie, or perhaps simply because he knew I wasn't Helena. He tried to squirm out of my grasp and nip at my fingers. I hear Dolores chuckle and Helena's excited voice, a feel a fury that makes me feel hot all over. I start to squeeze and squeeze, until I feel, more than hear, something snap.

Coco-Pop stops wriggling.

I put him back in his cage and close the latch, then lie on my bed, staring at the ceiling. About an hour later, Helena comes upstairs to our room, I sit up onto my elbows, her screams seem to fill every inch of the house and I watch as she rocks the broken hamster in her hands.

Dolores runs up the stairs, her footfalls heavy, her eyes filled with panic. She caught sight of Coco-Pop and then our eyes meet. I see the look I had often seen in my mother's eyes, and I knew I had lost Dolores too.

Two days later, Millie was dead too. She had somehow drowned in the bathtub.

A lesson learned.

I had pushed Helena too hard this time, and she had pushed back.

"I am sorry. I am so sorry." I sobbed, trying to shut the images of the past out of my mind.

I opened my hands. Coco-Pop was moving again, and I felt a flash of relief, but then I was hit by a wave of revulsion as I realised he was now a mass of writhing maggots. A few matted bits of black and white fur were all that remained of Helena's hamster.

I screamed and dropped him. His stomach burst open, spilling maggots in every direction. I scrambled backwards and hit the sofa. I felt bile rise in my throat and I forced it down again.

"Enough, Isabel!" I begged through my tears. "Enough."

The light flickered and returned, and then there was nothing dead on the floor. I breathed a sigh of relief, but I knew it would be short-lived. Isabel, I realised, seemed to know all about me, my deepest, darkest secrets, and if I wanted to even the score, I would need to know hers too.

Chapter Twenty-Three

"I am very sorry to hear about your father," Dr Roberts told me as he ushered me into his office.

"Thank you," I said.

I knew he would prefer to discuss this recent event before we began therapy, so I decided it would be expedient if from the start I simply said everything he wanted to hear.

"I knew he was ill and that I was going to lose him. Still, it was quite a shock that it happened so soon, but I was glad I managed to reconnect with him before he died."

He nodded sympathetically.

We hadn't really reconnected at all, but I didn't want Dr Roberts to focus on my father's death. I had more pressing matters to deal with.

"At least he's resting now, and no longer in pain," I added, when I realised Dr Roberts was waiting for me to continue.

As much as I was aware that therapists stretch out silences to get their patients to speak, it still annoyed me how well it worked. Often I felt I was grasping at straws to say the correct thing so that he would think of me as 'normal'.

You may ask what was the point of coming to see a

therapist if I wasn't being truthful, but Dr Roberts did help: he helped me perfect the new Beth, who had regular issues such as a phobia of water. Granted, seeing Isabel was not normal, but I had tempered even those experiences a little.

"Yes, indeed, he was suffering from a very terrible illness, both the alcoholism and the cancer. Still, even though we take comfort in knowing that he is no longer suffering, we cannot ignore our other feelings. The hurt, the loss, the missing."

This time, I was the one to simply nod, and I turned my attention to the window. I focused on the raindrops as they slid down the window pane, filling me with a sense of calm. I had to be strong enough to face the past, both mine and Isabel's.

"How have you been since our last session?" Dr Roberts continued, notepad and pen at the ready.

He could sense I didn't want to talk about my father at this moment. It was another reason I liked him as a therapist: he wasn't one to push. I had seen other therapists before, briefly, who had all seemed to have a preconceived notion of how the session should go, and were loath to deviate from that path.

"Since we attempted the past life hypnosis last week, I've had more dreams of Isabel," I told him.

"That's understandable. By bringing forward experiences from prior lives into our current lifetime we are opening up memories into our conscious awareness. Connections between past and present lives can be subtle and it isn't always easy to connect the dots. It can take time to be able to do this. Time is also required to release or diffuse the energy and emotional blockages from our past experiences." He let that sink in for a moment before adding, "Are you ready to begin?"

"Yes," I said resolutely, shuffling a little on the sofa to make myself as comfortable as possible.

"Right, we will begin much like we did last time. Just allow yourself to rest." His voice became softer and more monotone. "Shrug your shoulders and let them go, lift your arms slightly and then drop them down. They are feeling heavy... Release any tension in your neck and back, tense your legs and then let them relax... Your whole body now feels relaxed. Become aware of your breathing, take a deep breath and just let it out... Take another deep breath and release it. Become aware of how your breath is moving slowly in and out of your lungs. With each breath you feel even more at ease, feeling yourself fall deeper and deeper. With each breath you let go of your anxieties, any worries, anything that weighs you down. Now imagine a quiet, peaceful spot. You are sitting in a meadow, surrounded by beautiful flowers on a warm sunny afternoon. Can you smell the flowers, Beth?"

I found that I could. I breathed in the scent of buttercups, violets, poppies and daffodils. An array of yellows, reds, purples and whites, like an iridescent rainbow in my mind.

"It's beautiful," I murmured, feeling my body melt into the grass.

"Just let yourself drift away. When you are ready, you will see a door appear. A door which is pure white. When you are ready, move towards the door and step inside. You are now in a room. The room is completely white and there are stairs going down. You can go down those stairs now, knowing you are perfectly safe and secure, warm and comfortable. With each step you feel more relaxed. There are ten steps. Ten, nine, eight…keep going…seven, six, five…you are almost weightless as you descend the final steps…four, three, two…one. Now, Beth, think of an important time in Isabel's life. When I snap my fingers, you'll be there."

I reached the bottom of the staircase and then heard his fingers click.

I was enveloped in darkness. A cold, pale hand reached out and grasped my wrist painfully. I didn't have time to scream before I was propelled forwards, through what felt like a wind tunnel. Air pummelled my skin, and suddenly it all came to a halt.

The sound of chatter made me open my eyes instantly. I clutched at my wrist with my free hand, but I was no longer being held. Five welts the shape of fingers were now burned on my skin; I touched them gingerly.

I found myself in a busy market. Men and woman in old-fashioned clothing milled around, bartering at various stalls of dried fish, baskets of oranges, oil and olives, as well as embroidered sheets and homemade dresses. I spun in a circle, fearing Isabel might be lurking right behind me, She wasn't, but I knew she was near. Her presence was like a foul smell lingering in the air.

"Beth, tell me who and what you see," I heard Dr Roberts say, his voice oddly muffled.

I described the market square. I caught sight of the church tower and knew where I was. I was in Tarifa's old town. The air was warm, heat rising from the cobbled streets, the sun a blazing ball of yellow in an otherwise blue sky, but I realised I was invisible to everyone, occupying a time and space of my own.

I felt happy here, amongst the townspeople. I felt like I was one of them, partaking of their busy lives and enjoying the sounds of their laughter and a sense of community. Or rather, that was how I assumed Isabel felt. It was as if her thoughts and emotions were pressing into my own.

That was when I saw her handing some jars to an old lady behind a stall. My first instinct was to recoil, but after a brief moment I realised it was not the vision of Isabel I had come to abhor: she was now just a young woman. She was no more aware of me than any of the other people at the market.

I moved towards her and simply watched her, appraising every inch of her as if I was studying an exotic butterfly that might fly away at any moment. She was wearing a flowing emerald dress which accentuated the green of her eyes. Her auburn-brown hair fell across her back in light waves, her skin the colour of honey. She seemed so happy and full of life, which jarred against the image of the woman who willingly gave up her life to the sea.

A couple of boys dressed only in brown shorts bumped against her. She dropped one of the containers filled with orange preserve, but before it hits the ground, a young man grabbed it – the same man who had given her the ruby ring. He offered Isabel the jar, and when their eyes met he stopped. The look they shared was unmistakable. It was the same look Nathan had given me the first time he saw me, as if I was the most beautiful woman he had ever seen.

Isabel blushed. She too was transfixed by this handsome young man. As he handed her back the jar, his fingertips grazed her hand lightly, and I could almost feel the jolt at his touch, the happiness and excitement that bloomed in her heart like a huge sunflower.

I understood why I was being shown this meeting. This moment marked a change in Isabel's life, and it was something I had to witness in order to understand what came next. This man had tilted her whole world off its axis, and in this brief moment it was as if Isabel knew that her life would never be the same again.

I think love at first sight can only really be believed by those who have experienced it, as I had with Nathan. The old Beth would have sneered at such an idea, but the new Beth was a little more open to possibilities.

They exchanged a few words, but I couldn't hear them. Isabel smiled and flicked her hair over her shoulder as this young man lingered by her side. He was tall, his skin tanned from the sun and his eyes dark blue. Isabel and the young man stood out from the crowd, as if bathed in a different light.

After a few moments the edges of my vision begin to darken, as if I was in a theatre watching a play and the lights are being dimmed just before they are switched off completely, plunging me into shadows.

I experienced a sudden and sharp sense of falling, and I closed my eyes against the horrid feeling in my stomach as it drops. I re-opened them once I could feel the ground underneath my feet again. I was now on a beach. The sand was hot between my toes and I could smell the ocean. I saw Isabel and the same young man walking along the shore. They stand a little apart, perhaps still too shy or nervous to venture closer.

The image darkened once more and now I know I was back in the hacienda, which felt so familiar. I was in Isabel's room. She sat at her desk, writing by candlelight, a gown as thin as gossamer hanging loosely on her young body. I ventured closer. Her writing was looped and elegant. I saw the letter was addressed to Alejandro.

"*Alejandro*," I whispered, sounding out his name. I felt an echo of love for this stranger.

Next to Isabel lay numerous letters addressed to her. I heard footsteps approach and she quickly gathered up the letters and hid them in a box beneath the bed.

A knock at the door.

"Come in," she said brightly, opening a book and pretending to read.

Francisco stepped inside.

"Hello, Papa. I missed you at dinner," Isabel said, giving him a kiss on each cheek.

"I know princess. We had a problem with one of the fishing boats and I had to stay late at the port. All has been sorted now," he said with a sigh, sounding tired. He took a seat in an armchair by the unlit fireplace.

"You work too hard, Papa."

"I like to keep busy," he told her with a smile. "Plus, I have a surprise for your birthday."

"What is it?" she asked excitedly.

Again, I was struck by how young she was, probably no more than nineteen or twenty. She had her whole life ahead of her.

"Ah, that would spoil the fun for me. You will just have to wait. I will retire to my room for the night. Do not stay up too late," he told her affectionately, kissing her on the cheek before leaving and closing the door behind him.

At the click of the door, the scene changed once more and I was now in the orange groves. It was dark and a cold breeze caressed my skin. I felt my heartbeat quicken, reminded of the dreams in which I dashed through the orchard because someone or something was hounding me. I peered around fearfully, but that sense of danger did not pervade the air this night. Instead, I heard excited whispers, filling the air with a sense of happiness and expectation.

I stepped closer to the sound. Behind the next row of trees, Isabel and Alejandro were bathed in the light of the moon. They were wrapped in an embrace and kissed each other, tentatively at first and then more passionately. Through our shared connection, I knew this was both Isabel's first kiss with Alejandro and her first kiss with anyone, ever.

The scene was familiar to me: I realised I had dreamt of this night before. After a few moments their lips parted.

"Alejandro," Isabel started a little breathlessly, "I must get back before Rosa or Papa realises I am gone."

He reluctantly pulled away and reached into his pocket, retrieving a ruby ring and kneeling before Isabel. "Isabel would you do me the honour of becoming my wife. Be mine until the moon and the stars no longer shine in the sky. My life means nothing to me if I do not have you."

"Yes Alejandro, of course I will be your wife. Nothing would make me happier than that!"

They embraced each other once more as if they never intend to let go.

Suddenly, the stars began to die out one by one, as if

someone was stealing them from the night sky, until finally even the moon was extinguished. All I could hear was my breathing, and I wondered why I hadn't heard Dr Robert's voice in so long. I feared I was in a place where not even he could reach me. Could I be stuck here forever? A mere shadow drifting between the past and the present, belonging to neither?

I reached out into the pregnant darkness, fearful to step forwards lest I fall into an interminable abyss, but suddenly I was pushed by cold, bony fingers and felt myself falling through nothingness, until I hit the ground with a harsh thump.

With a little effort, I raised myself up and found myself at the bottom of the staircase in the hacienda. I looked down at myself and see that I am wearing Isabel's long grey dress. Nightfall seemed to press at the windows as if desperate to get inside. I knew I shouldn't be wandering the halls at night: *Father doesn't like it when I do that.* I needed to hurry to my bedroom, but I was overcome by a sense of apprehension that I couldn't quite explain.

I was feeling Isabel's emotions as if they were my own, each move I made an echo of her own movements, and with each quiet step I took, the cold, coiling sense of dread in my stomach grew. Whatever sight awaited me in her bedroom it was the reason Isabel chose to end her own life, and she wanted me to know why.

I was now standing outside her bedroom door. It was shut, but I could hear voices coming from inside. Could it be Rosa and Papa wondering where I have gotten to? I had no control as Isabel placed her hand on the doorknob and slipped inside. The room was cast in the diffused silvery light of the moon. It was almost as dark as the rest of the house, but I could make out two people on my bed... well, Isabel's bed.

I recognised the murmured whispers of Alejandro interspersed with moans of pleasure, and my heart shattered, unimaginable pain tore and slashed through my mind and body. There was another person, a woman. I couldn't see her face, only her slim body, a mane of dark hair spilling across her bare back as Alejandro took her fervently from behind.

Isabel tried to cope with what she was witnessing, not wishing to believe what her eyes were telling her. The wave of horror, of heartbreak, of feeling like her whole world has imploded, was agonising. I didn't want to feel her agony and despair. I wanted to leave, but I was trapped inside her, to see what she saw, to feel what she felt. I cried out but there was only silence, my screams resounding only in my mind.

A small sound of sorrow escaped Isabel's lips; so light, given the turmoil bubbling in her head like a raging river. Yet it was loud enough to distract Alejandro from the fervour of sex. He turned and our eyes met for the briefest of moments. His face one of absolute shock, confusion and disbelief.

Isabel did not ponder this, however, and bolted from the room. She thundered down the stairs and out into the night as fast as a gazelle in flight. Her long grey dress clung to her legs, but she raced on regardless. I wanted her to slow down, to ease the beating of her heart. She ran and ran. She reached the sand dunes, her lungs burning, but she did not pause to rest. Instead, she continued until she reached the shoreline.

The water lapped against her legs as she began to move

further and further into the sea. I screamed at her to stop, but I did not exist in this time and place. Isabel continued to push herself out, using her arms to propel herself forwards. Her dress was now soaked, slowing and weighing her down. Soon she could not touch the seabed and she kicked with her legs, allowing the current to take her further out.

The water was so dark, so different to the inviting hues of blue during daylight hours. Now it was black, treacherous and deadly. It was also cold, stealing the heat from Isabel's body and smothering her breath, yet all she felt was the pain in her heart. The piercing dagger of betrayal wielded by the man she loved more than life itself.

Her arms began to tire. She only wanted the misery to end, and so she stopped moving. She allowed herself to sink. I felt her life ebbing away, her pain and anger like a flame in the dark. Just before it was extinguished, I caught sight of the ruby ring as it slipped off her finger and landed gently onto the seabed below.

Isabel

Chapter Twenty-Four

"Isabel! Isabel! Where are you, girl? Come back and finish your lesson!" I heard Rosa cry from the kitchen window.

Rosa had a very loud voice which always seemed to reach me no matter where in the grounds I was. I looked up the hill, towards the hacienda, which stood proudly against the backdrop of the green hillside and the pale blue sky, like a soldier protecting and watching over our groves.

Papa told me that one day I will run the hacienda with my husband, and we would continue supplying the towns around us. He said it was a great responsibility. I didn't tell Papa this, but I wasn't sure I wanted a husband. A husband meant babies, and babies could mean death.

It did for my mother.

I wished I could remember her, but of course I couldn't. I had seen paintings of her, created by an artist in the village who painted her soon after she married Papa. She was very beautiful, with hair the colour of the sun, and pale skin. She looked so different to me.

Rosa said my mother had always wanted a little girl and that she watched over me from Heaven. I hoped that was true. I missed her very much, but I had Rosa and Papa. So I was lucky. Rosa told me of little girls and boys in the village who had no mama or papa, and who lived on the streets. She often told me this when I hadn't finished my dinner, like last night when I didn't finish all my potatoes and vegetables, but Rosa didn't realise I had then put them away in my handkerchief.

I skipped to the end of the row, to the corner where the pines trees stretched until they almost reached the beach. It was here that I un-wrapped my parcel, which I had tucked in my pocket, and emptied out the scraps of food.

I took a few steps back and sat.

I knew they won't be long.

And they weren't.

At first it was just one large crow which descended, hopping ungainly on the ground, but it was followed by another and then another. They gobbled up the food quickly and then preened their black glossy feathers. We sat for a while together, sharing the space at the edge of the forest. After a few moments they took flight once more, shrieking in the rapidly warming air. As I got up, I noticed a little shiny white rock on the grass. I picked it up and pocketed it.

It was a gift.

It had taken a couple months, but the crows were now my friends. I brought them food and they brought me things, like rocks and seashells. Rosa didn't like crows; she thought they were a symbol of death, but I didn't. I saw them as bold, smart and resourceful. Plus, I had to win their friendship. They were not so easily befriended as the cats and dogs that we kept at the hacienda.

It was still early morning, and the men and the boys from the village were arriving to tend the fields. We provided a lot of work for the town. Most of them walked – it wasn't far into town, maybe half an hour – and others arrived on unhappy-looking mules. Rosa sometimes let me add water to the trough for the horses and mules. The men worked until the sun set. In the summer they took a break during the very hot hours, and I had sometimes caught them napping, their hats covering their faces.

I preferred walking through the grounds than sitting up in the house writing, adding numbers together or learning how to crochet cushions and blankets. I would much rather go out and play with the other kids, but Papa preferred I stay at home, where it was safer –that was what he kept telling me: "It is safer here princess." I liked it when he called me that – his princess. It made me feel special. I thought because he lost Mama he worried even more about losing me.

I realised I had better make my way back, though, so I hurried up the slope towards the house.

"Isabel!" Rosa cried again, but she didn't sound angry with me –not yet, anyway. "Don't make me come out looking for you!"

"I'm coming, Rosa!" I answered.

"Isabel," she started as soon as I walked in, "you know your father prefers you getting all your work done before you go off *exploring*."

"I was only gone a little while, Rosa. I just went to feed the crows. Come, look, see what they brought me today!" I said, taking the stone out of my pocket and holding it up for her to see. "I think this one is my favourite yet."

"You know, your mother had a way with animals, just like you. She loved the horses and the dogs, but she didn't bother with crows!" Rosa said, but she was smiling.

"Am I much like her, then?"

I loved hearing anything I could about my mother. These snippets of information were all I would ever have of her, and I treasured them like gemstones. Father didn't like talking about her much because it hurt and makes him sad.

"You have a kind heart, just like she did. Lucia always had a good word and a smile for everyone. Even though she was the major's daughter, and very beautiful, she never acted superior to anyone. That's why everyone loved her so. When she left the north to come down here to marry your father, people were so sorry to see her go," Rosa said, staring out the window. I could see her eyes becoming teary.

Sometimes I was jealous that Rosa had known my mother so well and that I never would, but that feeling didn't last long. It was because of Rosa that I had a connection to my mother, even if it was just via stories.

"Come on – let's get back to work," Rosa said. "The sooner you start, the sooner you'll be finished."

"Yes, Rosa," I said, helping myself to a glass of water and sitting down again.

I brushed the hair from my face impatiently. The day was warm and humid, and I hoped we would have a day at the beach tomorrow. I reasoned it was too hot for learning, but it was an excuse Rosa wouldn't allow, so I returned to my sums and to the story I had started that morning.

After a little while, soon getting tired of what I was doing and wanting to stretch my legs again, I had the uneasy sensation that I was being watched. I glanced towards the open doorway that led to the living room. For a split second I thought I saw a child move past.

Rosa must have noticed my perplexed frown. "What's distracting you now, Isabel?" she asked, putting the vegetables she had been chopping for the past half hour into a big black pot.

"I thought I saw someone walk by –a child..." I stammered.

"Don't be silly, girl. You and I are the only ones in the house. Just get back to your lesson. Lunch will be ready soon."

Although Rosa sounded dismissive, I noticed a slight edge to her voice. She busied herself cleaning up the kitchen, but she had a strange look on her face which I couldn't describe. Rosa didn't like me speaking out of turn or contradicting her, so I finished my story and helped her set the table.

After a lunch of stew and beans, I was allowed to go outside again. Normally in this heat I would play in the courtyard, which was shaded and filled with plants and flowers of all colours: I watered them and helped them grow. Papa said I have the gift of green fingers, but I wasn't sure what he meant: my fingers were not green. The courtyard was also where I played with the cats and dogs we kept on the grounds, who were also looking to escape from the afternoon sun. But today, Rosa ushered me out the door and told me to play in the groves this afternoon, muttering something about having to sweep the courtyard.

"Sweep the courtyard? Why now?" I asked, but Rosa told me not to argue and to just go on out and play.

So I did, before she asked me to tidy my room. I'd left a number of toys scattered on the floor, wooden animal figurines that the carpenter in town had made and which Father had given me for my birthday a couple of years ago. I had two horses, a cat, a dog, a cow and two sheep. I even had a wooden family: a father, a mother, a young girl and a little boy.

The mother figurine was the one I treasured most, of course. I'd spend hours making up conversations between the girl and her mother, sharing confidences, experiences and stories. I'd try to imagine things that my mother might say; some anecdotes had been so ingrained in me that I could almost believe my mother had really told them. I had also left my nightgown unfolded in my bedroom, so I hurried out before I was called back.

I spent the rest of the afternoon running through the grounds, making up games as I went along. I pretended to be an adventurer exploring a jungle, keeping an eye out for man-eating monsters, and then a pirate looking for buried loot on a deserted island.

Our two cats, Blanca and Zara, had come looking for me. I often gave them scraps of tuna, so I was one of their favourite humans. They came and lay next to me, where I was resting under the shade of some palm trees. Their soft purring mixed with the sound of the wind rustling through the leaves.

I must have fallen asleep, and it was the sensation of being watched, being exposed, that woke me. I looked around. I could hear the men shouting and laughing in the distance, but they were in the next field over, picking olives for oil. The thought of dipping warm bread into freshly-made olive oil would normally make my mouth water, but not today. Today I felt scared, and it was the worst kind of fear, the kind in which you are not sure of what exactly you need to be afraid of.

I couldn't see anything, but both Blanca and Zara hissed viciously before skittering away. The breeze flowing through the trees, which before had been so relaxing, now sounded like evil whispers. The sun was now lower in the sky, casting longer shadows that grew and merged together. I picked myself up quickly and, with a final look into the fields, I hurried home along the sun-dappled path.

When I got home, Rosa was nowhere to be found. I called out for her but got no response. In the kitchen I poured myself a glass of water from the large flower-painted jug and drank it down rapidly. I wiped my mouth with the back of my hand. The house was quiet, which wasn't strange in itself, but I was on edge now, and every sound I made seemed magnified a hundred times in the stillness.

I went up to my room. The first thing I noticed was that my toys were no longer on the floor but lined up on the shelf. My nightgown wasn't where I had left it either, on the foot of the bed, but was now hanging neatly on the back of the chair beside my small dressing table. It was a little strange, as Rosa always made me clear up my own mess: she said that Mama would not want me growing up to be spoilt and lazy.

There was some water in the basin by the window. I washed quickly with a flannel and changed into my nightgown. I felt a little better now that I was cooler and my belly was filled with water.

The window was smothered in creepers. Rosa had told

Jose the gardener to cut them back, but he still hadn't got around to it. I thought of going in search of Rosa, as we would normally have had dinner by now, but decided against it. If she wasn't here then she must be busy doing something important. So, instead, I gathered my toys and laid them on the bed to play. It only took me a moment to realise that the mother figurine was missing. I felt a little jolt of panic, and I ran around the room, checking in the cupboard, under the bed and in the drawers, the smell of cedar wood now cloying in my nostrils.

"Where could she be?" I cried aloud, feeling tears prick at my eyes.

She must be somewhere —she'll turn up, I told myself. She couldn't have gotten lost. I played with the father figurine and the little boy, imagining Papa teaching him to fish. A short while later, Rosa came into the room, carrying a plate loaded with bread and goat's cheese, and a large glass of milk.

"Isabel, I brought you something for dinner. Did you have fun this afternoon? You can eat here in your room tonight if you like, as I have some cleaning to do in the kitchen." She handed me the plate and kissed me on the top of my head.

Rosa was smiling, but she looked sad. She never let me eat in my room, saying that ladies always ate at the dinner table. She also looked tired, her eyes red as if she had been crying.

"Are you OK, Rosa? I was looking for you," I said softly, taking the plate and placing it on my dressing table.

"Yes, I'm fine, it's just been a long day. You know I am not built for this heat," she said, trying to sound dismissive, but I know her too well. She was hiding something.

"I can't find the mother."

"What can't you find?" Rosa asked, perplexed.

"The mother doll," I repeated, holding up the figurine of the young girl. "I've looked everywhere, but she's gone."

"Don't fret, I am sure she will turn up. She can't have gone far," she reassured me, giving me a good-night kiss. "Now have your supper and get to bed. Just bring down your plate in the morning."

"Will Papa be home later to tuck me in?"

"Maybe. We'll just have to see what time he gets home from trading in the next village."

"Good night, Rosa. I love you."

"Good night, Isabel," Rosa whispered. I caught her wiping a tear from her eye. "Love you more."

I ate my dinner in silence, accompanied only by the crickets chirping outside. Their loud *cheep-cheep* sounds were incessant during the night-time, as they tried to woo females. Their noises did not frighten me; they were the sounds of the night and I was not afraid of the dark, but I was now afraid of the other unknown things that lurked there.

Some of the moon's light filtered through the dense foliage around the window, bathing the room in a strange glow. I thought I heard whispers. I strained my ears but now I heard nothing, so I must have been mistaken. I put the toys back on the shelf and got back into bed, pulling the covers high up over my head. I didn't know why I'd got into the habit of doing this lately, but it made me feel safer.

I was desperately trying to fall asleep when I heard the door click open. I felt my whole body stiffen and I held my breath.

"Are you sleeping, Isabel?" The faintest whisper.

I breathed out again. It was only Rosa.

"I can't sleep," I replied.

"Shall I sing to you?"

I pulled the covers down to my neck and nodded gratefully. Rosa took the seat by my dressing table, her face covered in shadow so I couldn't see her expression. She began to sing. Rosa had a nice voice; I'd told her this before but she said her voice was too croaky, not like Mama's, whose voice was envied even by the birds.

Rosa sang to me an old lullaby, one she had sung to me since as far back as I could remember, on nights when I couldn't sleep because the thunder roared or because I was sad thinking about the mother I had never known. She said that Mama would have sung it to me too.

Duermete mi nina, de mi corazon, ya no llores mas,
Duermete ya, que viene el cuco y te comera,
La, la, la... la, la...

The song, as well as the voice, was so familiar and comforting that after only a few minutes I fall asleep.

A short while later, I heard something scrabbling across the tiled floor, *click-click-click*, sounding like when the dogs needed their nails cut. I had been hot and had thrown the covers back, but now I wanted to grab them and pull them back over my head, but I was too scared to move, like a mouse frozen in the glare of a hungry cat.

Then I heard the click of a door. Had someone just *left*? Or had someone or *something* come into my room?

"Rosa?" I croaked feebly.

Silence.

Then more clicking sounds, *click-click-click,* and then like scratching sounds, closer still.

Something was tugging at the sheets!

I was now trembling in fear as the sheet was pulled further down my legs, but I still couldn't move or cry out.

Something heavy was now on the bed.

I was acting like a scaredy-cat, I knew that, and I was angry with myself – but I couldn't help it. It was only when I felt sharp pains on my hands and legs that I cried out and scrambled out of bed and onto the floor.

I felt as though I'd been bitten by something. I began to cry both in pain and in fear. In the moonlight I saw three large brown rats on my bed, their beady black eyes focused on me.

I shrieked.

Their tails twitched.

With trembling hands, I lit the large candle on the bedside table, hoping the rats would flee from the light. I scanned the room and the floor, anxious that there might be more of them around. When I glanced at the far wall, I screamed again.

Grotesque stick figures with rictus grins had been drawn roughly on the wall, arms too long and eyes too large. A father, a mother and two children.

Two little girls.

Chapter Twenty-Five

Morning sunlight streamed in through the window, golden and bright. I awoke, still tired. It had taken me a very long time to get back to sleep after what had happened last night. I saw that the candle on my bedside table was now nothing more than a deep pool of wax. I had been too scared to snuff it out.

Rosa and Papa had both come bursting in my room when they had heard me scream. I yelled for Blanca and Zara, who had come running and chased off the rats, and even managed to kill one of them. I thought I could still smell its blood, even though Rosa had cleaned it all up, her face so pale that it frightened me just as much as the rats had done.

I looked down at my blood-encrusted fingertips. Rosa had carefully cleaned the wounds on my legs and hands and covered them in a salve made with herbs from the garden. Reluctantly, I looked at the wall, expecting to see the horrible stick family staring back at me, but there was nothing there.

I rubbed the sleep from my eyes. The wall was still as white and bare as it had always been. For a split second I wondered if I had simply imagined the whole thing. Rosa had always said that I had a wild imagination – but I knew it was real. I could recall it too well.

I washed my face and changed out of my nightgown, and was halfway down the stairs when I heard my father and Rosa in the kitchen. Papa sounded angry. I was surprised to hear him like this, so I paused and listened. I knew it was wrong to eavesdrop, but this was so unlike him.

I could only remember him sounding this angry when one of the stable boys had come to work drunk. He had startled one of the horses who had then attempted, and failed, to jump the fence. The poor gelding had injured his back leg so badly that he had to be put down.

I took a couple more tentative steps down, hoping the creaking staircase would not betray my presence, and sat down on the second to last step.

"Enough, Rosa! I am tired of excuses! I want an end to all this, do you hear me? The only reason I have let this go on for as long as I have is because of Lucia! Understand that Isabel is my first priority. I have to think of her, so make *this* go away once and for all!" Papa yelled. Then he came stomping out of the kitchen.

For a moment, I thought he was going to come upstairs and catch me red handed, and I didn't want him directing that anger at me. I breathed a sigh of relief when he turned to the front door and slammed it so hard behind him that the paintings on the wall shook.

Once the beating of my heart had calmed down, I tip-toed to the kitchen. Rosa was by the kitchen sink, her back turned to me, but I could tell she was crying by the way her shoulders were shuddering.

Rosco, one of our dogs, lay next to her feet, but yelped happily when he saw me and trotted to lick my hand. Rosa turned around, perhaps fearing that my father had come back to yell some more, when she saw it was only me she turned away again instantly, wiping her face.

"Morning, Isabel. I am just making you some magdalenas for breakfast."

"What's the matter, Rosa? Why are you crying? And why was Papa so angry?"

The kitchen smelled of oranges, as it usually did. It was usually a smell I loved, but not this morning, not when there was so much anger and sadness in the air. Rosa continued working at the sink and I thought that perhaps she wasn't going to answer me.

However, finally, she said, "You don't need to worry yourself about it, Isabel. I just got upset over something. Your Papa and I think differently on what is best, that's all."

I took my usual seat at the breakfast table. Rosa gave me two magdalenas and a large orange, cut into chunks.

"Have I done something wrong?" I asked after taking a bite. The cakes were warm, moist and sweet, and I felt a little better already.

"You? Of course not, but you do ask too many questions. Let's just have our breakfast and we can get started on your lessons," Rosa replied, trying to muster a smile, though it was not convincing in the least.

I didn't like to see her upset, so I ate all my breakfast. Eating all my food made Rosa happy, as sometimes I could be a bit particular – her words, not mine. I washed up my plate so Rosa wouldn't have to, and sat at the table again, where

Rosa continued teaching me how to subtract large numbers.

"This is important," she told me. "One day, when you are running the household, you will need to know how much you have left of one particular good, and how much you have left to trade."

I simply nodded, but then said, "Rosa, after what happened with the... rats, I thought I had seen something drawn on the walls. Something – *someone* – must have drawn it. But nothing was there this morning, so I'm not sure if it was part of a bad dream."

"I see. Well, if it was gone this morning, then perhaps it was just a dream. We all have bad dreams from time to time."

"But I also thought I'd heard horrible whispers..." I added, not wanting to ask if she had wiped the drawings away.

She didn't respond. To avoid the silence stretching on, I asked, "What are your bad dreams about?"

"Well..." she began. I held my breath, hoping she'd open up and tell me some grown-up stuff, but she simply said, "Oh, nothing in particular. I often forget about them by the time morning comes around."

I could tell she was lying. She turned her face away from me, but I caught the haunted look in her eyes. She could remember her nightmares, and by her reaction –Rosa was a strong, brave woman – they must be pretty scary.

The day continued much like the morning before, but instead of spending the afternoon playing in the fields, Rosa promised she would take me down to the beach. The beach was one of my favourite places, and I went to gather some toys to take with me, including an old bucket so I could build a sandcastle.

Once I was ready to go, I went in search of Rosa but couldn't find her anywhere. I searched through the hacienda and even went outside and called for her amongst the orange groves, thinking she may have gone to pick some oranges to take to the beach. That reminded me to get some old bread from the kitchen to feed the seabirds. I ran back to the kitchen, hoping Rosa would now be there and that I had simply missed her whilst searching for her in the fields, but the kitchen was empty.

Taking some of the bread and wrapping it in a piece of cloth, I put it away in my bag and headed to the courtyard, but Rosa wasn't there either. A flash of colour caught my eye and drew my attention to the tower.

The square tower was the tallest structure in the hacienda, located at its northern end. It rose into the sky and could even be seen from down in the village. Like the hacienda, it was made of white stone, but its top was wood. I had never been inside the tower: I was not allowed. The structure was not safe, or so Rosa and Papa always told me – but if that was true, why was Rosa up there?

It was definitely a flash of her blue dress that I had seen through the hexagonal windows that were dotted around the tower, following the curving staircase within.

There. There she was again.

I went back to the kitchen and waited for her.

"Rosa, where were you? I was looking for you," I asked her as soon as she set foot inside.

"I was only gone a minute, child. I just needed to pass on some instructions to the men about where to leave the oranges once they have finished picking them," she replied.

I knew this to be a lie, but I decided to leave it be... for now.

We headed towards the beach. There was a nice breeze today, helping to mask the heat of the summer sun, but I was still feeling too hot by the time we reach the seaside. The sand was as golden as always, and I hurried down to the water. Rosa trailed slowly behind me. She had been quiet during our walk, which was unlike her, but she seemed to have a lot on her mind recently, so I stayed quiet too.

The easterly winds had brought in fronds of seaweed and pieces of driftwood which now lined the shore like a narrow, brown carpet. I kept my eyes peeled for any washed-up treasure. I once found a very old coin; I cleaned it as best as I could and kept it in a small chest in my room, where I stored all my riches.

Today there was nothing to be found, other than the washed-up white shells of cuttlefish. I put my feet into the translucent water and looked towards the horizon, where the sun met the sea. It seemed as if the ocean had no end, and I wondered what lay beyond the beyond. I breathed deeply, filling my lungs with the ocean air, and listened to the music of the waves. Without hesitation, I plunged into the water, so blue it reminded me of peacock feathers.

"Don't go out too far, Isabel!" Rosa called after me as I swam and splashed about.

I stayed close to the shoreline to keep Rosa happy, or else she would be nagging me all afternoon. I was a good swimmer, although the sea could be treacherous at times. The currents and rip tides could pull you out, no matter how much you tried to swim back to shore, but Papa had always told me to follow the current if that were ever to happen.

I pretended to be a mermaid lost at sea, looking for my mermaid family. It was at moments like these that I wished my family was whole. Mama would help me dig holes and build sandcastles in the sand. She would try and brush my messy hair, made wild by the sea, and I'd have a sister or brother to race across the sand dunes. I felt like I was just a quarter of a broken apple, fragmented and incomplete.

Rosa had made some cakes the day before —*torrijas* soaked in honey — and we feasted on them, sitting on the blanket watching the sea, as the winds picked up and it became rougher. I threw a couple of pieces to the seagulls, which they devoured in seconds. Rosa pretended not to notice. She didn't really like seagulls either.

We headed home as the sun began to dip, and dark clouds brooded over the skyline. Rain was not usual for this time of year, but it did happen. Rain would make it cooler for a little while, at least, and was good for the fruits we grew, but today I looked at the clouds wearily, as if they were messengers of something bad. I stopped in my tracks, not wanting to go home.

"Come on, Isabel, don't drag your feet," Rosa told me. "It's been a long day for me and I must get home before your father does. You know how grumpy he gets when he is hungry."

We both laughed at this, and I told myself I was being silly. Clouds were just clouds and even though I'd been sensing a peculiar *feeling* around the hacienda recently, it didn't mean anything bad was going to happen.

I picked up my pace, only stopping to shake a stone from

my sandal, and soon we were home. Rosa headed into the kitchen but I ventured into the courtyard. I spotted Blanca hiding behind a large terracotta pot.

"Blanca!" I called out. Usually she came running, but today she just sat there as if trying to make herself small.

I approached her, but she only shot out and ran away like an animal on fire. It would have seemed funny if it wasn't so unlike her. Disheartened that Blanca was in no mood to play, I started to head back inside, but then I saw a tip of a tail hanging from the lip of the bucket beside the well. Zara was the most multi-coloured cat I'd ever seen. Her soft coat was black, white, cream and orange, as was her tail.

I felt something cold and heavy settle in my stomach as I inched closer to the well. My eyes were locked onto the tail, willing it to move, but I could soon see that Zara would no longer do any such thing.

Her eyes were open, as if in shock that she was no longer alive. The bucket was three-quarters full with water, and Zara's body lay half-submerged in it.

"Zara! No!" I cried finally, followed by a noisy sob and a sharp pain in my chest.

I fell to my knees and picked her out of the water carefully. I held her cold body to my chest and stroked her almost absentmindedly. I must have been in shock, because I was just staring at a point on the wall as I continued to pat her matted fur.

Rosa must have heard me wail: the next thing I knew she was kneeling next to me and attempting gently to take Zara away. After a few moments I let her. I continued staring at that dark patch on the stone wall as if it was the most interesting thing in the world.

I thought back to when I first found Zara, then only the smallest ball of fur. It appeared she had been abandoned by her mother, so we took her in. I gave her some goat's milk for a little while, until she could eat some fish. She was my friend, and I couldn't understand how she had drowned in a bucket.

A little while later, Rosa was back, wrapping a shawl around my shoulders, even though it wasn't cold, and guiding me upstairs. She heated water on the fire and she prepared a bath for me.

As I saw the level of water in the bath rise as she poured in another bucket, I take a panicked step back, and then another, until I hit the wall. I pictured Zara's dead eyes, how horrible they looked when there was no life behind them. I didn't want to go in the water, and Rosa had to peel off my clothes and put me into the bath. She was being gentle with me, but I wished she would just leave me alone.

"Isabel, child, let's get you washed. You have half the beach on you. I know you are very sad to lose Zara, but sometimes accidents happen," Rosa entreated.

"How—" I started to say, but couldn't finish.

What I had felt like screaming at her was, *How can you say that was an accident?* But I held my tongue. It dawned on me that Rosa couldn't possibly believe that Zara had somehow drowned. Unlike Blanca, who didn't mind it too much, Zara hated water.

No, someone had grabbed Zara and set out to harm her. To kill her. But who? Who would do such a thing? I knew the young women who came to help Rosa clean the house and wash the clothes – they all seemed nice enough, and wouldn't risk their job doing something so evil. Could it have been one of the men from the village? But why would they do something like this?

I was still in a sort of daze as Rosa washed me, something I was too old for her to do, but I knew she was trying to be kind. I just couldn't understand why she was acting as if what had happened to Zara was just some unfortunate mistake. What was she hiding from me?

I wanted to demand an answer from her, but I knew how stubborn she could be. I got out of the bath, the water now tepid, and allowed myself to be wrapped in a large towel and then guided to my room. I changed into my nightdress and sat on the bed. Rosa left, saying that she would bring me up some food in a moment, but I couldn't stomach the thought of eating, not when I could still feel Zara's dead body in my arms.

As promised, Rosa brought me some soup she had made earlier, with a thick slice of bread. I forced a few spoonfuls down, but refused to eat anymore and instead lay in bed staring up at the ceiling, feeling too awake and too sad to sleep.

"Would you like me to sing to help you get to sleep?" Rosa asked softly.

"I think I'm getting a little old for that," I said, more sharply than I had intended.

"Perhaps, but it always helped when you were little. It's OK to be upset, Isabel. I know you loved Zara, and I'm sorry..." She trailed off, looking visibly upset.

"It's not your fault, Rosa." I didn't like seeing her unhappy. She was like my mother, after all. "You can sing if you want to."

She looked a little less sad as she began to sing.

Duermete mi nina, de mi corazon, ya no llores mas,
Duermete ya, que viene el cuco y te comera,
La, la, la... la, la...

I closed my eyes and pretended to be drifting off, but I knew I wouldn't fall asleep for hours yet. Something had been going on inside this house recently, and I had to find out what. I had a sinking feeling in my gut that if I didn't discover it soon, it would be too late.

Beth

Chapter Twenty-Six

I was gasping for breath but nothing happened; it was as if I was in a vacuum. The burning in my lungs intensified. It was only when I heard Dr Roberts voice that I seemed to gather my senses and air reached my lungs.

"Beth... Beth, you are in a safe place. You now feel a sense of calm wash over you. There is nothing to fear. Nothing can harm you here." I noticed the sharp edge of unease in his tone, even though he was trying to mask it. "Beth, it's now time to leave the past and return to the present. I am going to count down from five, and when I get to one, you will back in the present feeling completely calm and at ease. Five... four... three... two... one."

The world which had turned dark now brightened. I opened my eyes and my vision adjusted to the light streaming in through the window. I blinked away the blurriness until the face of Dr Roberts came into focus.

"Beth, how are you feeling?" he asked, sounding and looking a little relieved.

"I'm... OK," I reassured him, taking another deep breath. "I was drowning."

"I couldn't reach you," he admitted. "I've never had that happen with a patient before. You were describing a marketplace, and then suddenly you stopped talking. I could see you were experiencing something unpleasant, but no matter what I said, you weren't reacting to my words."

"I was in too deep," I offered by way of explanation.

"Can you tell me what happened?"

"It's a little fuzzy, if I'm honest. I remember the marketplace, then standing in an orange grove, and then I was drowning," I replied, deciding that a half-truth was better than a complete lie.

"Our ties to the past offer us glimmers, emotional resonances, of past events. It can take some time to understand the significance of what we have seen. We must also remember that human memory is fraught with errors and incongruities. Reality is also coloured by our perspective." Dr Roberts leaned back in his chair. "What do you think you have learned from this session?"

"I learned that Isabel loved someone very deeply and that she decided to end her life in a moment of extreme emotional pain." I paused. "I guess I'm finding it hard to draw parallels between her life and my own."

"Like I said, Beth, these things take time," he repeated as he jotted down a few notes.

There was one important thing I had come to understand, even though I didn't share this with Dr Roberts: that some wounds cut so deep that they mark our soul for all eternity.

When I let myself back into our flat, I decided to run a bath. The session with Dr Roberts had only lasted an hour but I felt utterly drained, both emotionally and physically. I took off my clothes, leaving them in a heap on the floor. I was about to slip into the scented hot water when my phone buzzed. I consider ignoring it, but figured it could be something important, so I retrieved it from my bag. It was a message from Helena.

I felt a slight pang of regret that I hadn't been in contact with her since the funeral. My past attempts at reconciliation had failed and, if I was really honest with myself, I'd gotten past the point of trying. Helena would always see the Beth of our childhood.

I tapped in my code and brought up her message. Like most of the correspondence between us, it was short and to the point.

The reading of the will is taking place at the law offices of Bishop & White at 10am tomorrow morning.

I knew I had to go, that I was expected, but I really didn't want to. I assumed my father had left everything to Helena; it would be his last and most passive-aggressive move towards me. As if I had ever been in any doubt as to what he thought of me.

After experiencing Isabel's life, I felt I had no energy left to deal with the drama in mine, but the new persona I had created for myself stuck to her responsibilities and so I found myself replying:

OK, thanks for letting me know. Will see you there. Hope you are OK.

I wasn't expecting a response, so I tapped on the Amazon

Music icon, chose an acoustic pop playlist and placed the phone by the sink. I then went back to the tub, having added a generous glug of rose and geranium bubble bath. I stepped into the bath. The water was just a tad too hot, but I knew once I was in I'd welcome the heat.

I lowered my body, releasing a sigh as the hot water helped to leach some of the tension from my body. My mind seemed to be resisting the memories, pushing back, but I made myself recall the experiences of the session. I had learned that Isabel had fallen deeply in love with a young man called Alejandro, a man she planned on marrying. He had then betrayed her with another woman and Isabel, in a moment of utter despair, had decided to take her own life.

So what was the point of all this? What was Isabel trying to tell me? Was this about Nathan? Was it merely a coincidence that Nathan had proposed around the same time I found the ring? Was she trying to imply that Nathan couldn't be trusted? That he had been or was going to be unfaithful? Was this the reason behind her *haunting* me?

I was clutching at straws to find parallels between our lives – but Isabel had grown up in a loving home, she had Rosa and a father who doted on her. So there were clear differences between us, but also some similarities – but couldn't that be said of almost everyone? If you look for a pattern hard enough, you'll find it.

I recalled reading about the 'law of attraction' when researching past lives. It stated that like attracts like, and that our subconscious emotions, thoughts and beliefs are carried over from previous lives, creating the circumstances of our present lives. We can even be surrounded by the same people.

Was Nathan Alejandro? The more I explored the theory, the less credence I felt I could give to it. Perhaps Isabel had unfinished business because her life had ended so abruptly. But she had lived so many years ago – what difference could it make now?

So many thoughts were running through my mind, like a kaleidoscope of colours, shifting and altering my perceptions. I didn't know what to think anymore. Perhaps I was trying to rationalise and understand something that simply couldn't be understood; it just *was*.

I closed my eyes and tried to empty my mind and focus solely on the warm water on my skin. Everything was quiet until I heard Mittens begin to mewl from outside the bathroom door, probably just seeking some attention.

"I promise to play with you in just a little while, Mittens. Plus I'll give you a treat. That sound like a deal?"

The only response was a faint scratching at the door, but I really wanted to unwind a little longer so I allowed myself to sink fully into the tub. The water filled my ears and all I could hear was the sound of the water lapping against the edges of the bath, and my own heartbeat.

Then I heard it, as if the voice was originating from the water itself –that accursed lullaby.

Duermete mi nina, de mi corazon, ya no llores mas,
Duermete ya, que viene el cuco y te comera,
La, la, la... la, la...

I lifted myself up but found that I couldn't break the surface of the water. I opened my eyes but couldn't see anything above me, yet I was coming up against an invisible barrier. I could hear the *thud, thud* as my hands and knees connected with whatever was keeping me beneath the water. As my lungs began to burn and the edges of my vision began to darken, I experienced, for the second time that day, what it felt like to drown.

I could feel my consciousness ebbing away when suddenly the surface became liquid once more and I managed to sit up. I felt exhausted and weak, and in-between great lungfuls of air, I began to weep. It was a cry of self-pity. I had never felt so alone. I felt like if I was standing on the edge of the cliff and a powerful wind was trying to push me over.

Did Isabel want me to suffer the same fate as her? But in God's name, why? I couldn't talk to Nathan about this – I wasn't even being completely truthful to Dr Roberts. I was alone in this, and I was still no closer to learning how to make Isabel stop.

I got out of the bath and wrapped a large towel around me.

"Please, Isabel, just leave me alone," I said to the empty bathroom. "I still don't know what it is you want. I'm sorry Alejandro hurt you, but I love Nathan and he loves me. I am going to marry him."

Still in my towel, no longer having the energy to change, I padded to the living room and lay on the sofa, cuddled up with Mittens. After a few moments I drifted off, reluctantly, to sleep.

I found myself at the kitchen table, fork in hand and sipping a glass of chilled white wine. I looked down at myself: I was wearing one of my little black dresses. It was one I had usually worn to go clubbing during my years at university, but hadn't worn since.

I looked across the table. Nathan was saying something about a new client. He was still dressed in his suit, but the top button of his shirt was undone and his tie was bunched up next to him on the kitchen table. I felt sick and disorientated and, with a shaking hand, I put the wine glass down on the table and dropped the fork. It landed on the plate with a loud clank. My ears were ringing and for a moment even my vision blurred.

"Honey, what's wrong?" Nathan asked, surprised.

I bolted up from my seat and ran towards the bathroom, for once glad that Nathan had left the toilet seat up, and vomited the wine and rice which I apparently had just ingested. The acrid taste and stench made me heave again until I was spent. I reached out blindly with one arm and flushed the toilet. Nathan, who had chased me into the bathroom but then had stood quietly beside me, now knelt down and rubbed my back lightly.

"You were absolutely fine just a moment ago. I wonder what brought that on so suddenly. Don't try to get up just yet, Beth –you look so pale. I'm gonna get you some napkins," Nathan said quickly, and rushed out back to the kitchen.

I made myself get up on shaking legs, and stumble to the sink to wash out my mouth. I would have screamed, but all the air escaped from my lungs before I had the chance. The eyes that stared back at me in the mirror were not my own. My own hazel-green eyes had been replaced by a green the colour of emeralds.

Isabel's eyes.

I now understood that fear is a kind of madness; I felt my own sanity slipping away. A raging feverish fire of dread flared painfully in my chest. A sudden wave of understanding flooded my mind, but the horror of such a realisation was too much too bear, and I felt myself shutting down, my body making a fruitless attempt to protect itself. I couldn't even call out for Nathan before the ground rose up to meet me.

Chapter Twenty-Seven

I felt pain radiating from the left side of my body as I turned in bed, so I stopped and stared up at the ceiling instead, watching the wild shadows dance across it, and I felt a prickle of unease. I vaguely remembered Nathan picking me up, helping me change into my pyjamas, tucking me into bed and washing my face with a damp flannel. We spoke but I couldn't remember what either of us said. It was like replaying a scene in my mind with the sound on mute.

I had grasped at something, a notion, before passing out, and even though my thoughts were a tangle of vague outlines, one idea was bolder than the others and began to solidify in my mind, chilling the blood in my veins.

Isabel may have started this to show me something from my past, but what if that was no longer enough? What if now that she had seen my life with Nathan, she wanted it for herself? *What if she could become me?*

Ignoring the pain, I turned and curled myself around Nathan's warm body. I was playing a perilous game, one I was not willing to lose but I was so, so tired, I felt sleep tugging at me and so I closed my eyes against the night.

I suddenly become aware of Nathan's weight above me,

the feel and smell of him so familiar, as he kissed my neck passionately, his hands running expertly over my body. My fingers clutched at the bed sheets and something else – my discarded pyjamas – only then did I realise I was completely naked.

I jerked upright and pushed Nathan away.

"Beth what's the matter? I didn't hurt you did I?" He asked a little anxiously, sounding slightly hoarse.

"What's happening?" I replied, my voice shaking.

"What do you mean?" He said sounding confused.

"I was sleeping." I said lamely.

"No I was sleeping, you woke me up and started to well you know..." He said, not sure whether to be amused or concerned. "Not that I'm complaining or anything, you know I love it when you make the first move." He continued and moved to kiss me again.

I pressed myself against the headboard and he stopped. I could just make out his expression in the gloom and he looked hurt.

"I'm sorry." I blurted and the fear I had experienced earlier twisted at my insides again and I had to stop myself from sobbing. "I think I was still half-asleep, I don't remember-"

"Hey it's OK honey." Nathan said when he realised I was trembling. "Hey, it's fine, let's just lie back down. I'll hold you till you fall back to sleep."

I slipped my pyjamas back on, feeling suddenly frightfully cold and let Nathan cuddle into my back. Eventually I must have fallen asleep again, because the next thing I knew, the sun was streaming through the window. Nathan was no longer in bed and for a moment I felt like weeping at his absence. Then I noticed the note lying on his pillow. I reached out for it.

Morning beautiful, I didn't want to wake you and thought rest was the best thing for you. Call me as soon as you are up. I love you xx

I looked at the time and realised I would need to hurry if I was going to make it to the reading of my father's will on time. I got ready on autopilot, focusing only on getting myself showered, dressed and fed, my mind empty.

I cuddled Mittens before I left. I believed she was safe now. Isabel toyed with her to make me remember what the old Beth had done to Coco-Pop, to unsettle me and to make me relive my past. I recalled Dr Roberts saying how past lives were like fragments, but Isabel was more than that – there was something powerful and dangerous about her that made me fear for my life, for my soul.

I needed to visit the past again, to discover more about her, but I couldn't do it in a session with Dr Roberts; he would pull me out at the first sign of trouble. I'd have to do it on my own, but it would have to wait.

I raced out of the flat and to my car. The traffic was a nightmare, which always seems to be the case when you are in a rush, but I was lucky enough to find one of the few remaining parking spots in the underground garage in the city centre. Hurriedly, I made my way to the offices of Bishop and White, and after speaking to the receptionist I took the lift to the seventh floor and caught a glimpse of Helena entering the lawyer's office.

I knocked on the door and it was opened by a man in his fifties with a mane of thick, white hair. He greeted me with a smile, introduced himself as Mr White, and ushered me inside to take a seat next to Helena. His suit, as well as the lavish office decor, screamed *money*.

I gave Helena a small smile, which she returned with a polite nod, acknowledging my existence. She looked a little thinner and paler, as if she wasn't eating or sleeping well. Not for the first time, I wondered if she had someone special in her life. I would never share in Helena's joys, but I wished them for her nonetheless.

"Again, morning, Helena and Beth. I am sorry we have to meet under such circumstances, but I will not keep you long. I've known your father ever since your mother passed away, and as the executor of his estate, I confirm this is his last will and testament, which he revised soon after his diagnosis." Mr White cleared his throat and paused for a moment to open the sealed envelope before him, before reading aloud, "I, Mark Ellis, residing at 8 Anchorage House, declare this to be my last will and I revoke any and all wills I made previously. I also direct my executors to pay any outstanding debts, funeral and medical expenses. I leave my said residence to my daughter, Helena, and leave my capital assets in the sum of £187,000 to my daughter, Beth."

I was so surprised that my gasp turned into a cough, and it took me a moment to compose myself. I glance at Helena, she seemed completely nonplussed, perhaps he had discussed this with her.

Mr White began to talk about the transfer of deeds and assets, but I was no longer listening. My father left me something…well, not just something —quite a bit of money – but why? Was it guilt for all the years he wished I wasn't his daughter? Did he feel remorse for the state of our relationship? Or perhaps he just felt obliged. I could try and fathom his reasons, but without him around to ask, it seemed pointless.

Mr White was wrapping up the meeting. "If either of you have any questions or if there is any way we can assist you going forward, please do not hesitate to get in touch with our office."

"Thank you, Mr White," Helena said, standing and picking up her handbag from the carpet.

"Yes, thank you," I repeated.

Helena and I walked out of the office together and headed towards the lifts. I scoured my brain for something to say, but thankfully Helena beat me to it.

"Beth, look—" she began, but faltered.

The silence stretched on between us, so I decided to say something I had said a very long time ago, but which was worth repeating.

"I am sorry, Helena, for everything," I said, so softly that I wondered if I had even said the words out loud.

It was Helena's turn to look surprised. I didn't blame her: I was alluding to the past, which was something we never did.

"I am sorry for everything that I was," I continued. "That *I* did... I cannot explain or justify it, but I have tried to be a different person, to be better."

Just a few words said out loud was all it took to cause the walls I had built my entire adult life to crumble around me. That, coupled with my father's death, experiencing Isabel's torments and reliving one of the happiest moments of my life – Nathan's proposal –had shaken the foundations of the life I had created.

The memories I had tried so hard to bury in the deepest recesses of my mind now played themselves out like a horror-movie reel in my mind, but one in which I could not turn away from the scary parts.

The time I broke all of Helena's toys on Christmas Day.

The day I pushed her down the stairs when we were only four years old and she broke her arm.

The time I pulled at her hair so hard a clump came away in my hand.

The time I was so jealous of her I grabbed a baseball bat and could have killed her had my father not intervened.

The afternoon I scalded her with a mug of hot tea.

The countless times I told her I wished she would simply disappear.

I had made Helena's life a living hell. There had only been so much even sweet Helena could take.

Finally, I recalled the *thwack, thwack* of the stick on my grazed knee on that fateful day. Helena had pushed me only to get back at me for having thrown a rock at her face. At eight years old she was no longer a passive victim to my anger. Even now you could still see the mark on her cheek. It was why we had left the seaside early that day – because I had hurt Helena once more – and it was why my father had been so angry.

I didn't know why I had been like that, but since as far back as I could remember, I had been filled with anger and malice. They say no child is born with hate, but I believed I was. I had been born of darkness, envy and misery. My father had seen me for the monster I truly was, as had Helena and Dolores. My mother had loved me but had also feared me.

To think of that child, to think that was me, made me recoil in disgust and despair. I had spent so many years trying to be better than that. So many years burying that child and pretending she no longer existed, that I could almost believe it hadn't been me... almost. Perhaps Isabel and I were more alike than I cared to believe. I had seen the malevolence in her eyes, so similar to that which I saw in the mirror as a child. Could I have been born carrying the anger and pain that she died with?

"I know you have," Helena replied softly, tugging me away from my awful recollections.

I felt as if I'd just been punched in the gut, and I steadied myself against the wall. Helena reached out to me, but hesitated before touching me. Even now, when the past had all played out in my mind, my brain still wanted to refute the reality of those memories. I may have created a new version of myself, but I would always carry the corpse of the old.

Then tears begin to fall, a flood of overwhelming emotions, self-hate, self-loathing, loneliness, anger, and the desire to have been different. I wanted to say more to Helena but I just couldn't. I felt like a fragile piece of glass already cracked in places. One more word or thought would shatter me into a million fragments.

Instead I ran as soon as the lift doors *pinged* and opened. I ran towards the stairwell and thundered down them. I didn't stop until I was in the confines of my car. Only here did I allow my silent tears to turn into heart-wrenching sobs. How long I stayed there weeping and wishing I could erase the memories which darkened my childhood, I didn't know. If I could, I would have erased myself, so that Helena, and both my mother and father, could have led the lives they deserved.

I had always thought it was one of the greatest tragedies of the human condition to recall bad memories so much more vividly and intensely than the good. How our moments of hardship and pain, eclipse the ones we cherish. Like a towering rock casting shadows over the landscapes in our minds.

I took my phone from my bag and thought of calling Helena to try and explain why I had run away, but couldn't think how to even begin. I checked the time: I had to pick up Nathan soon. He had managed to take a long lunch break so we could drive down to view the Old Manor House as a potential venue for the wedding reception. I felt so unbelievably tired, as if I had lived a lifetime since Nathan's proposal, and I just wanted to go home and sleep – but I couldn't. I didn't want Nathan to worry about me more than he already was.

I drove out of the underground parking lot, my sore eyes blinking against the brilliant sunshine as I emerged. Nathan was waiting for me outside his office building and jumped in as I parked in the lay-by.

"Hey, sweetheart– how did it go with the lawyer and Helena?" he asked, kissing me on the cheek and squeezing my hand, as he took in my bloodshot eyes.

"Yeah, fine really. My dad... he left me some money," I said, already indicating and driving back out onto the main road.

"Really?"

"Yeah, he left the house to Helena and left me just under £190,000."

"Wow. That must have come as a bit of a shock? Is that why you've been crying? Was Helena upset that your father had left that to you?"

"No." I took a deep breath before continuing, "I think she knew, and I've always thought Helena should have the family home. I've never wanted it. I guess I'm just a little shell-shocked, that's all."

Nathan nodded and seemed to sense that I needed time with my own thoughts. He tuned the radio to my favourite R&B station, the volume down to a soft background hum as we drove out of the city centre and towards the countryside.

I knew that Nathan viewed my father and Helena as cold and indifferent and, although that had never been my intention, it was easier than the truth. The truth was that they had every right to want to exclude me from their lives. If a tree branch is infected and rotten, you have to cut it off to save the rest of the tree. That is exactly what my father did. He cut me off to save Helena; he didn't believe I could change.

The satnav was directing me to take the next exit. We would soon reach the Manor, so I forced all these poisonous thoughts behind the wall in my mind and faked a smile for Nathan's benefit. A man who appeared to be in his sixties was waiting for us at the bottom of the drive, and he greeted us as soon as we got out of the car.

"Welcome, Nathan and Beth."

"Good afternoon, Mr Turner. Thanks so much for fitting us in during my lunch break," Nathan told him.

"Not a problem at all, young man," he replied with a wide smile.

Mr Turner was dressed in a classic blue crew-neck sweater, brown chinos and a light jacket. He gave me the impression he was one of those older gentleman that was always dressed smartly no matter the occasion. I took in the flowering meadows that surrounded the Old Manor House, which sat atop a rolling hill. For just an instant, I recalled the hacienda, but I shut that thought down, fast.

"The grounds look beautiful," I commented.

Mr Turner beamed proudly. "I'm glad you think so, Beth. My family has owned this property for generations, but it has become a little too much for me and my wife to manage now that we are older, and our eldest son suggested we downsize and keep the Manor as a venue for hire. Have you looked at many places for your wedding?"

"Actually, this is our first. I came across it online and I guess I fell in love with it," I told him honestly.

I allowed the sunshine, the crisp fresh air and the smell of flowers to lift my spirits as we walked towards the house. I was choosing to focus on Nathan and my future in this moment. The fact that I was now inheriting a large sum of money meant we could now afford a place like this for the wedding.

I held onto Nathan's hand as Mr Turner showed us around. He explained that the Manor was a Grade II listed building and they had renovated it around six years ago. After the quaint reception hall, the first thing we saw was a large dining room in which we could host the dinner. Adjacent to this was a large, circular hall, complete with a sparkling chandelier on the vaulted ceiling, an inglenook fireplace and large windows, through which we could see a natural swimming pond flanked by a sun terrace.

The Manor had been wonderfully refurbished, yet retained its character. I loved the oak timber, the flagstone flooring and the decor. Back in the entrance hall, two large winding staircases led to the upper floor where there were eight en-suite bedrooms. Taking a quick peek inside, it seemed like a perfect place to spend our first night as husband and wife.

It hit me just how few people I would be inviting to this wedding. It would be mostly Nathan's family, friends and co-workers, but I supposed I was OK with that, because this next step in my life represented a whole new chapter. Going forward, I would allow myself to make new friends, to no longer feel ashamed about the person I once was.

Mr Turner showed us the outside space, mentioning the potential to hold the service on the terrace or by the pond, should we decide not to go with a church service, and if the weather wasn't great, we could shift the ceremony indoors to the renovated stables, which I thought would look spectacular covered in fairy lights and Calla lilies.

"What do you think?" I asked Nathan quietly when Mr Turner was out of earshot.

"I'm thinking *wow*."

"I know, right? I think this place is perfect. I love it. I don't think I want to even look at any other venues," I said.

"The Old Manor House it is, then. Well, that was easy," Nathan said with a laugh. "It's nice to see you looking happy, Beth," he whispered, his tone more serious.

"There's actually something I've been meaning to talk to you about," I began. "I thought I could handle it on my own, but I'm not so sure anymore..."

"I knew something was up, but I didn't want to push you – and then we heard of your dad's illness..." he said, taking my hand and giving it a squeeze.

"I know, and I'm sorry. Let's go rejoin Mr Turner and tell him we would love to hold our wedding here. Now we just need to decide on the date!"

I was surprised at myself for deciding to open up to Nathan about Isabel, but seeing this place made the fact we were soon to be husband and wife all the more real. I didn't want to start this new chapter in my life with this *thing* eating away at the back of my mind. It was one thing to keep my past secret, but the present was a whole different matter – and what if I couldn't ever rid myself of Isabel? What would I do then?

Chapter Twenty-Eight

I dropped Nathan off at his office. The city centre was busy with afternoon shoppers, tourists and students. I was keen to get back home and start working on my latest project, which I had just been commissioned by a local newspaper, off the back of the Water-Well Media project. I had been asked to contribute photographs to their in-depth expose of homelessness in Bristol. I was looking forward to the opportunity to work on a human interest story, and to develop photos which would resonate deeply with the public and help raise awareness.

I was just about to head back out into the traffic when I thought of Helena and, before I could second guess myself, I whipped out my phone and sent a quick text message asking if it was OK for me to stop by the house to see her. Surprisingly, she replied instantly and said yes. I made a U-turn and started heading towards my childhood home. I parked at the bottom of the drive to find Helena waiting for me at the door. Her hands were wrapped around a mug as if for warmth.

"Thank you for seeing me. Sorry for the short notice," I

told her as I hurried up to the door.

"It's no problem. I didn't have anything planned. I've just made myself a tea – would you like one?" she asked.

"Yes, thank you," I replied gratefully.

I followed her into the kitchen. The house was so silent, a stark reminder that Helena now lived here alone. I hoped she would put her own mark on the place, paper over the past and create a happier future.

"Is it strange being here without Dad?" I asked before I could stop myself.

She paused halfway through making the tea. "Not as much as I would have thought. Seeing him suffer like that, the pain he was in… I couldn't see him like that."

"Helena, I'm so sorry for everything—"

"Beth, not now. We've all done things we're not proud of, things we could have all done… differently. I'm not saying I understand you… but if I could have looked past my own hurt and anger, perhaps I would have been able to see that you have tried to change."

"I know I can never make up for the past, but I want you to know that I only wish good things for you."

Helena simply nodded.

I looked towards the hall just in time to catch a glimpse of someone walking across the threshold. The smell of death now permeated the air, and I struggled not to gag.

"What's wrong, Beth?" Helena asked.

I turned back to face her and stumble backwards. Isabel was standing directly behind Helena. Helena didn't notice, but looked both alarmed and annoyed.

"Beth, for God's sake, what's the matter with you? If this

is some sort of game, I really am not in the mood," she said bluntly, and stormed towards the living room.

Isabel kept her eyes focused on me. Her corpse was mottled and green, the skin hanging off in places, bones exposed where sea-dwelling predators had feasted on her body. I tried to recall the image of the little girl in the vineyard, of Isabel's beauty at the marketplace. She may have been like that once, but death, and whatever she had become since, had stripped her of what had made her human.

I could sense the depth of her malice, almost as if it were something tangible. This wasn't a game or a message she wanted to deliver. She had transcended the grave seeking retribution and vengeance – I just couldn't yet grasp why. As if suddenly bored with me, she leapt up and onto the ceiling. Scuttling on all fours, like an abhorrent demonic creature, she followed Helena out of the room.

"Leave her out of this," I hissed vehemently, and followed.

I regretted having come here. The last thing I wanted to do was cause Helena any more hurt or place her in danger.

"Beth, I need to lie down. It's been a long few days," Helena said dismissing me as soon as I'd walked into the living room.

Isabel was sitting right next to Helena, a skeletal arm raised as if to touch her face, a look of something like fascination on her decomposed features. Before I could restrain myself, I launched myself at Isabel, but in a split second she vanished and I just crashed into the sofa. Helena looked at me as if I was crazy.

"Beth, please leave. I don't know what's wrong with you.

I never have. But I want you gone now."

"I'm so sorry. I don't expect you to understand or to ever forgive me," I blurted hastily, gathering myself up.

Her silence spoke volumes. I ran from that silent room, from that silent house. I jumped into my car and sped home. I needed to regress again. It could be dangerous, but I had to. I let myself into the apartment and Mittens sauntered over instantly for a cuddle. I gave her soft coat a few long strokes and then closed myself off in the bedroom.

I pulled the curtains to block out the light and lay down on the bed. I slipped the ruby ring off my finger and held it tightly in my fist. I emptied my mind and began to breathe slowly. I recited Dr Roberts' words and repeated them in my mind like a mantra. I found myself relaxing, my body becoming heavier and sinking deeper into the mattress with every exhalation.

I pictured the empty room once more, the staircase to a dimly-lit corridor with doors on either side, and proceeded to the door which seemed to be almost thrumming with energy. I repeated the same question in my mind: *Why? Why? Why?* That was what I needed to know. To understand the real reason why Isabel was here. I opened the door and stepped through.

I landed heavily on the cold, hard ground. The room was lit by the glow of the moon, bleak and sombre. Once more I wasn't simply a spectator - I was trapped in someone else's body, someone else's mind, seeing through their eyes as if their face was a mask, and feeling their emotions as if they were my own.

But I did not like what I was feeling, and I wanted out of

this body. The feelings of anger, hate and pain were all too familiar. I saw my hands, my legs in front of me. I was not much older than a child, but these emotions that welled inside me had no place in someone so young. I looked around the room I found myself in. It was both familiar and unfamiliar at the same time. It was circular in shape and made of white stone, but the roof above me was made of wood and there was only a small window high above me.

There was a small bed in one corner, a night table with a basin of water. A small cupboard, its doors open, filled with a few items of clothing, a couple of blankets and some toys. Her thoughts —now my thoughts —turned to Rosa. She —I — loved and detested her in equal measure. Loved her because she was the only person I had known outside these walls. She had fed me, washed me and clothed me, but she had also kept me prisoner.

For years she had told me it was not safe to leave this room, telling stories of bogeymen that took and ate children, but now I knew that she was a liar. That everything she had told me was a lie, and that was why I hated her.

I cradled a sharp piece of metal in my hand. I had been using this for the past few days to unlock the door to this prison – as I had come to think of what I had always considered to be my home —and venture out.

Not too far, mind, as I was afraid there could be a monster waiting to rip me to pieces and feast on my bones when I left the sanctuary of this place. But each night I had gone a little further, and then a little further after that, and discovered how many other rooms there were here. There were other people, too. I could sometimes hear other voices, but Rosa said they came from far away. From out *there*, where it wasn't safe.

I had spied on Rosa. Seen the other little girl that she loved so much, and the man the girl called Papa. I was quiet; I had learned to sneak around like the rats that sometimes entered my room. I fed the rats scraps and they were my only friends. But I had grown tired of simply sneaking around. I set my rats on their beloved Isabel but I was too scared to run away, to go any further than the grounds of the house, and so, like a coward, I came back here.

Did Isabel know I was here? That Papa had chosen to love only *her*? Did she realise all she took for granted whilst I was all alone with *nothing*?

Hate bubbled within me but I froze when I heard footsteps on the stairs. Rosa would know that it had been me. What would she do now? She would take away my key and I would die in this room – perhaps dead is better. I heard the click as she turned the key in the door.

"Sofia..." Rosa said as she entered. Her face was a mask of sadness but I knew now that she was just pretending; she was nothing but a liar.

I edged away from her and towards the basin. I could just make out my reflection in the water. I tried to focus on the left side of my face, which was so much like Isabel's, but inevitably I fixated on the right. As always, it pained me to see myself.

How my mouth twisted, the abnormal growth crushing my right eye, scar tissue where my right ear should be, my face smaller, pinched and contorted, like that of a troll. I covered the right side of my face with my long, dark hair.

I was filled with self-loathing and disgust. That was why I was kept here – not because there were monsters out there, but because *I* was the monster.

"Sofia..." Rosa said again, and I couldn't bear to hear the pity in her voice. "It is not safe for you to leave this room. Please hand over what you have been using to open the door."

I took a step towards her, but I felt myself falling, as if the ground beneath my feet had disappeared.

I woke up with a start on the bed.

I was still in the circular, sealed room. Sunlight now seeped through the small overhead window. I was older now. Years have passed and still I was tucked away in this room like a dirty secret.

Rosa had been spending more and more time with me lately. Over the years I had got her to talk about the other people who lived in this house. People she could no longer deny existed. I knew Isabel was spending more time on her own now, so Rosa had more time to sneak up here and keep me company. I wheedled out of her that Isabel had met someone and hoped to be married soon.

I pretended I was happy for her, I pretended I was content to live like this, to live through Isabel, pretended that I had come to accept that this was my fate. I knew Rosa loved me; I had come to understand she was the reason my father didn't drown me like an unwanted animal when I had barely lived, the moment I came into this world and cost my mother her life. But I am not.

Soon they will all experience the hell I have lived these many years.

Very soon.

I bolted upright in bed once more, but this time I was back in the present, home and far away from that dreadful room. I held my hand to my chest, the forsaken ring still clenched in my palm, my heart beating too fast, like the wings of a hummingbird.

It takes me only a moment to realise how wrong I had been all along; how wrong I had been about everything. Like a thundering wave crashing upon the rocks, I understood. I finally understood why Isabel had been haunting me, but I wished to God I didn't. There was no coming back from this. You cannot un-know the truth once you have witnessed it.

I was not Isabel.

I never had been Isabel in a past life.

In a past life I had been Sofia, Isabel's twin sister.

I –Sofia– had spent years locked up in that tower. I had seen and felt that existence through my own eyes. Despite Rosa's continued attempts to keep me hidden, to keep me alive –if you could call that existence living– I had still managed to leave my cage even if only for little snippets of time. Time enough for the hate within me to blossom, time enough for me to plot, to envy Isabel for the life she had been granted and the one I had been denied.

That sense of rejection, of inferiority and self-loathing, had smothered Sofia's soul in darkness, and she had finally lashed out by taking away Isabel's happiness, by taking away Alejandro.

Covering her face and under the cover of night, she had tricked Alejandro into thinking she was Isabel. Perhaps she had not intended for Isabel to walk in on them, perhaps she had. Either way, her actions had led Isabel to take her own life.

How could Sofia's father have kept her locked up like that?

"Isn't that what your father had wanted to do to you, Beth? Lock you up for your own good? Perhaps if he had, your mother would still be alive," Isabel's voice whispered inside my head, venomous and cruel.

"Stop it, Isabel!" I cried out to the empty room. "I get it now! I know why you are so angry, at Sofia, at me! But that wasn't my life! I am not responsible for Sofia's actions! Or your father's!"

I had heard it said that envy is the most futile of emotions, because you are often envying the idea of something rather than the reality. However, in Sofia's case I could understand how envy had grown inside her and stripped her of every good thing that made her human. She had existed in a labyrinth of misery and the myriad of her life's lost moments and unending pain had culminated in this single act to inflict the hurt she had experienced her whole life, onto Isabel, who was also innocent.

"What do you want from me, Isabel?" I asked, tired and deflated.

"Only what is mine, only what you took from me!" the hellish voice rebounded across the room.

I –or Sofia; it no longer mattered – had been the cause of Isabel's death. Isabel had drowned herself, believing that

Alejandro did not love her. The ring I held in my hand wasn't mine from a past life; it represented the future I had stolen from my own twin sister.

This show Isabel had orchestrated had been to make me suffer but also to show me that she hadn't been aware of my existence. Sofia's hate and anger had been unjustly unleashed on someone who hadn't deserved it. Isabel was as innocent as Helena had been throughout all the hurt I had caused her as we grew up.

Whatever had happened to Sofia in the end, I may never know, but all that vileness she had inside her, I had carried into this life and continued to hurt those closest to me, Helena, my mother and my father. If Helena was also Isabel, I hoped the better part of Isabel lived within her and that she would experience some peace and happiness in this life.

In the shores of Tarifa I had walked in Isabel's footsteps and had inadvertently awoken something that had been buried for a very long time. What Isabel had become in the years since her death was only an echo of what had made her human. She had become something sinister, perhaps even demonic.

Isabel wanted to live a life once more. She wanted my life, she wanted Nathan, perhaps even Helena too. The life she feels she is owed.

No one was safe from what Isabel had become.

I felt another piece of me die inside as the happiness I had so wanted for myself, for the person I had tried so hard to become, slipped away from me. There were just too many pieces of me now, too broken to ever make whole again.

If Isabel managed to push me out again, would I be able

to come back? Or would I be lost forever, tucked away in a prison in my own mind, whilst Isabel was unleashed on the world through me?

I simply couldn't let that happen. Through both the ring and opening myself up to the past, I had invited her in, and she had worn me down, made me relive my past, to punish me, to make me aware of the past we shared. In that way Isabel had also weakened me, making it easier for her to take over my body.

I had tried to rewrite my own past, but perhaps I hadn't done enough. I had caused too much pain already. The same story was being played out, centuries apart: twin sisters, one carrying too much pain and hate. Could I really have expected a different ending?

I only hoped Nathan could forgive me and find happiness —he deserved that much.

I got out of bed slowly and went into the bathroom to run a bath. I moved into the kitchen and grabbed a bottle of wine from the fridge and drank. I cuddled Mittens and prised all my sleeping tablets and my anti-anxiety medication from their plastic sleeves.

I wasn't giving up, not really. I still had hope. After all, when all appears lost, some semblance of hope must remain, like the embers of a dying fire that may still reignite. It was just a different kind of hope – hope that whatever came next and that whatever our souls were made of, I had paid my penance for this life and my past one.

I would sacrifice myself to save Nathan, to save Helena, to sever this link I had created with Isabel and to atone for what Sofia had done. Perhaps with my death Isabel could also find peace.

I grabbed my phone and sent a couple of messages. I pictured Nathan's smiling face, the feel of his lips when we kissed. I pictured us growing old together. I created those images with such colour and detail that they could almost be real; they could almost be memories. These were my final thoughts, my last feelings filled with nothing but love, as I slipped into the warm waters and allowed them to engulf me.

Nathan

Chapter Twenty-Nine

I checked my phone again but I still had no messages from Beth. I had been trying to reach her all afternoon, but she hadn't answered my calls or my texts. I knew she was starting a new project and that she could sometimes get lost in her photography for hours, but she ought to have replied by now.

I looked up from the mound of paperwork on my desk at the half a dozen people milling about the office. Pretty much all of them looked stressed and tired. I knew I had been extremely lucky to get a position here, but the hours I'd be putting in over the past few months had been gruelling. Still, we had bills to pay, plus the wedding, and I wanted to be able to save enough for a down payment on a house once Beth and I were married.

Beth had now inherited quite a bit of money, but I didn't want us to be relying solely on that. I also wanted us to travel – the trip to Tarifa had been great, and I was so proud of Beth for overcoming her fear of the water. Now I wanted us to travel to Hawaii, the Maldives, the Caribbean, and a whole host of other exotic locations. Beth deserved that.

Ever since the night I'd met her, I had seen something in

her that made me want to protect her. No other girl had ever made me feel like that, not even Kat, the only other serious girlfriend I'd ever had. The more time I'd spent with Beth, the more *alone* I realised she was: no family, few friends, but that made me want to be there for her all the more. There was an air of fragility about her, as if she had spent her entire life walking a tightrope, careful not to put a foot wrong lest she fall. I put it down to her childhood, which couldn't have been easy. She never spoke much about it, but I knew her mother had died when she was eight years old and her father had become an alcoholic as a result.

Even after more than three years together, I still felt there was a side of Beth I didn't know, but I trusted she had her reasons and would confide in me when the time was right. I was concerned for her now, though. She had seemed *off* for the past couple of weeks. Obviously, the death of her childhood nanny and the news of her father's illness and his subsequent death had been bound to affect her, but I think it had started before then, soon after we got home from Spain. She had seemed more preoccupied than usual, perhaps even a little distant.

I checked my inbox. Another five emails had come in, three of them from my senior associate referencing an upcoming case, but I couldn't concentrate on any of it. I wished I could spend more time at home with Beth rather than spending my evenings here. I hoped the kitten I'd got her made up for my absence a little.

I checked my phone for the umpteenth time, even though I hadn't heard a notification. Still nothing. For the next ten minutes I focused on work. Feeling fidgety, I got up and walked to the photocopier machine, and scanned copies of the documents my boss had requested and then emailed them over.

When I checked the time, it was a little after 5pm. I usually didn't leave the office until 6pm or 6.30pm – no trainee lawyer wanted to be the first to leave – but I felt something wasn't right. I shut down my computer, grabbed my jacket and hurried out the door to the adjacent parking lot. The clear skies of the morning had turned into a blanket of cloud which hung low and menacing as night set in.

I was starting the engine when my phone pinged. I took it out of my jacket pocket and released a sigh of relief when I saw it was from Beth. As soon as I opened it up I felt my stomach drop and my heart begin to race painfully.

I am so sorry Nathan, please forgive me but I had to protect you. Know that I love you more than anything in this world. Always have, always will xx

I jammed the car into reverse and sped home as my mind screamed questions at me: *Sorry for what? Protect me from what? Why does the message sound so final? Surely Beth wouldn't do anything like... that... We have our whole lives ahead of us.*

I parked haphazardly in front of our apartment block, took the stairs two at a time, and burst through our front door. Trepidation hit me like a wave as I found the apartment in utter darkness. *What if she's not even here? But where would she go?*

"Beth?" I called out as I flipped the light switch.

I darted to the kitchen. Mittens ran up to me and began to wind herself in and out of my legs, mewling loudly.

"Beth!" I repeated, more loudly this time, and I started

dialling her mobile as I raced to the bedroom.

I heard a ringtone shatter the silence. It was coming from the bathroom. Through the closed door I could hear the *drip-drip* of water. I gripped the door handle with a shaking hand, turned it, and pushed the door open. The only light was that from the mobile on the floor as it rang. I dropped my phone and the call disconnected.

The room plunged into darkness, a split-second reprieve from the horror I had just seen: Beth lying motionless in the tub beneath the surface of the water, her hair floating around her like a dark halo.

The only word that escaped my lips like a strangled groan was, "No!"

I turned on the light and burst forward. I felt as if I was moving too slowly, as if I was wading through a torturous nightmare and this wasn't real. I grabbed Beth and hauled her out of the bath in a single swift motion, then laid her as carefully as I could on the bathroom floor.

She didn't react, but the bathwater was still tepid, so I didn't think she had been in there very long. Hope flared inside me and I pushed my fear aside. I checked whether she was breathing. She wasn't.

I reached for my phone and called 999, blurted out that I needed an ambulance and gave my address, then tossed the phone onto the floor without disconnecting the call. I tilted Beth's head back slightly and lift her chin. I placed my hands in the middle of her chest, one on top of the other, and begin to push hard and fast. I administered compressions that were at least two inches deep, delivered at a rate of at least 100 compressions per minute. I tried to focus solely on what I was doing, grateful that my mates and I had signed up for a first-aid course when one of us had almost drowned out in Cornwall whilst surfing.

I pinched Beth's nose shut and placed my mouth over her own and breathed. I did this twice, watching her chest rise and fall, and then continued compressions.

"She's not breathing!" I shouted to the operator. "Please hurry!" Then I delivered another set of breaths.

As I continued the compressions I glance away, unable to look at Beth's expressionless face any longer. My eyes caught sight of something in the mirror.

I took in a sharp breath as I saw a face – a corpse-like face – with an expression of absolute fury – but then it vanished. My mind was already overwhelmed with despair and so I rejected that horrific, fleeting image and concentrated on Beth, who needed me.

I needed her too. I felt tears course down my cheeks. It seemed like hours had passed since I had pulled her out of the water, but it had probably been only minutes. I felt desperation threatening to break me, but I persevered.

I breathed into her again, and was about to do it once more when she jerked and then began to cough. I turned her onto her side as bathwater and half-digested pills spilled out onto the bathroom floor.

"We're in here!" I yelled as I heard the paramedics at the door. "It's going to be OK, Beth. I've got you," I whisper to her, holding her gently to me. "I've got you."

Two paramedics rushed in and took in the scene. They ask me to step back and, reluctantly, I did so. They wrapped Beth up in blankets and placed her onto a stretcher, then checked her responses quickly and carried her outside. She seemed so weak, but she was alive, and that was all that mattered. I followed and got into the ambulance with them. As we pulled away, sirens blaring, Beth blinked and then looked at me, a faint smile on her lips, her eyes a flash of brilliant green.

THE END

Printed in Great Britain
by Amazon

60108595R00193